LIVING IN

WATER

A NOVEL

ALEX Z. MOORES

This is a work of fiction. All of the characters, organizations, and events portrayed in this novel are either the product of the author's imagination or are used fictitiously.

LIVING IN WATER. Copyright © 2017 Alex Z. Moores.

Printed in the United States of America.

Author website: alexzmoores.com
Cover painting by Yoju, "Portrait of Cloud", artbyoju.com
Novel edited by Robbi Sommers Bryant, robbibryant.com
Cover design by Leo Baquero, leo_baquero@hotmail.com

Permission for Reproduction
Elizabeth Coatsworth, "Swift Things Are Beautiful", with permission from www.bethlehembooks.com

Terje Oestigaard, *Water, Christianity, and the Rise of Capitalism*, with permission from I.B. Tauris & Co. Ltd.

ISBN 978-0-692-77476-2 (IngramSpark Paperback)
ISBN 978-1533585325 (CreateSpace Paperback)

Dedicated to my family, especially my wife and two sons.

PART 1

FOG

God perches above heaven
Viewing the world
Through the eyes of the fog

"All the wild world is beautiful, and it matters but little where we go, to highlands or lowlands, woods or plains, on the sea or land or down among the crystals of waves or high in a balloon in the sky; through all the climates, hot or cold, storms and calms, everywhere and always we are in God's eternal beauty and love. So universally true is this, the spot where we chance to be always seems the best.

— John Muir

THE FOG SWEPT IN on a torrent of wind like a god riding a gray stallion across the sky. The ocean's surface writhed, clamored, and crashed against gigantic rocks, returning white spray into the belly of the fog. Rising above steep cliffs, the dense mist climbed gentle slopes of grassy hills, passing over ranches of cattle, horses, and sheep as smoothly as the day turns to night.

Racing down the other side of the coastal mountains in threads, the fog collected itself and slowly wandered through the valleys. It overtook forests of redwood and oak trees without even breaking a twig, rocking the silky strands of tattered lichen dangling from the branches. Sliding along, it engulfed the neatly manicured rows of apple orchards and vineyards.

Slow in its approach, the fog drifted over downtown Santa Rosa, California. It crawled into housing developments blanketing parked cars and swallowing an assortment of kids' play equipment. People clambered out of nightclubs, restaurants, and cinemas disappearing into the milky mist. Tricked-out cars cruised the streets, blaring loud beats and creating spectacular halos through the fog.

Gaining momentum, hazy strands of fog moved quickly as they forged ahead of their main body. They shot around the edges of the houses, somersaulted over rooftops, and surrounded a young man named Stacey Shepherd.

CHAPTER 1

Heaven has beautiful things
Fog and love
Enticing, yet elusive

"True love is like ghosts, which everyone talks about but few have seen."
— François de La Rochefoucauld

STACEY WATCHED as the summer fog invaded his city. Like a cloud of ghosts, the fog huddled around Santa Rosa, holding everything hostage. Its mysterious origins and haunting movements intrigued him. He likened the scene to a Judgment Day when God's dewy breath sent angels streaking over the land in search of righteous souls.

Does God move in and out of our lives like fog? Sporadically engulf us for short moments at a time? Love is the same. Will I ever find "the one"? Does God even care? Questions bombarded Stacey as he stood on the patio of a hillside restaurant.

"Hey," Reece called out, interrupting Stacey's meditation.

Turning around, Stacey saw his brother walking towards him. Reece and Stacey were both tall and handsome. While the family resemblance was obvious, the character seen in their facial features differed. High cheekbones and a strong jawline provided Stacey with an expression of leadership. Appearing chiseled from ivory, his face had a serious edge with taut, clenched jaws. Reece's carefree smile demonstrated ease and relaxation. Dimples, rounded cheeks, and bushy hair contributed to his juvenile-like cuteness.

Their friend, Brian, joined them on the patio. Although it was August, the fog added a chill. Brian zipped up his light jacket. Only a few years older than Stacey, he was already the principal at the elementary school where Stacey taught. Brian flew up the ranks from teacher to principal, partly due to his large, burly stature. He used his size to intimidate the superintendent, teachers, parents, and students — at least that was Stacey's theory. Aside from his robust outward appearance, Brian was one of the kindest and funniest people Stacey knew.

"Stace, whatcha doing out here in the fog?" Reece asked, handing Stacey a glass of Zin.

"I'm taking a break from the party." Stacey kicked at the grass bordering the upscale restaurant's patio.

"Is something wrong?" Brian rested his hand on Stacey's shoulder. "You've got that look in your eyes."

"No, not really," Stacey replied. "After all, what could be wrong when you've been chosen for a teaching exchange in Munich?"

"Hopefully, not a damn thing." Brian took a swig of beer. "You're a hell of a teacher, Mr. Shepherd. You deserve the honor. And I'm not just saying it because you're my friend."

"Thanks, but I've only been teaching a few years. I don't feel like I deserve it yet. You know? It should go to a veteran teacher." Stacey shifted the wine glass from one hand to the other.

"You're one of the most innovative teachers I've seen. We all think you're doing a spectacular job," Brian said. "I wasn't on the committee that made the decision, but I can tell you that age can be a hindrance in these cases. We want young teachers with high energy to travel to Germany and return with fresh ideas to share with our school."

"Thanks. That means a lot to me. I feel honored . . . I do. I work hard for those kids," Stacey said.

"I know you do. Hence, the honor," Brian said, patting Stacey on the back.

"I hope *our* school gets a great teacher from Germany," Stacey said.

"I'm not worried." Brian shrugged. "The teachers that've come to our district in the past have been hard working, dynamic, and great with the kids. I'm expecting the same from this next group. So don't worry; your class will be in good hands. If not, I'll have to throw a little of this weight around." He chuckled as he pinched his waist.

"I still can't believe you get to live in Bavaria with free accommodations and still get your regular salary. What a damn good opportunity," Reece exclaimed.

"It's a sweet deal. That's why I couldn't pass it up. I'll do some traveling and bike in the Alps," Stacey said, letting loose a slight smile and taking a sip of wine. "Speaking of accommodations, I wonder where my apartment will be and what it will look like. I'm hoping it isn't in student housing."

"I've talked to a few people who've done the exchange, and they said that it varied," Brian explained. "They said that they needed to be their own advocate. So, if you don't like the housing, let them know and they'll try to get you a new place to stay. You'll get all the details and your questions answered at the orientation meeting in a few weeks."

"That's good to know because I have a lot of questions," Stacey said. "I'll feel more comfortable about this trip once I talk with the organizers and some of the teachers that have already taught in Germany. That way I'll have a realistic idea of what to expect."

"Is this the reason for the ruffled brow and *Thinking Man* pose?" Reece asked.

"Yeah, I guess I'm just wondering if this trip is what I really want," Stacey admitted. "It's a four-month commitment. That's a long time to be gone. My friends, my job, and the house . . . Why would I want to leave all of this?"

"*Why?*" Reece raised his voice. "Only last week you hoped to get chosen so you *could* get away, gain a new perspective, and have an adventure. Remember?"

"Oh, I remember," Stacey said. "But now that it's a reality, it's hard to believe I'll leave you all behind."

"We'll be fine. Shit, I'll be too busy winning golf tournaments, mountain biking, and dating the ladies to worry about your sorry ass in Germany," Reece teased.

"I'm sure you're right. You're always an example of brotherly love," Stacey said with a quick laugh.

"*Yes*, I am," Reece raised his bottle and drank a mouthful of beer. "When do you have to leave?"

"School begins the second week of September," Stacey answered.

"And you'll be gone for how long?" Reece asked.

"It's supposed to be for the semester, until Christmas. But, I could stay for the entire year if the German teacher wants to stay in California," Stacey replied. "I don't think I could stay longer than a semester, though. I'll miss you guys too much."

Stacey turned to Brian. "Since our mom and dad died, Reece and I haven't been apart for more than a few days."

"The person you'll *really* have to worry about is Sara," Brian warned. "She wasn't too happy when you applied for the position. Now that you've been selected, I wonder how she'll react."

"No need to wonder. I broke up with her today." Stacey swirled the Zin in the glass.

"Whoa. Why didn't you tell me?" Reece asked, suspending his bottle in mid-air before taking a sip.

"I guess I didn't want to ruin the moment," Stacey confessed.

"That's a good thing, Stace. Just the other night you admitted that she wasn't the girl for you,'" Reece said. He raised his bottle. "So, kudos to you."

"Thanks," Stacey said. "Even though she wasn't 'the one', it would've been nice to have a date tonight. No disrespect to you two."

"Stace, you're hardly ever alone. In fact, Reece wishes he could date as many women as you do," Brian teased.

"I *am* jealous," Reece said with a laugh.

"I know I date a lot of women," Stacey confessed. "But Reece, we're in our twenties now. Brian is married, and Jeff is getting engaged. I'm the big brother. I should set a better example. I used to love everything about dating: the chase, the romance, the sex . . . damn, even the breakup. I don't get that same rush anymore. I want to find that one woman that holds my attention. A woman I can build a future with."

"Now you're beginning to sound like Jeff. He's in love with Patty and that's *all* that makes him happy," Reece said.

"Jeff and Patty remind me of Mom and Dad when they were still alive; two people happily in love," Stacey offered.

"You're right, Mom and Dad did have something special and so do Jeff and Patty," Reece replied. "But both Dad and Jeff would give up almost anything for their women. I don't know if you've got that kind of commitment."

"Maybe you're right. Maybe I don't. Or, maybe, I just haven't found the right woman," Stacey said.

"You wish you were still dating Patty," Brian joked. "Luckily, my sister has good taste in men. That's why she's dating Jeff."

"I'll drink to that," Reece said. They all clinked their glasses and bottles together again.

"I did get a sense of love when I dated your sister in high school. But, that was a long time ago," Stacey said gloomily. "Now, love feels like this fog. It slinks in from some hidden place and silently overtakes me. It seems so dense, but when I reach into it, there's nothing of substance. Then, before too long, it simply vanishes. That's my perception of love."

"So you've fallen in love before, but you couldn't sustain it?" Brian asked.

"Yeah, that's exactly it. The excitement of a new relationship slowly fades. I swear boredom stalks me, and eventually, I'm overcome," Stacey replied.

"You're right. Love is an illusion," Brian said. "We trust that love is a real entity. That's the story we tell ourselves. But, we never *really* know what the other person truly feels. My advice? Make sure you keep making new memories so that the intensity builds beyond the initial crush. Find someone who will be honest about their feelings. It adds intimacy. I found that with Beth."

"I know how it works. It just hasn't happened yet." Stacey felt the familiar knot of frustration in his stomach.

"Can we continue this profound conversation later?" Reece asked. "I'd like to hook up with some women tonight."

"Sure. Let's make one last appearance before we leave," Stacey said.

"Where are you goin' after this?" Brian finished his drink and placed it on an outside table.

"We're gonna meet up with Jeff and Patty at our house. Then, we're all goin' out to the bar. Wanna come?" Reece asked.

"Nah, I have to lay this party to rest. Maybe another time," Brian said. "I promised Beth I'd come straight home. Say hi to Patty for me."

"Sure," Reece said, gulping down the rest of his beer. "Now, let's go back into that party, find my brother a wife, and a woman for me."

Reece put his arm around Stacey, and the three of them went back inside the restaurant, leaving the fog to loiter on the patio.

Stacey felt relieved that he had given words to his thoughts and feelings, and they were now out of his head and into the world. They launched like bubbles into the air, floating up through the enigmatic universe, preparing to burst open, and releasing the wishes to a listening ear. What a miracle if his parents or a higher power heard him.

* * *

LATER THAT EVENING, Stacey and Reece drove home in the convertible. The cool wind pushed streams of fog past them at a furious pace, obscuring their view of the stars. The chill didn't keep them from driving with the top down. Heater cranked high and music down low, they cruised in comfort.

As they neared a four-way stop, a roar came from the left. A startled Stacey and Reece whirled around in the direction of the sound. The halo of two bright lights sped toward the crossroads. Stacey slammed to a stop just as the other car screeched through the intersection. As if flying on tornado winds, the careening car zoomed by; its tail lights disappearing into the fog.

The brothers turned to each other and shook their heads in dismay.

"Shit," Reece said. "That was fuckin' close."

"What are people thinking, driving like that in this weather?" Stacey didn't bother to hide his irritation. He released the brake pedal and slowly moved through the intersection.

As they continued home, the fog seemed to magically drift upward, like a lace curtain lifting on a waft of air.

As they rounded a corner, the fog inexplicably faded around a billboard with the words ADVENTURES IN EUROPE printed across the top. Pictures of magnificent locations in Europe glowed under the yellow spotlights. Four squares depicted people hiking, skiing, biking, and hang gliding in the Alps. The image of mountain bikers riding on a lush, single-track trail caused an unexpected surge in Stacey's adrenaline. Across the bottom, a directive insisted that Stacey needed to call or email HS Travel for more information.

Stacey fell into a fantasy of traveling to Europe and biking the Alps with his brother and friends.

Lost in the ad, Stacey slowed to a crawl.

"Hey, Stace," Reece said, shaking Stacey's shoulder. "You're in the middle of the street, dude."

"Shit." Stacey pulled out of his trance and pressed on the gas pedal. He turned to Reece and said, "Have I got a proposal for you and Jeff."

CHAPTER 2

Less elusive is life's meaning;
Happiness for yourself and others

"There is a tide in the affairs of men, which, taken at the flood, leads on to fortune; Omitted, all the voyage of their life is bound in shallows and in miseries."

— William Shakespeare, *Julius Caesar*

STACEY TURNED onto their street, passed Jeff's parked car, and pulled into the driveway. Jeff was a best friend to both Stacey and Reece. Frequent visitors to the Shepherd household, Jeff and Patty knew to let themselves into the house with a key hidden in the garage. Stacey's exhilaration mounted as he jumped out of the car, hopped up the steps, and opened the door.

After the death of their parents in a car accident, Stacey and Reece became co-owners of their childhood home. Although only in high school at the time, the brothers managed the house and kept up with their grades.

At this point, the house was a perfect metaphor for where Stacey and Reece were at in their lives. Both brothers were in their mid-twenties. Reece still had a carefree teenager's view of life. Stacey, on the other hand, was more sophisticated than most men his age. The house reflected these two differences in lifestyle.

Decorated to convey elegance, the living room was furnished with matching couches and chairs, paintings of the Italian countryside, and replicas of *Cupid and Psyche* and *Apollo and Daphne*. Stacey had kept most of his parents' decorations in place to maintain a sense of maturity in the house.

The décor in the kitchen and attached family room, however, showed a different side. Reece's dirty dishes lay on counter tops and piled in the sink. The windowsill held a collection of assorted beer bottles. Framed posters of sports stars and pennants of their favorite teams hung on the walls. Sports trophies lined the mantle above the fireplace. A video game system lay on the floor with wires and controllers strewn about. These two rooms represented the threads that tied them to their days of youth.

Stacey burst into the kitchen, with Reece close behind. Patty sat on a barstool at the counter sketching on a discarded envelope, while Jeff mixed her a drink in the blender. Patty, a slender brunette, radiated girl-next-door good looks with her yellow sundress, white cardigan sweater, ponytail, and freckles that sprinkled across her nose and onto her cheeks.

Jeff had a tuft of curly, brown hair that gave him an inch of height, though still a few inches shorter than Stacey. His smile brought out his dimples, a contrast to his sleepy eyes. His tight, short sleeve shirt showed off his lean, muscular body.

"Wait until you hear my idea," Stacey blurted.

"Whoa, Stace. Slow down," Jeff said with a laugh.

"How was the party?" Patty interjected.

"It was . . . Great. They chose me to go to Germany for the teacher exchange program," Stacey replied. "But—"

"That's awesome news," Patty interrupted, clapping her hands. "Now we *really* have a reason to celebrate tonight."

"Congratulations. You've been hoping you'd get this opportunity, and BOOM, here it is," Jeff said, giving Stacey a friendly hug. "I can't believe you're going to teach in Germany. Are you stoked, man?"

"I was shocked and pretty damn nervous when they called my name. I didn't think they were going to choose me," Stacey said. "But now that I've had a glass of wine and time to adjust to the idea of going to Germany, yeah, I'm excited."

"When do you leave?" Jeff asked.

"Two months," Stacey replied. "I have a couple of orientation meetings scheduled. Directors and teachers who've formerly been exchange teachers will be there to answer questions. The first one is this Monday. I'm supposed to get a shitload of paperwork to sign and packets to read about the schools, my teaching assignment, my housing, and the customs in Germany."

Glancing at the blender, Reece asked Jeff, "Hey, is there enough left for Stacey and me to get a glass?"

"Sure, I'll pour you a tall one," Jeff replied, reaching into the cupboard for a couple glasses.

"What about the language?" Patty asked. "You don't know anything about German. You barely know English."

Patty threw a wadded piece of paper at him.

"That's not exactly true. My grandmother spoke German with us. I still remember a number of words," Stacey explained, tossing the wadded paper back at Patty. "Plus, we're required to take an online course, probably something like Rosetta Stone. During the first orientation meeting, they help us register for the course. I'm sure I'll be a master after that."

"Will you be teaching in German?" Patty asked.

"No, or else I wouldn't have taken this job," Stacey said, chuckling. "I'm going to teach literature and math to primary students in English. The nine and ten year olds should already be fairly fluent in English."

"What does Sara think about this?" Jeff asked, pouring the margarita into the glasses.

"Um . . . We broke up today," Stacey said, his adventurous idea now interrupted.

"Oh, I'm sorry," Patty said.

"We're officially done," Stacey said.

"Sounds like you could use a drink," Jeff said. He handed drinks to Stacey and Reece. "What happened between you two?"

"Oh, same as usual," Stacey said. He took a sip and gave Jeff a nod of approval. "I date these girls for a while and then get bored. Luckily, Sara made it easy. God. Was she high maintenance, or what?"

"Even we could see that," Patty added.

"Enough about that," Stacey said, happy to change the subject. "Do you guys remember when we biked in the Cascades a couple of summers ago, and we stopped at that rest area about half way up our climb to the summit?"

"Yeah," Reece and Jeff said in unison.

"Those quotes motivated me to keep pushing myself," Reece said.

"Exactly," Stacey exclaimed. His excitement began to mount. He reached into his back pocket, pulled out his wallet, and took out a piece of paper. "I want to read this quote I saved from that ride. James Hill said, 'Most men who have really lived have had, in some share, their great adventure.' Guys, it's time for ours."

"You kept that all this time?" Jeff asked, surprised.

"Yeah, I did. It felt important. And then tonight, as we drove home, there was this serendipitous break in the fog that revealed a billboard, and, I swear, the message seemed specifically aimed at me," Stacey said. His enthusiasm caused his words to run into each other. After a suspenseful pause, he continued, "Listen guys, I'm going to teach abroad because I need an adventure. *You* need an adventure, too. What do you say to a few weeks of sightseeing and mountain biking in the Alps, before my school starts? We could take our bikes or rent them there. France, Italy, Germany? Shit, it's the holy land of mountain biking."

"You're kidding, right?" Reece asked, chuckling. He glanced at Stacey, who couldn't have looked more sincere if he tried.

"No. It'd be a blast," Stacey said. "You guys always talk about going to Europe, right? Here's our chance. It's meant to be. Let's do it."

"Stace, that's *crazy*," Jeff commented. "We can't just go to Europe. We need passports. Plus, who has the time off?"

"You forget, bro, that you're the only slacker that gets umpteen weeks of vacation," Reece added.

"Reece, come on," Stacey pleaded. "You have fewer responsibilities than me. You play golf for a living, for god's sake. You've got twenty reliable clients per week. Reschedule those golf lessons for another time. The only other thing you do is practice, and you play in a dozen tournaments a year. None that I know of are coming up in the near future. You had more responsibilities in college. So, you can't use that excuse. I know you can get time off from work."

"Maybe," Reece said, looking perplexed. "You're wrong about the tournaments, though. Remember, you're caddying for me in the PGA qualifying tournament at the end of July. When I win that, I take my first tee on the PGA tour at Silverado Resort in Napa in early September."

"How could I forget? My brother's debut into golf's storied PGA tour," Stacey said, giving Reece a high-five.

"Nonetheless, I'll look into getting time off," Reece said.

"Yes, you will," Stacey stated. He turned to Jeff and Patty. "Jeff, buddy, I know you have a gazillion hours of vacation and sick time accrued. Didn't you say that your bosses were pushing you to take your vacation time instead of cashing it in at the end of the year? I'm sure you can go if you *really* wanted to. What about you, Patty? Wouldn't you love to go to Europe?"

"Yeah, you know I would, especially for the art. I . . ." Patty hesitated. She put down her drink. "I don't know if the timing is right, though, and I don't know about going with you guys on a mountain biking trip. No offense."

"Come on, guys," Stacey pleaded. "Think of it. A real adventure. Mountain biking in the Alps. I mean, *imagine* being able to say that we've biked in the Alps. That'd be so cool, right? And while we're biking, Patty could go hiking or check out the art at some of the museums. Then, we could go to the major cities and hang out. We could see Paris, Munich, and maybe Rome. We'd be like the group of friends in that Hemingway novel."

"If you recall, they were all mysteriously wealthy with no jobs," Jeff replied, pulling out a chair from the table and sitting down. "I don't know, Stace. How much would something like that cost?"

"I'm not sure," Stacey answered. "It'll probably be around fifteen hundred for a plane ticket, and another hundred a night for twenty nights. That's about four thousand dollars. Rail tickets would probably be another thousand. Food, bikes, and miscellaneous might cost a thousand more. So, what is that, about six or seven grand a piece, or so?"

"Shit, that's a lot of fuckin' money for the same kinds of mountains we have in the U.S.," Reece said, his eagerness waning. He hoisted himself up to sit on the kitchen counter. "For that kind of money, we could ride all over the Sierras, the Rockies, and even go to Alaska."

"We can go to those places anytime we want. I'm talking about a once in a lifetime trip," Stacey said as he paced across the kitchen. "We're not going to have this opportunity much longer. Soon, we won't be in as good as shape as we are now, and Jeff and Patty will be married . . . if Jeff ever proposes."

"Yeah, right," Patty muttered with attitude.

"Damn, Stace. Why'd you have to bring that up?" Jeff fumed.

"You two will be married with kids in a few years. Who knows where everybody will be living? This is the right time, regardless of the money," Stacey argued.

"I don't know, Stace. Six or seven grand a piece? Damn, that's a good percentage of our savings. Mucho dinero." Jeff took a swig of his margarita.

Stacey stopped pacing midway across the kitchen. "I know it's a lot of money, although Reece and I could use some of our inheritance. If you need some assistance, we could help out," Stacey offered.

"Why does it have to be now? I know it's convenient for you because you'll already be there. But, for the rest of us, it's a little impractical. Why not wait until next summer?" Patty suggested, looking up from her sketch of flowers. She slid the envelope away and asked, "Do you guys have any real paper that I could sketch on?"

Reece walked to his room and returned with a few pieces of computer paper. Patty took the paper and resumed drawing.

"Listen, it's probably the only time we'll all be able to have an adventure like this. Like I said, it's meant to be," Stacey said. He took a drink of the margarita and then stared out the window as if looking into the future.

"Plus, our ten-year high school reunion is in a couple of years," Stacey continued. "I've been thinking a lot about the fact that I'm behind in my timeline of success. I haven't done what I'd hoped when we graduated.

"I mean, I earned a finance degree from college. I thought I'd be making a shit load of money by now and be the envy of everyone from our graduating class. Who knew I wouldn't like the business world?

"So here I am in a teaching job that I love, but sure as hell can't buy me a lavish lifestyle. The realization has slowly sunk in that life isn't going to be as glamorous as I had once hoped. I have a regular job. I'm not going to be on the cover of any magazine. I have no idea how to judge if my life is a success."

He plopped down in a kitchen chair.

"Stace, who are you comparing yourself to? We're all trying to get by the best we can," Jeff said.

"I'm comparing myself to what I think I should be," Stacey said. "I've been thinking quite a bit about what we've done since high school. At our reunion, everyone will have the same stories about college, work, family, and vacations they've taken. I want a story that'll set us apart. I want to have a *real* adventure that people will envy and admire. *And*, I want my brother and best friends to come with me."

"An adventure is nothing but a story, Stace," Patty argued. She had drawn a field of flowers and was shading the grass. "After the adventure ends, it's nothing but a memory; a shadow of a life you lived. People will envy you for the time it takes you to tell the story. But after that, what then? I think people admire you more for becoming a teacher. I really do."

"That might be true, but an exciting adventure on the side doesn't hurt," Stacey replied. "My whole existence is work and hanging out with you guys. I need more. I want an experience that will make me feel alive. I want to compete against nature. I want to compete against myself."

"I think we all understand that. But your time for an adventure might not be the right time for us," Patty declared.

"I get that," Stacey said. "But, we need to do something to force our destiny. If the time we spend on this adventure just blends into our life, then we won't notice that the timing is wrong or right."

"Well, we've always talked about following in Mom and Dad's footsteps through Europe," Reece commented. He opened the cabinet and pulled out a bag of tortilla chips. He poured some chips in a bowl and placed it on the kitchen table.

"That's right," Stacey agreed, reaching for a handful of chips. "They always said life is about learning new things, seeing new places, and meeting new people. This is our chance. After sightseeing during the day, we could party at night with the Swiss, or Germans, or whomever."

"Damn." Reece exclaimed. His face lit up. "That could be awesome. I could take my guitar and play at the hostels. Think of the European women we'd meet. Okay, I'm in."

Stacey turned his attention toward Jeff and Patty. He took a big gulp of the margarita and said, "Okay, Reece is in. How about you two? Jeff, you could bring your new high-powered camera that cost as much money as this trip."

They all chuckled over Stacey's comment.

Stacey played the room like a nightclub act. He knew in his heart that he had no choice. There was a reason that the dense fog had curiously lifted at the very moment he approached that billboard. His brother and friends were destined to go with him, so he tried his best to charm them into saying yes.

"Jeff, you'd get spectacular pictures of the Alps and think of the shots of cities like Paris and Rome," Stacey said.

"I have always wanted to take pictures while riding the Portes du Soliel in the French Alps and then try to get them published in *Mountain Biking* magazine," Jeff said.

"Patty, is there a better place to study art than in Europe?" Stacey asked. She nodded while doodling. "Your life here blends perfectly with this trip. Imagine all the history and inspiration you can dig up in the museums; paintings in the Louvre, the Prado, and maybe the Uffizi in Florence. Bring your sketchpad and draw the masterpieces in person. Plus, you could hike in all the gorgeous landscapes in Europe. What do you guys say?"

Patty stopped sketching, put down her pencil, and turned to face Jeff. "I ca—"

"Yes. We'll go," Jeff interrupted. "I'd love to see the Alps. I'm sure the mountain biking is unbelievable. Remember that guy who rode through Berchtesgaden in Germany. He said it was the best riding he'd ever done. I bet I could get some great pictures from the trails. Plus, this will be Patty's graduation present. You know we've been saving for a vacation. She'll simply get it early."

"Jeff, wait," Patty said, sternly. She put both hands on Jeff's legs. "I don't know if I can go. Remember, I'm taking my last two classes, and my big art project is due at the end of the semester, so it all depends on when you guys plan to go."

"Shit. I forgot all about that," Jeff said.

"When do you start school?" Stacey asked, looking concerned.

"I start at the end of August. The only time I could go would be after I finish classes in early December," Patty said.

"Sorry, Patty. If we went at Christmas, we couldn't mountain bike because of the weather," Stacey said.

"And *I* can't go in August because I'll be in class. I'm sorry, but I'm out," Patty apologized. She shrugged and shook her head. She made eye contact with all of them and continued. "You guys know how much I want to get my masters. I don't want to have to wait until spring semester to take the classes."

"Come on, Patty. Can't you be a little late for classes?" Jeff pleaded.

"Jeff, I *can't* go," Patty insisted. She straightened her posture and stared intensely at Jeff.

Jeff could read her eyes but blindly continued. "Listen, you could probably take a couple of weeks off. That'll be about three or four actual classes. I'm sure you wouldn't miss much in a couple of weeks. Then, you'll be back in time for midterms and finals."

"I *can't* go. Shit. If you want to go that much, then go!" Patty said, sharply. She waved her hands in frustration.

"Fuck. I guess I'm *not* going," Jeff said, aggravated. He paused a moment and then said in a soothing voice to Patty, "You know I can't go without you."

"I'm sorry, Jeff. I just can't," Patty maintained. "I can't miss these two classes. I'm so close to graduating. I want more than anything to graduate on time."

"It's okay. You two can go with us next time," Stacey offered.

"Yeah, you and Jeff won't be missing anything except watchin' me do my thing with the ladies," Reece joked.

"I don't know about that, Reece," Patty replied with a smile. "Thanks anyway for trying to smooth it over. I really would like to go, but the timing isn't right."

Stacey knew how much her education meant to her. She had worked two jobs for one year after they all graduated high school so she could afford college. Then, she had to postpone college to take care of her mother during cancer treatments. Stacey suddenly felt guilty for putting her in this situation.

There was an uncomfortable silence. Stacey guessed everyone was considering all that had recently transpired. Stacey, Reece, and Jeff drank their margaritas, looking aimlessly around the room. Patty returned to her sketch.

After some time, Patty put down her pencil and broke the silence. "Let's go to the bar now. Okay? I told Heather that we'd meet her there by 9:00," Patty said. She glanced at her watch. "Damn, it's almost 9:00 now. You guys can talk about the trip later."

"That sounds good, except I want to check out some things about Europe online. Reece?" Stacey asked.

"Yeah, I'll stay to help," Reece said.

"We'll catch up with you guys in a while," Stacey added.

"Okay. We'll see you later, then," Patty said. She and Jeff stood up and placed their glasses near the sink. "Have fun dreaming about Europe."

"Yeah, see you later," Jeff said,

"All right, see you guys in a while, but remember to keep thinking about the trip. I'm going to keep after you," Stacey teased. He stood up from the chair and shook hands with Jeff. "Maybe you'll think of an idea so you both can come."

Jeff shrugged his shoulders, took Patty's hand, and they walked out the door.

After Jeff and Patty left, Stacey turned to Reece. "Hey, Reece, let's toast to our adventure."

"Okay, we'll drink to following our passions." Reece dropped down from the counter.

"I'll drink to that," Stacey said. He picked up the pitcher and poured the rest of the margarita into their glasses. He placed his other arm around Reece. "This is to our adventure. To following our passions."

"We'll ride our bikes, explore the land, and score with the women," Reece stated with a laugh. They clinked glasses and took a sip. "What do you think will be your favorite place to visit?"

Stacey paused before answering. "I don't know, maybe the hills of France where they do the Tour de France or the Alps of Germany."

"Great mountain biking spots, I'm sure," Reece agreed.

"Remember when Dad made us read *Candide* that one summer before we traveled across the U.S.?" Stacey asked.

"Yeah, he was always into that French philosophy shit," Reece said.

"Like Candide, we'll probably travel all over the place and realize our favorite place is right here in California," Stacey said with a chuckle.

"You're probably right. Nothing beats the rides here and in the Sierras," Reece agreed.

"That's what we're about to find out," Stacey said. They finished the last of the margaritas.

"I've got a great idea," Reece announced, cracking a smile. "How about we go for a night ride up into Annadel? It'll kick off our adventure. We'll ride up to the lake and back; something quick."

"What about meeting up with Jeff and Patty? We're supposed to be at the bar soon," Stacey asked.

"I'm way too jacked to sit at a bar," Reece explained. "Leave a message on Jeff's cell. Tell him you're too tired. They're meeting other people down there, anyway. We'll go out with them another night."

"Okay, I'm in. Mountain biking is better than drinking in a bar any day," Stacey commented.

Stacey texted Jeff, *Reece and I won't be able to meet you. Have fun without us.*

Jeff wrote back, *No big deal. Heather and Paul are trying to convince Patty to go to Europe. :)*

Maybe they'll go after all, Stacey thought.

After changing their clothes, Stacey and Reece pumped up their bike tires, oiled their chains, and checked their brakes. They put on biking shoes, helmets, and headlights, and walked their bikes out the side door of the garage. With a nod, Stacey and Reece climbed on their bikes and rode off into the fog.

CHAPTER 3

Happiness comes from
Freedom to follow passions,
Ambition to start

"Swift things are beautiful: Swallows and deer,
And lightning that falls bright veined and clear . . .
And slow things are beautiful: The closing of day,
The pause of the wave that curves downward to spray."
— Elizabeth Coatsworth, "Swift Things are Beautiful"

T HE FOG EMBRACED Stacey and Reece, dampening their faces and clothing. The wind chilled their skin. They rapidly pedaled on the flat streets. Their speed increased and lights streaked. Cars zoomed by. Houses and buildings blurred. Tires skimmed and hummed over the asphalt. They were on a mission. The faster they rode, the quicker they'd arrive at their destination. They pushed their legs. They guided themselves with their arms. Their eyes focused five feet ahead. Their peripheral vision circled ten feet around them. They were in the moment. Silence enveloped them as if in a vacuum. They experienced every second that time held them captive.

I love riding: the excitement, the freedom, the adventure, the exercise, and the wind. I love it all, Stacey thought. This is when I feel the most alive. Each ride brings new possibilities, new decisions, and new trails to take.

Stacey and Reece entered Annadel State Park, slowing their speed considerably. They transitioned from the pavement of the streets to the loose dirt of the trails. The topography became flat and curvy. The two riders changed their cycling tempo from street quickness to trail durability. On the street, their legs held a steady, fluid rhythm. On the dirt, their legs moved in a constant start-stop motion.

They rode along on a smooth stretch of trail until they ran into a rocky, rutted patch of ground and had to change their pattern of cycling. Mountain biking on the trails fluctuated between riding in a smooth, rhythmic cadence and an erratic, lurching action.

Stacey and Reece began their steep climb on the Canyon Trail to the lake. Stacey always used his meditative practice to reach the top of the mountains quicker than his riding companions and without any sense of pain or loss of breath. His secret was to concentrate on counting his breaths from one to one hundred, repeatedly. It kept his breathing at a steady rate, allowing the rest of his body to function properly on those difficult climbs. A consistent, stable breath regulated the thoughts, pain, anxiety, and adrenaline of Stacey's body. This practice allowed his soul the freedom it so hungrily sought.

He kept his focus on the light ahead of him, pedaling slowly and methodically. His eyes sought out the path of least resistance from rocks and ravines. Reece was somewhere behind him, but Stacey wouldn't have known it. Only Stacey, his bike, the trail, and the fog existed in this moment.

After the strenuous uphill climb, Stacey and Reece reached the top. They teetered on this tipping point between a vigorous climb and a fun downhill.

I am on the precipice in which the opposite action is about to occur, Stacey thought. Nothing in the world sustains the same action forever.

Several deep breaths later, Stacey and Reece pushed off and started down the hill. The trail leveled off and meandered down a short distance to a darkened lake. Stacey couldn't see the water of the lake, only fog and blackness.

They rode in complete solitude around the edge of the lake until they spotted the trail that led back down to the park's entrance. They stopped, sucked down sips of water, ate a fruit bar, buckled their helmets, and sprang forward on their bikes.

"Be safe, Reece," Stacey called out behind him. He received only a grunt in acknowledgment. Stacey and Reece picked up speed. The terrain became steep and rocky. The air rushed by. Their eyes watered. Their faces were wet with dew. They jostled. They braked. They flew. The light from their headlamps flickered. They saw only 20 feet ahead. In a second that twenty feet had vanished. Rocks and ravines whizzed beneath. The trail came out of nowhere. It disappeared just as quickly. They steered and leaned. They braked again. Gravity accelerated them. They could feel it in their gut. As their speed increased, the rush of adrenaline consumed them.

Focus, he thought to himself. One mishap and wham.

After five minutes, the steepness of the trail lessened. The path became less rocky. From a mountain biker's perspective, it seemed smooth. Stacey and Reece gave in to the power of gravity. They took their fingers off the brake levers allowing their bikes to zoom down the hill unimpeded by any obstacles in their path. The two brothers had time to plan their path. This portion of their ride developed into a tranquil drive through the countryside. They balanced on a razor's edge over a slick surface. They leaned carefully, their two wheels spraying dirt off to the side. They took off through the air on jumps, turning their bikes in mid-flight. They were art in motion.

Finally, the trail leveled off. As they passed the entry gates, Stacey and Reece gave each other high-fives and then continued their ride home through the thick, dewy fog.

* * *

DURING THE NEXT TWO MONTHS, Stacey's life ebbed and flowed like a mountain bike ride as he prepared for his adventures in Europe. In the beginning, he achieved his tasks quickly. Taking an online course, Stacey began brushing up on his German. He attended orientation meetings, studying the German society and their education system. He searched his classroom and packed teaching materials. He got his passport, picked his hotel arrangements, and bought rail tickets. He created an itinerary and packed his travel gear.

Stacey spent hours online and on the phone contacting the teacher exchange coordinator, housing coordinator, European hotels, agencies, and bike stores. He went to the library and bookstores looking for info about Europe and the Alps. All of this preparation made him giddy. He craved the taste of freedom that travel brings. As he planned, his excitement reminded him of the eagerness he felt as a child when his parents were arranging a family trip.

. Meanwhile, Reece, Jeff, and Patty were busy, too. Reece played a lot of golf practicing for his upcoming tournament. Jeff and Patty were still contemplating joining Stacey and Reece on the trip. Patty left messages with her master's advisor and the university about taking a leave of absence. Jeff requested the vacation days from his work, just in case.

In the middle, the pace of preparation for Stacey's trip slowed. There weren't as many items on his to-do list anymore. Time seemed to drag. Consequently, he hung out with his brother and friends to keep him busy.

Caddying in Reece's first PGA qualifying golf tournament, Stacey helped Reece train for the event and then capture a fourth place finish. Watching and assisting Reece in hours of intense training, Stacey felt proud of his brother's performance. Reece, though, was extremely disappointed because, by not placing in the top three, he missed earning a spot in the next qualifying tournament called 'Qualifier

Monday' and a shot to play in the real PGA Tour, alongside the likes of Jordan Spieth and Phil Mickelson.

The big news was that Jeff and Patty decided to go on the trip. After a week of long discussions with her master's thesis advisor and university official, Patty received a reprieve from attending the first couple weeks of classes. Instead of the classes, she would have to keep a journal of the art she saw in Europe, and she'd have to work on a paper and her portfolio. She also was advised to check the availability of her classes online every day of her trip. If the classes were close to being full, she'd have to fly home to secure her spot in the class.

In the final weeks leading up to the trip, Stacey became overwhelmed. He mailed seven boxes of his teaching materials and personal items to the address of the program coordinator in Germany. Researching online, he devoured information about German history, culture, educational curriculum, and philosophies. It seemed like a frantic time, but also exhilarating. He couldn't wait to see what adventures awaited him in Europe.

CHAPTER 4

A smile, like the poet's muse,
Inspires passion in the lover's heart

"Love, she thought, must come suddenly, with great outbursts and lightning, - a hurricane of the skies, which falls upon life, revolutions it, roots up the will like a leaf, and sweeps the whole heart into the abyss."

— Gustave Flaubert, *Madame Bovary*

WAITING ONBOARD A TRAIN in Zurich, Switzerland, Stacey prepared himself for the train's early morning departure. After stuffing his backpack onto the overhead shelf, he fell limply into one of the six unoccupied chairs. Peering out the window, he hoped to see the Zurichsee. Encountering only darkness, Stacey tried to envision the foothills of the Alps sprawled around the aqua-blue water of the lake. He could picture the trails that meandered and plunged their way down the edge of the mountains.

After his eyes adjusted to the lack of light, a grayish mist came into view. Wispier than the fog in California, the vapor rising over the lake appeared to Stacey like a spider web dancing on the breeze. The fog reminded him of how far away from home he had traveled. Pondering the vastness of the world, he suddenly felt melancholy. He forced himself to think about other things. His mind wandered through images of his first week in Europe.

* * *

THEY HAD ARRIVED in Paris and spent a few days exploring the city. The Cathedral de Notre Dame and the Basilique de Sacre Coeure were some of Stacey's favorite sights, but nothing compared to the Louvre. Its Baroque architecture stood alone as a massive piece of art in its own right.

Mandated by Patty, their first bike ride had taken them through the Loire Valley. Thinking the ride wouldn't be challenging because the roads were mostly flat, Stacey had initially opposed it. After the ride, however, he couldn't stop fantasizing about the castles they'd toured along the way.

Once in Blois, they had rented bikes that came accessorized with touring racks on the sides and back. They put their belongings in the storage compartments on their bikes, leaving items they didn't need in a locker at the bike shop.

Each day of the ride, they toured picturesque, stone castles, such as Chateau de Cheverny, Chambord, and Chenonceau. The chateaus shared similar architectural styles—their white, Tuffeau stone walls, turrets, and roof windows. But they differed in their interior design and outside gardens.

They walked through, noting the grandiose styles of some chateaus. Furnished from floor to ceiling with paintings, sculptures, clocks, and gold plated mirrors, they exuded wealth. Other chateaus were decorated in a more modest, medieval style. Tapestries hung from stone walls, and large, wooden furniture pieces sat like wallflowers in cavernous rooms. They strolled through opulent gardens of expansive lawns, perfectly manicured hedges, and vibrant fountains. They toasted their glasses of wine at illustrious vineyards. All the while, they leisurely pedaled along some of the most scenic roads in the world.

Stacey recalled their first mountain bike ride in France. After leaving the Loire Valley, they'd taken a train to Chamonix in the heart of the French Alps. They rented mountain bikes and spent a couple of days exploring the parks. The terrain, under the looming presence of Mt. Blanc, was incredible. Exhilarating jumps, quick berms and switchbacks, and dangerous drops pervaded the trails.

Finally, and most recently, they'd traveled to Switzerland. They strolled through Zurich with its fabled blue waters of the Limmat River and the Zurichsee.

One of Stacey's most enchanted walks began from their hotel near the University. He walked down to the Grossmunster Church with its iconic, dual towers and imagined the historic leader, Charlemagne, riding his horse nearby. Following the Limmat to a walking bridge, he watched the water spill into the Zurichsee. He then wandered along the lake path to the Burkliplatz Park. As he tasted samples of fondue foods at restaurants near the park, he watched the swans and sailboats meander around the river. He ended the walk by window shopping his way through the Bahnhofstrasse, a street housing some of the trendiest and expensive stores in the world, such as Cartier and Tiffany.

Nevertheless, Stacey felt disappointed in Zurich. They'd spent two days riding in hills that looked similar to the rolling hills of Northern California. The trails weren't as challenging or scenic as he had hoped. He looked forward to getting to Salzburg and the Bavarian Alps. The ride along the steep, granite cliffs and lush, evergreen forests were sure to be challenging and the views spectacular.

* * *

THE SUN'S MORNING LIGHT STREAKED across the eastern sky gliding into the train compartment where Stacey sat. A ray of light flickered upon his face, lifting him out of his reminiscence of the first half of their adventure in Europe. The sunlight grew brighter as it radiated off of a thick layer of ruffled clouds set low in the Zurich sky. As it climbed out of its glorious dawn robes of pink, yellow, and blue light, the sun instantly reminded Stacey of surfing at sunset. The red glow of the sun disappearing into the horizon would turn the ocean's white-water into a coral froth.

This is beautiful, Stacey thought. I wonder if it means anything that I'm here witnessing such an incredible sight. To see something this stunning is a gift.

Suddenly, Reece popped his head through the compartment door. "Stace, what are you still doing in here? I thought we were meeting in the dining car?"

"I wanted to rest for a bit. Someone had to save our seats in this compartment," Stacey answered.

"I don't know why you're so tired. We kicked those girls out at 9:00, and you were asleep by 10:00," Reece said.

"You knew I didn't want to hang out with them all night. They weren't exactly the type of girls I'd go out with, anyway," Stacey said.

"Dude, you should've been honest about it and told me last night. I could've gone to their place or something," Reece said, dispersing the residual frustration from the night before.

"Fuck that," Stacey called out, quickly. "I would have gladly let you try your magic act with those girls if it had been earlier in the evening. But I wasn't about to give up my last remaining hours of sleep so you could have your way with some Swiss girls."

"Okay. Okay," Reece said. He chuckled and his eyes twinkled. "I'm only saying that you could have helped out your little brother."

"Sorry," Stacey offered. "I didn't even want to take those girls home last night. We have a big day today; you know? And, I wanted to get some sleep so that I'd be ready to ride that gnarly Austrian Deadly Downhill."

"Yeah I know. Oh man, that's going to be awesome. I can't wait." Reece gripped his hands around imaginary handlebars and pretended to steer a bike up, down, and around trails.

"Anyway, there's more where that came from," Stacey said. "Tonight I'll get you four girls. Okay?"

"That's why I love you, man," Reece said. They gave each other a high five. "I'm sure those girls are *so* disappointed. They wanted me for a couple more days."

"I'm sure they did," Stacey said, grinning.

"Didn't you think those girls were hot, though?" Reece asked.

"Yeah, they were pretty," Stacey replied. "But, like I told you, I'm not interested in hooking up with women on this trip. I'll leave that to you. Plus, we're leaving today."

"Well, it meant something to me," Reece stated. "Fast and furious, Stace. It brings a thrill to my world. I mean, you never know where these things will lead you. You look the other way, and poof, a great opportunity vanishes. That's what I think."

"Good philosophy," Stacey said. "By the way, why'd you have to lie to them with those ridiculous stories?"

"I don't know. I guess it makes me look better in their eyes and it can't hurt anyone if they think I'm richer than I am," Reece replied.

"But you don't need to say those things. You're a great guy regardless of whether you can afford a sports car or not," Stacey said.

"Hey, bro, you were the one who wanted to come on this trip so you could impress people at your high school reunion," Reece countered.

"I'm making an impression on them with things I've *actually done*. Besides, I'm trying to amaze myself more than anyone else. Whereas, *you* are lying," Stacey argued. "You don't always need to be this whirlwind of a guy who leaves girls awestruck for a few moments and then disappears into thin air. Mom and Dad didn't raise you that way and neither did I."

"Well, fuck you, too," Reece snapped back. "I'm only having fun. That's what those girls were doing, too. I'm not hurting anyone's feelings. They knew we were only here for a night. I'm enjoying myself. That's more than I can say for you. And don't ever mention Mom and Dad like that again. They would be proud of who I am."

"I know. I'm sorry. I shouldn't have said that," Stacey apologized. "They *would* be proud of you. I am, too. Sometimes I think that since you are family I can tell you anything on my mind, whether it's good or hurtful. Sorry."

"I accept your apology. Just don't say that again," Reece warned. A feeling of satisfaction swept over him.

"This traveling thing is a relationship oven. The meaning of every statement or gesture is intensified by the stress of traveling in a foreign place," Stacey said. "I guess I've always admired you for being so casual and lighthearted with women while I'm the one who overanalyzes."

"Thanks, I guess," Reece said.

Looking into the hallway, Reece spotted Jeff and Patty walking toward the compartment. They were hunched over with the weight of their packs slung over their backs. "Speaking of ovens, here comes the couple who is way overdone."

Looking haggard, Jeff and Patty entered the compartment.

"Well, well, well. If it isn't the two lovebirds of Europe," Reece teased.

"How was the hostel? Did it get any better from the first night?" Stacey asked.

"You know what? Those guys were rude the whole time," Jeff replied, shaking his head and struggling to take off his backpack. "They wouldn't move us to a new room, they wouldn't give us directions to anywhere, and they wouldn't answer any of our questions."

"The walls were so thin, they seemed separated by paper. You could hear everything. Plus, the bathrooms we had to share were disgusting. I couldn't wait to leave," Patty said with a disgruntled look upon her face. "So, how was the hotel?"

"It was nice. It's much better than a hostel, let me tell you," Stacey replied.

"Was it cheaper?" Patty asked.

"Yeah, this one only cost 75 Euros," Stacey said.

"And, we had our own bathroom and a TV in the room," Reece added.

"I don't know why people say that hostels are the cheapest places to stay in Europe," Stacey commented.

Patty turned abruptly towards Jeff and said, "See, I told you we should have gone with them to a hotel. But, no, *you* wanted to check out the hostel first."

"You could have told me that you wanted to stay in a hotel and we would have gone," Jeff replied. "I thought it'd be cheaper to stay at the hostel. We're trying to save money, remember?"

Jeff flung his backpack onto the shelf that hung over the seats, helped Patty slide her pack off, and threw it next to his.

Trying to end the bickering, Stacey asked, "Did you guys have fun yesterday at the museum?"

"Yeah, we had a good time," Jeff began. "We went to a few museums. Patty wanted to see some famous place downtown. It was this cool museum of Swiss history. It had some paintings, furniture, armor, old globes and shit."

"Jeff, it was a little more than that," Patty offered. She plopped into the window seat. "It was their entire history in one building, even from the time of Charlemagne. I can't believe how old things are in these museums. It's hard to believe that someone spent so much time making the paintings, or clocks, or the furniture. They spent years putting the tiniest of details on these works of art.

"It reminded me of what we try to do with ourselves. We spend years trying to paint our personalities to look a certain way or to carve memories into our souls. Anyway, I thought it was amazing."

"Honey, you're right," Jeff said, apologetically. "I didn't mean to downplay it. I enjoyed the intricate details, too."

"I wanted them to know it involved a little more than just old crap at the museum," Patty retorted.

"I thought you made it sound pretty cool. I think we should go to a museum like that in Austria or Germany," Stacey said.

"So Jeff, did you at least go for a ride? Stace and I went on an awesome trail at Uetliberg Park. It sent us through some sweet, single track," Reece said, changing the conversation to something of his liking.

"Nah, we didn't go mountain biking, but we did go to the park. We walked up to Uetliberg Mountain, and I took some great pictures of the lake." Jeff replied. "My adrenaline is building up as I imagine riding in the Alps."

"We're excited, too. We had a few good rides here, but the mountains aren't very tall or forested like I thought they'd be. You didn't miss anything," Stacey said.

"Did you guys meet any Swiss women?" Jeff asked and winked at the guys.

"As a matter of fact, before we saw you guys, we'd just said good-bye to two girls we partied with last night," Reece bragged.

"And did you . . ." Jeff paused and whispered, "Did you guys get some?"

"You dork. You think I don't know what you just said?" Patty chided. She turned to Reece. "So Reece, did you get laid last night?"

"If you must know, no I did not. And do you all want to know *why* I didn't score in Switzerland?" Reece said with attitude.

"Because European women have taste?" Patty teased.

"Funny, but that wasn't the reason. It's because of him," Reece said, pointing toward Stacey.

"Because of me?" Stacey exclaimed. "Who cares? I'm too tired to bother with what you're going to say."

"That's good because I'm not too tired," Reece said, swaggering around the compartment. "I'm goin' back down to the dining car and explore today's options. One of the girls wanted me to play a couple of songs. She's this cool German girl with rockin' blue hair and a nose ring. Just my type. Anyone wanna join me?"

Silence.

Reece reached up onto the shelf and grabbed his guitar. He strummed a few chords and sang, "A cool girl I wanna see, and she's waitin' just for me."

With that, Reece slipped out the door.

Jeff handed Patty her backpack and pulled his own off the shelf. Patty got her sketchpad, and Jeff took out a book.

Putting in his earbuds and listening to music on his phone, Stacey perused a mountain biking magazine. He enjoyed hearing good music when he traveled and looked forward to relaxing for the seven hours on the train.

Jeff took his seat next to Patty. Stacey and Patty had claimed all window seats for the entire vacation. Stacey felt entitled to his seat because the trip was his idea. One of Patty's many stipulations before agreeing to go to Europe was that she'd get to sit by the window on all modes of transportation.

Stacey now had his chance to vent his frustrations to Jeff and Patty. He tugged out his earbuds and mumbled, "Reece pisses me off sometimes, you know? He never takes the initiative. He's always waiting for me to help him out. You can't yell at him because he acts as if nothing's wrong. He takes what he gets and he's happy with that. Doesn't it piss you off?"

"I know what you mean," Patty said, turning to Jeff. "Sometimes Jeff won't follow through with things he says he'll do. And look at Reece, he doesn't have a girlfriend. I wonder why?"

"What's that supposed to mean?" Jeff barked. "Just because I didn't get all excited to go to your museums with you, huh?"

"Yes, I *do* want you to be a little more enthusiastic about it," Patty stated. She took Jeff's hand. "I came here to study art and work on my portfolio, but I haven't been able to do that very much. My master's professor gave me specific assignments to complete instead of attending his classes, and I haven't done them. I can't miss the classes and then show up without producing any art."

"I'll make sure you get time to finish the assignments. I promise everything will be better, and I'll be more supportive of your interests," Jeff whispered. He gently patted her leg.

"Good, because you're not the only one who wants to have fun on this trip. I'm trying hard to have a good time with you and get my degree at the same time," Patty said, leaning back in her seat and pouting. "It seems like you only want to hang out with Stace and Reece. You need to treat me better, at least as well as you treat them. No, better than you treat them. I'm supposed to be your best friend. Instead, I'm the reason you're not having any fun. I'm sorry I came along."

"I'm sorry, Patty. I know I've been a jerk this weekend. I apologize. I'm sorry. I promise everything will be better. I love you, honey," Jeff said. He leaned over to kiss her.

Stacey never knew what to do or how to feel when they spoke to each other like that, especially when he was alone with them. He used to think it was cute, but the sweetness of it diminished many years ago. He put his earbuds back in and peered out the window, waiting for their disagreement to end. When he looked back at them, Jeff's eyes were closed, and Patty stared blankly out the window.

Stacey knew Patty wasn't enjoying herself. He felt guilty for pressuring Jeff to go on this trip, which led to Jeff coercing Patty. He knew they would resolve their differences eventually, but he wanted to nudge them along in the process.

Stacey removed his earbuds again and said, "When we get to Salzburg, let's take a day to relax in the city. We could all go sightseeing or maybe to a beer garden. What do you think?"

Jeff opened his eyes. "That would be cool. I want to visit the huge castle that overlooks the city. What do you say, Patty? That'd be fun, huh?"

"I guess we could do that," Patty said. "And afterward we could go to the Dom Cathedral where Mozart used to play. I read somewhere they have a choir concert every night."

"We could do that, too. Good ideas," Jeff said. He gave Stacey a quick nod as a gesture of appreciation for the act of kindness.

"I agree," Stacey replied. Jeff and Patty still weren't talking together, but at least it was hopeful that she might have a better time. Feeling relieved about that situation, he put in his earbuds and resumed listening to the music.

A few minutes later, Stacey glanced out the window and caught a glimpse of a young woman with a pack on her back and a mountain bike at her side. He always felt an automatic attraction to women who ride. Wearing workout clothing and her hair in a ponytail, the woman looked as if she had stepped out of the cover of a fitness magazine. Even from the train, Stacey saw loveliness and natural beauty in the woman's features.

The woman stopped in front of Stacey's window. A worried expression crossed her face as she peered in one direction and then the next. Stacey thought she might be looking for someone or confused about what train she needed to board. In a split second, he made the decision to meet her.

"Jeff, what time is it?" Stacey asked.

Jeff was on his phone already and answered, "Almost 6:00. The train should leave in about fifteen minutes. Why?"

"Just wondering. I'll be right back," Stacey replied. He jumped up, stuffed his phone in his pocket, and rushed out the door.

As soon as Stacey exited the train, the fog completely encompassed him and the woman into its world. Time seemed to slow. He stood staring at her, not knowing what to say. She smiled coyly, triggering a rush of heat through his body.

Was she intentionally hiding her radiant smile because it would give away the thoughts in her head? Stacey wondered. God, I certainly hope so, he thought.

His heart beat faster, his muscles tightened, and his breathing became heavier. He felt strangely invigorated. It was as if the first rays of sunshine had awakened his soul following a long, cold hibernation.

"*Grüß Gott. Können Sie mir bitte helfen mein Fahrrad in den Zug laden?*" the young woman asked.

"Sorry. English?" Stacey said, hoping she could understand at least a little English.

"Ah, sorry," she said, her German accent strong. She paused a moment. Again, she smiled coyly.

Stacey's mind raced. Did she bat her eyes? Is she attracted to me?

"A man told me to put my bike on the front engine of the train. You can help me put bike on train, ya?" she asked.

"Of course," Stacey said. It took everything he had to avoid gazing dreamily into her doe-eyes.

"Thank you much," the young woman said. She smiled once again, swung her bike around, and started walking further into the fog.

A blast of desire swept through Stacey. Not wanting to lose her in the mist, he quickly followed her. He realized he had become so flustered that he'd momentarily lost the knack of small talk. Self-confident with women, Stacey usually could lead a conversation in whatever direction he chose. Perhaps he was nervous because of his immediate attraction for her. Maybe he felt rattled because of the fleeting amount of time he had to make a connection.

They passed a few train cars designated as second class and then came upon cars for first class passengers. They had arrived at the train's engine. Not paying attention to where he walked, he almost knocked the woman over. Instead, he ran into her bike, and it fell to the side.

"Oh, *Bitte*," Stacey apologized. He helped her pick it up.

"I am all right. You know small German, ya?" she asked.

"Ja, ein wenig," Stacey answered. Then he extended his hand and said, "My name is Stacey."

"Anneliese," she said, shaking his hand.

Her touch sent sparks up his arm.

"Anneliese. Lovely name," he said, carefully. He tried to keep from stuttering.

"Thank you," Anneliese said. "This looks like the front of train. You walk in and see if any bikes are there?"

"Absolutely," Stacey said.

He hopped up the stairs, entered the train car, and saw a large space with several bikes chained to the railings. Stacey got off the train and told Anneliese that she could store her bike there. She took a U-shaped lock off the bike and then led the bike into Stacey's open hands. He heaved it up on his shoulders, wanting to get the bike on the train as soon as possible so that he'd have more time to talk with Anneliese.

He climbed the short stairway that led into the car. Anneliese followed. Stacey rolled the bike to an open area and pushed it into a vacant space. Anneliese locked the bike to a metal railing. They both quickly exited the train car and then simply stood there staring at each other.

"Thank you," Anneliese said, breaking the silence.

"My pleasure . . . What do you do now?" he asked, trying to form his sentences in a way that she would understand. He took a moment to admire her shoulder-length, dark brown hair. Her alluring eyes resembled pools of amber. Her skin glowed a summer's bronze. The top of her curvy, yet lean body reached Stacey's shoulders. It was her radiant natural beauty that had been so striking when Stacey had seen her from the train.

"I meet my friend on the train," Anneliese said. Her words interrupted Stacey's trance. "I have to go find my friend. Thank you." She smiled one last time and walked into the nearest first class train car.

"Bye," Stacey said, watching her walk away.

The train whistle blew, forcing him back to reality. The conductor stepped out of a train car and shouted directions. Passengers flocked around him on their way toward their seats.

Departure time, Stacey thought. He did a quick scan, but Anneliese was not in sight. He jogged back to the rear of the train, climbed into the passenger car, and headed to his compartment.

For the first time since his high school days, Stacey felt giddy and nervous about a woman. This kind of excitement had disappeared at age seventeen when his parents died in the car accident. Their death had shut down his sense of elation for romantic relationships. However, thinking about those minutes with Anneliese made his heart flutter.

He stopped in his tracks. He wanted to look for Anneliese, but knew that the chances of finding her, talking to her, and beginning a romantic relationship with her before the train left the station would be futile. Instead, he decided to finish his walk to the compartment.

Jeff and Patty slept holding hands. A good sign, he thought. He quietly eased himself back into his seat, put in his earbuds, and pushed play on his phone. He fell asleep listening to classical music and daydreaming about the mysterious woman with the honey-brown eyes.

CHAPTER 5

Like a bee and flower
When two hearts touch
They are nourished and transformed

"I live my life in widening circles that reach out across the world."
— Rainer Maria Rilke, *Rilke's Book of Hours: Love Poems to God*

THE TRAIN SPED THROUGH the short, meandering valleys outside of Zurich, dispersing the thin layer of fog like the wake of a speedboat skimming over water. After a brief moment, the fog slipped back together.

Miles past Zurich, the train reached the majestic Alps. Dark green forests covered the mountains. At the top loomed the Alp's distinctive chunks of white granite. The train traveled along a glassy river through the steep alpine valleys. The chilly air above the river kept the fog alive. On either side of the river, homes and farms of lush vegetation extended hundreds of feet from the valley floor to the upper slopes of the Alps.

As it climbed a small hill that distinguished one valley from another, a shadow shrouded the train. Darkening cumulus clouds hovered above the Alps, ascending high into the air and banishing the sun from the eastern sky.

The train eased down the other side of the hill covered by the last of the fog. The fog condensed on the train's windows and seeped through an open screen. It trickled down Stacey's window and slid along the glass until it came to his outstretched arm. The water tickled his arm as gravity pulled it down, waking him.

Stacey checked his watch. 7:00 a.m.

As if he had never stopped thinking of her, Anneliese returned to his mind. Stacey became fully aware of his surroundings, realizing that Jeff and Patty were still asleep, and Reece was most likely at the dining car.

Through the thinning fog, Stacey had sporadic views of the Alps. He sat in astonishment. He had fallen asleep while the train pushed through the dull green, rolling hills of Zurich and awakened to the lush, jagged Alps. The train traveled near a small village of farmhouses and church steeples. The bright-green grass meadows appeared to go on forever in either direction. Mountains of granite seemed to climb straight into the sky. Off in the distance, snow-capped peaks jutted up, even higher. He stood up, reached into his pack, and grabbed his camera. Stacey took his seat hoping to get a few good pictures of the unbelievable scene that lay before him. He wanted to awaken Jeff and Patty to show them but decided they'd be in a better mood after a good sleep.

He put the camera to his eye, but quickly took it away. He wanted a better view, maybe one where he could see from both sides of the train. He decided to check out the vestibule between the cars. Perhaps, from there, he could view the outdoors through unobstructed windows on each side.

Stacey stepped into the vestibule, praising himself for choosing the perfect space for taking pictures. Two large windows were on each side, plus windows in the doors.

The view was astounding. A river cascaded over large boulders, flowery meadows flirted between pine tree forests, and the granite cliffs sat like stepping-stones for the gods. A smile grew large on Stacey's face. He clicked on his music and marveled over Mother Nature at her best.

"Excuse me," a woman said, stepping into the vestibule.

Stacey turned only to see Anneliese. The sight of her awakened his body. Her proximity caused his blood to pump furiously, sending his body chemistry into disarray. A mass of thoughts spun in his mind. He could see the sentences he wanted to say, but just as quickly, they disappeared. He would have stood there dumbstruck if Anneliese hadn't spoken first.

"Hello," Anneliese said.

"We meet again," Stacey said, wishing his reply had been clever.

"Where do you come from?" Anneliese asked. "You are from America, ya?"

"Yes, I live in the U.S. Do you know California?" Stacey asked.

"Ah. You live in Hollywood. Movie star, ya?" Anneliese exclaimed. They both laughed at her comment.

"No, I live near San Francisco," Stacey said.

"I see pictures of San Francisco. It is a nice city. Someday I go for holiday," Anneliese said.

"Where are you from?" Stacey asked.

"I come from Bavaria in Germany," Anneliese said. "It is beautiful. You can imagine."

"I'm sure it is. My name is Stacey, remember?" he added. They shook hands again.

"I remember your name. I am Anneliese," she replied. "Why are you here in the door?"

"I'm here taking pictures of the Alps. I couldn't see well from the compartment, and my friends are sleeping in there," Stacey answered. "What are you doing out here?"

"I walk around the train because I not have much to do. Awful to be in a train for so much time. I like to meet new people," Anneliese replied.

"What about your friend? Did you ever find her?" Stacey asked.

"Ya, I find her. But, she is with a man somewhere," Anneliese replied, rolling her eyes at the thought of her friend's behavior.

"Would you like to hang out and talk with *me*?" Stacey asked, holding his breath and hoping she says yes.

"Ya. I am glad we meet again," Anneliese said. "What word is *hang out*?"

Stacey thought her accent distorted the words in a lovely way.

"It means we could be together to talk," Stacey explained. A charming smile dawned. "If you want?"

"Okay. I would like to hang out because I have much time to be on the train," Anneliese said. "Where do you stop?"

"We're going to Salzburg. We've got five more hours. Where are you going?" Stacey asked.

"I stop in Rosenheim, Germany. It is four hours more away. My town is near München," Anneliese said.

"Great. We'll have time to talk," Stacey said. His heart pounded when he heard that she lived near Munich. It was a perfect lead-in to telling Anneliese that he was going to be a teacher in Munich. But, he hesitated. He didn't want it to seem like he was jumping to the conclusion that they would see each other after the train ride. So instead, he asked, "Are you here *only* with your friend?"

"Ya, I am with my friend, Wendeline. You will like her if you meet. All men like her. She is much funny. She is in dining room," Anneliese said. "Who do you travel with?"

"I'm with my brother and two friends. My brother, Reece, is talking with a girl and my friends, Jeff and Patty, are sleeping," Stacey said. "Why do you have your bike with you?"

"We were on holiday in the French Alps. We camped near a lake. We took many rides on the mountains. Also, biking is good sport for meet boys," Anneliese exclaimed. They both laughed. "We did not meet boys. But it was much fun, you can imagine."

"That's cool . . . I mean great," Stacey tried to avoid using slang as he spoke. "My friends and I love to mountain bike, too. That's why we are traveling in Europe. We rode through the Loire Valley in France on road bikes, and then went mountain biking in the French Alps and Zurich. Now we're going to ride around the mountains near Salzburg and then in the Italian Alps. I can't wait."

"Why do you like to ride mountain bikes?" Anneliese asked.

"I love to reach the top of a mountain and look down at what I've climbed. I get a feeling of great accomplishment," Stacey answered.

"I like to sit on a special rock at a trail near my home. When I look down at the river and tall trees of my town, I know I am far from people. I feel peace," Anneliese said. Stacey couldn't help but consider that he and Anneliese had much more in common than he thought. She enjoyed the exact moments and had the same spiritual feelings when mountain biking.

"I think that's super cool," Stacey concurred.

"What is this word, *cool*?" Anneliese mimicked. Her accent made the word 'cool' sound funny. As they both laughed, Anneliese brushed her hand on Stacey's. The flirtatious gesture showed Stacey that Anneliese was interested in him. His initial attraction deepened.

The vestibule doors opened, and people strode noisily through their conversation.

"We could go find a quiet place to talk?" Stacey offered.

"Ya. I like the idea. We *hang out*. It's *cool*," Anneliese said. They both laughed again.

"My friends are asleep in my compartment. We could go to the dining car, but my brother is there. Any ideas?" Stacey asked.

"We can go to my train car. It is empty. Wende is in the dining car and nobody has a seat in compartment," Anneliese said.

She led Stacey through the doors and hallways of three train cars. Along the way, they passed bearded men smoking near an open window, people walking with their eyes glued to their cell phones, and a group of teenage girls with headphones.

Anneliese stopped, opening the door to her compartment. She grabbed her pack down from the overhead rack, took out cards, a small gold box, and threw her backpack on the rack. They sat down in the seats next to the window. Anneliese opened the box and offered Stacey chocolate, which he gladly accepted.

"Do you know how to play the *Watten* card game?" Anneliese asked as she held up a few cards. The cards were brightly colored and depicted numbered hearts, acorns, bells, and leaves. There were also cards picturing men such as the king and ace.

"I recognize the cards, but I don't know the game," Stacey said.

"It is much liked game in Bavaria. We have a long train ride, so I teach you to play. Ya?" Anneliese asked.

"Sure. I'd love to play," Stacey said.

Anneliese shuffled and dealt five cards from the German suited deck. She passed out a handful of chocolates to use as bids for the winning hand.

"I think to teach you the rules as we play," Anneliese said. She passed out a handful of chocolates to Stacey. "My friends and I like to put money or chocolate as . . . What is word for money you play at horse racing or cards?"

"Oh, betting?" Stacey asked, unwrapping one of the chocolates and eating it.

"Ya, betting," Anneliese repeated. "You not bet in Watten, but we bet to make it more fun."

They played three sample games, sharing many laughs in the process because Stacey couldn't remember the rules or scoring. Finally, they played in earnest, getting to know each other in the process.

"Do you have any brothers or sisters?" Stacey asked, looking at his cards.

"I have one sister who finished university. Her name is Eva. She is a teacher of English to children," Anneliese replied, reviewing her cards. "I love my sister. But, she is older and tells me what I should do."

"I understand. Reece is my younger brother, and I always try to help him. But mostly, I try to keep him away from the wrong girls," Stacey teased. Again, they laughed. Stacey thought it unusual that they both understood each other so well, especially their sense of humor.

"Do you have more brothers or sisters?" Anneliese asked.

"No," Stacey replied. "My one brother keeps me busy enough. We live together in California."

Just then, Stacey's eyes caught sight of a grand, blue lake. Stacey motioned for Anneliese to look out the window. As they admired the spectacular view, Stacey reveled in the situation at hand. He couldn't believe that he was on a train through the Swiss Alps and sharing the experience with such a stunning woman. He felt his mind racing ahead in the relationship, but he had to tell himself to simply enjoy the moment.

Small steps, he thought.

Once they passed the lake, Stacey turned his attention back to Anneliese. "So, do you go to college?"

"I am in fourth year of university in München. I am much frightened because it is my last year of university. Then I take the exam for more study in higher university and hospital," Anneliese replied, picking up her cards once again.

"What do you study?" Stacey asked.

"I study medicine. I want to be a doctor for children. I not know if I am good enough to be a doctor, but I try much hard," Anneliese said.

She picked out chocolates from the bag and put them on the table. "I bid four chocolates."

"I'm impressed. I admire you for wanting to become a doctor, especially a pediatric doctor," Stacey said. He matched the number of chocolates from his bag and added two more.

"Thank you. Do you go to university in America?" Anneliese asked.

"No, I graduated a few years ago. I went to a local university north of San Francisco," Stacey replied.

"What did you study at university?" Anneliese asked, putting down one of her cards.

"I studied to be a stock broker. But when I graduated, I realized that I didn't enjoy the job," Stacey replied. He laid down one of his cards.

"What you do now for job," Anneliese asked.

"I'm a school teacher. I teach fourth graders. I love my job," Stacey said.

"I think teaching young children is much wonderful job. Teacher is a good job like doctor," Anneliese said.

"I agree," Stacey said. He thought the conversation was going well. Now that teaching had been mentioned, Stacey had the perfect lead-in to telling Anneliese he'd be teaching in Munich.

"Speaking of teaching, after we get back from mountain biking in Italy, my brother and friends will be flying home. I'm staying on, though, to teach at a school near Munich," Stacey added.

"Really?" Anneliese said, excitedly. "Which school will you teach for?"

"It's called Phorms. It's a bilingual school in Munich," Stacey said.

"I know Phorms. It is across Isar River from university and my apartment," Anneliese acknowledged, playfully hitting Stacey's arm.

"Maybe we can get dinner, once I'm settled," Stacey proposed.

"I would like that," Anneliese said. "How long do you teach at Phorms?"

"I signed up for a semester, but I can stay for another if I want," Stacey replied.

"I think you will like it here and want to stay," Anneliese said, continuing the game by calling out another trick and placing a card on the table.

"Do you live alone in your apartment, or do you have roommates?" Stacey asked.

"Ya, I live alone in apartment. Wende wants to live with me when she finishes college in Rosenheim," Anneliese said. She began to giggle. "My apartment is near Schwabinger Bach and the English Garden. It is only area in München where people can sit naked in the sun. I am sure you will like it there."

"That is funny, but probably not my style," Stacey said. Anneliese nodded in agreement.

Stacey placed the remaining trick of cards on the table and exclaimed, "I win. I have 15 points."

"Ya. You win. I think to let you win," Anneliese teased. They laughed.

During their conversation, Stacey's mind finally quieted. As if he were in a state of meditation, his words originated with ease and his movements were instinctual.

It felt as if the moment itself existed only because their two souls carved out a niche in the universe and willed their creation into reality. Their sentences formed streams of words. The speech flowed down into a sea of one world. Their smiles provided the warmth of a sun. The hidden thoughts were the stars that sat brightly in the heavens.

In the course of their conversation, Stacey learned many things about Anneliese's family life, relationships, personal interests, and travel. Stacey and Anneliese continued talking about helping children in their respective jobs. Stacey learned about Anneliese's quest to become a doctor. She told him that she thought she'd be a teacher, but as she took more science courses in high school, she fell in love with biology. She had a passion for the human body and for helping others, especially children.

Stacey learned that Anneliese's parents were still married, and they lived in the same home that she had grown up in. Her dad sold pharmaceutical products to doctors, and her mom taught dance to high school students. Anneliese had grown up dancing. She loved to ballroom dance and had even won contests throughout Bavaria.

Anneliese told Stacey that she was currently single. She had boyfriends in college, but nothing too serious. Her last relationship occurred during her second year at university. She broke up with him because the relationship affected her studies. She revealed that she would love to have a large family someday, but added later that she didn't know how she would have the time to raise a family if she became a doctor.

Stacey agreed, but postulated that maybe her husband could be the one to stay at home. Anneliese smiled at the comment.

Anneliese played the violin, which led to a conversation about her trips through Italy and France as part of a traveling orchestra. She had never been to America, but because of her dad's job, she and her family had been to Canada. Anneliese said that she'd love to visit America, as well as Africa. She had a real desire to volunteer her medical services to an African hospital once she became a doctor.

Before they knew it, over three hours had passed. The train whistle hissed. Stacey knew that they were almost at the Rosenheim train station where Anneliese and her friend would depart the train. The end of the moment between Anneliese and Stacey had come. What came next from Stacey seemed only natural.

"I've had a great time with you. Can I see you again?" Stacey asked. He had a coy smile on his lips.

"Ya," Anneliese whispered. Her welcoming smile lingered on her lips as if she was waiting for a kiss. She moved closer to Stacey.

Hand in hand, Stacey pulled Anneliese to his body. Her hands found Stacey's chest. He wrapped his arms around her waist, touching the curves of her body. His lips met hers in a kiss.

The train whistle hissed again. This time, the train began to slow down.

"I need to get bag and bike now," Anneliese said.

"I know," Stacey said. They both held their heads low in a hesitant silence. Stacey continued by saying, "Anneliese, I have to tell you the truth. I know you have to leave, but I don't want to part with you."

Anneliese must have sensed the urgency of the situation, as well, because she replied, "Please, you, your brother, and friends come to my house in Rosenheim to visit. My house is much big, and my family went away for holiday. The mountains are near my house. You come, ya?"

"I would love to stay with you, but I have to check with everyone first," Stacey said. "You haven't met my brother or friends. Are you sure it's okay?"

"Ya. Please come. You and friends will have wonderful time," Anneliese reassured Stacey. "Go get your backpack and friends. I get my bag, bike, and Wende. We meet you here soon."

"Thanks so much, Anneliese. My friends will be excited. I've had an incredible day," Stacey concluded. "See you soon."

"Ya," she whispered and kissed his cheek.

Stacey left and walked into his compartment, interrupting Reece in the middle of a story.

"Stace, come in. You've got to hear this story," Reece said, excitedly.

"All right, Reece. But, you have to hurry because I've got a story of my own," Stacey said.

"Okay, well I spent the entire time with this girl from the dining car that I told you about earlier," Reece explained. "She's amazing. You guys *have* to meet her. She lives in Germany near Munich. She said that we could come and visit. I think we could swing by on our way back, or maybe, I could leave you guys while I visit Wende and meet you guys back in France. What do you think? Isn't that cool? If we hurry, we can meet her. She's getting off at this—"

"Did you say that the woman's name is Wende?" Stacey interrupted.

Reece nodded.

Wende? Was this Anneliese's friend? Stacey wondered. The idea of the coincidence made Stacey more determined to stay with Anneliese.

"Reece, I met a woman on the train, too. Her friend's name is Wende. Does your Wende live in Rosenheim?" Stacey asked.

"Yes, she does," Reece said.

"No shit. I bet Wende is Anneliese's friend," Stacey said.

"Yeah, that's it! Wende told me about her friend, Anneliese," Reece exclaimed.

"Unbelievable," Stacey said. "Out of all the people on the train, we hook up with friends."

"I can't believe it, either. I thought you said you weren't going to pursue any women," Patty said, laughing as she glanced at Stacey.

"I know, but she pursued me, in a way," Stacey said. "She's the one who found me in the train. It's nice to have a girl who wants to know more about me and has the same interests."

"I know what you mean, Stace. I feel the same way about Wende," Reece added.

"Anneliese is fantastic. I really like her," Stacey said. "And get this. She invited us to stay at her house for a few days. Her family is out of town, so it's all good. I told her that we want to ride in Bavaria. She offered to show us some great trails.

"Then after a few days, we could travel on to Italy and resume our trip. What do you think? Should we get off the train now and stay with them in Germany, or should we go to Salzburg like we planned? We need to decide now because they're getting off this train in about ten minutes to catch the train to Rosenheim."

"I think I can speak for Stace. We're going to Rosenheim," Reece interjected.

Jeff and Patty were both speechless. An awkward pause blanketed the compartment for a moment.

"I'm sorry about changing the plans," Stacey said. "You can still go to Salzburg if you want. We could meet you in Italy in four or five days. Or, you two could come with us to Rosenheim. Anneliese said that it's near Munich and the Alps. It's a beautiful area and there's plenty to see. Plus, the train ride to Salzburg is short, so it would be an easy day trip to make from her house."

"Well, what's traveling if you don't have a few unexpected side trips here or there, right?" Patty replied.

Jeff shot a surprising look at Patty. "Hey Patty, I'm okay with still going to Salzburg. We could let these guys have their fling in Germany."

"No, it would be an adventure. We should go—I mean, as long as we have a private room. We'll still go to Salzburg, right?" Patty asked. Her tone was more of a statement than a question.

"Anneliese did say that her house would comfortably fit all of us and that her family wouldn't be back for four or five days," Stacey added.

"Okay. We better get going if we want to get off the train," Patty said.

A sense of urgency struck as they tried gathering their belongings before the train stopped. As they got ready, Stacey told them about his conversation with Anneliese. Finally, they exited the compartment and walked down the hall to Anneliese's compartment where they met Anneliese and Wendeline.

Stacey and Reece introduced the young women to Jeff and Patty. There were hugs and cheek kisses between the three sets of friends. As they waited for the train to slow, they talked about Anneliese's home and things to do in Rosenheim. Stacey glanced at all of the faces to gauge everyone's disposition. He was pleasantly surprised to see a large smile on Patty's face.

Maybe this detour will be good for Jeff and Patty, Stacey thought.

Once the train stopped, they all walked off together to pick up Anneliese's bike from the front of the train. Looking out into the distance, Stacey could see the Alps rising out of the misty valley. Above the Alps, in every direction, dark rain clouds brooded over the skies for as far as Stacey could see. A few drops of rain landed gently on Stacey's head as he walked hand in hand with Anneliese into the train station. From there, they would catch a taxi to their next adventure in Rosenheim.

PART 2

RAIN

The rains are God's hands
Wielding the power to transform
Through action

"My Sorrow, when she's here with me,
Thinks these dark days of autumn rain
Are beautiful as days can be;"
　　　　　— Robert Frost, "My November Guest", *A Boy's Will*

LOOMING OVER THE ATLANTIC like menacing battleships, rain clouds rumbled across France and into the German state of Bavaria. The agricultural lands and the evergreen forests that covered most of the Bavarian countryside were the first to be drenched. The endless rain sliced the Earth's landscape, slowly carving and sculpting the ground. New life flourished as the water penetrated scores of thirsty seeds.

Entering Munich, the gateway city to the Alps and the capital of Bavaria, the rain hit full force. Sheets of rain slid down rooftops, careened off buildings, and hitched rides on cars. In some areas, the rain pooled together into brisk streams, eroding streets and walkways on its way to the Isar River.

The rain clouds thundered out of Munich and approached the formidable Alps. The clouds' eerie underbellies swirled around the mountains and collected in the valleys. Heavy amounts of rain poured over the southern towns of Berg, Rosenheim, and Berchtesgaden. The water seemed to reach down from the sky and sweep life away, drowning unsuspecting creatures. Like an indifferent god, it wielded its power without concern as to whether it created or destroyed.

Shrouding the region like a net, the rain fell with such intensity that it affected everyone, including Stacey and Anneliese.

CHAPTER 6

Relationships are powerful stories
Deftly balanced and woven

"The fountains mingle with the river and the rivers with the ocean
The winds of heaven mix forever with a sweet emotion
Nothing in the world is single; all things by law divine
In another's being mingle; why not I with thee?"

— Percy Bysshe Shelley, "Love's Philosophy"

ARRIVING BY TRAIN in Rosenheim by 5:00 p.m., the group took a short taxi ride through the downpour to Anneliese's house near the Inn River on the outskirts of town. Wendeline, however, was picked up by her mom at the train station. She wanted to spend time with her family before partying with Anneliese or Reece.

Rosenheim seemed like the perfect location for Stacey and his friends. It was close to the bustling city of Munich with its wealth of German culture and the quiet foothills of the Alps filled with an abundance of recreational activities.

Upon arrival at Anneliese's house, they gathered their luggage, removed Anneliese's bike that had hung precariously out the back of the taxi's trunk, and waved off the taxi.

Anneliese took them on a brief walking tour of her parents' house. The outside looked like a quintessential European chalet with white paint, dark trim, wood shingles, roof windows, and flower boxes. Patty gushed over its outward appearance.

Entering the house through a door alongside the garage, they entered the mudroom. Two long, thin tables, several lamps, a wooden chair, a coat rack, and a shoe stacker filled the room.

Anneliese led them upstairs to the living areas. Decorating the walls, black and white photos in antique, silver frames depicted Anneliese's relatives. Other family heirlooms, like old fishing poles, signed memorabilia, and a record made by one of Anneliese's aunts, hung on the walls above the pictures.

The second story opened into a large living area consisting of a living room, kitchen, and dining room. Pine trim and flooring added to the chalet-in-the-Alps ambiance.

The living room was the largest of the rooms. Alpine paintings hung from the walls. Wood-framed couches and chairs surrounded a coffee table. Covering an entire wall, a bookcase with handcrafted designs carved around the edges housed hundreds of books. A small and inconspicuous television sat on a shelf next to a stereo twice its size.

With only a few appliances and an absence of knick-knacks, the kitchen appeared plain and minimalistic. The cabinets were painted glossy white. Uncluttered and bare, the butcher-block countertops glistened like honey. An informal dining table stood off to the side in the breakfast nook. A door opened onto a beautifully designed wooden deck and a lovely backyard. Dwarfed by a large tree on the far end of an oval-shaped patch of grass, a small studio or sunroom glistened in the late evening light.

In the dining room, tapestries hung from the walls, fine china filled the ornate cabinet, and a stunning chandelier presided over an antique table. Based on the opulent contents, Stacey surmised that Anneliese's family had made wise financial decisions.

Upstairs on the third floor, Anneliese showed her guests the four bedrooms and the two bathrooms. Jeff and Patty took the guest bedroom because it had a queen-sized bed. Stacey and Reece shared a trundle bed in her sister's room. Anneliese's sister had an apartment in Rosenheim, so her parents turned the room into an upstairs office area with a bed. Everyone went to their respective bedrooms, unpacked, and rested.

After nearly an hour, they slowly made their way downstairs to the living area. Reece asked Anneliese to turn on the television. The travelers enjoyed the challenge of watching the commercials and programming in the language of each country they visited. Flipping through the channels, Reece commented on the abundance of soccer on TV.

"There is much soccer on TV. I don't like the games on all the time," Anneliese complained.

Considering Anneliese's statement, they finally settled on watching a popular German series called *Stromberg*.

"It is like British show, *The Office*. You know this show?" Anneliese offered.

"Yes. We have the same show back home," Reece replied, eagerly. Now that they had a sense of the show, Stacey and Reece could follow the plot lines and sometimes understand the humor.

"I have much food for making dinner," Anneliese announced.

"We'll make dinner," Patty called out.

"That will be *cool*," Anneliese said, emphasizing her newly acquired bit of American slang. She pulled out a variety of ingredients, a couple of pots, and some cooking utensils.

Dinner consisted of diced sausages, potatoes, and zucchini. Tired from traveling all day, everyone was grateful that Jeff and Patty prepared such delicious food. As they ate, the conversation revolved solely around the topic of things to see and do around Rosenheim.

"In the next days that you stay here we could visit the Chiemsee or Neuschwanstein Palaces, museums in München, sights in Salzburg, or mountain bike parks near Berchtesgaden," Anneliese suggested. She glanced out the window. "Maybe, the storm stops tomorrow, but maybe no. We make plans when we know."

After dinner, most of the group adjourned to the living room. Jeff sat on the couch and thumbed through pages on his tablet. Laying her feet over Jeff's legs, Patty doodled in her sketchbook. Reece had retrieved his guitar from upstairs and strummed softly in the background of the conversation. Stacey and Anneliese, however, remained in the kitchen washing the dishes.

From the kitchen, Anneliese called, "Patty, what do you want to do tomorrow?"

"I'm not sure. I'm kinda bummed about the weather. Most of our plans are either outside on hikes or sightseeing," Patty complained. "I'd like to go to Vienna, maybe the day after tomorrow, to see paintings by Gustav Klimt. He's one of my favorites."

"Do not let the rain stop your plans. It rains most in summer and fall, so people in Bavaria are outside anyway," Anneliese said, putting dishes in the dishwasher. "Reece, what do you want to do?"

"Anything as long as it's with Wende." Reece stopped playing for a moment

"I tell her you say that," Anneliese teased. "Is she coming here tonight?"

"She texted me saying she'd be here in an hour. So, any time now," Reece said, picking up his phone from the table.

"Ah, my phone's dead. Does anyone know what time it is in the U.S.?" Reece asked, holding his phone in frustration.

"Yeah, it's almost 11:00 a.m. in the states. Why?" Jeff replied, not looking away from the screen of his tablet.

"I'm expecting an email. I might be working the PGA tournament in Napa the weekend we get back," Reece answered, slamming his phone on the coffee table.

Started by the sudden noise, Anneliese stopped loading the dishwasher.

"Whoa, I didn't realize my own strength. Sorry, Anneliese," Reece said.

"It is okay," Anneliese replied and resumed the dishes.

"Do you have a computer or tablet I could use to check my email?" Reece asked.

"Ya, we have a computer in den down the hall. I show you," Anneliese replied. She dried her hands on a towel and took Reece down the short hallway. Returning to the kitchen a few minutes later, she laughed and said, "I forget words on the computer are German. I find him Google in English on the internet."

Walking over to the living room to collect dirty cups, Stacey glanced over Patty's shoulder to peek at her sketching.

"What are you drawing, Patty?" Stacey asked.

"I'm sketching the rain as it hits the window and trickles down," Patty replied. She held up the paper so that he could see more clearly. "I've been struggling with a theme for my master's portfolio. I've had so many ideas over the past month, but I can't seem to settle on one, until just now."

"It would be difficult for me to be that creative. I can't imagine being an artist, a musician, or a writer because of the pressure always to be inventive and unique. I admire those qualities in you," Stacey praised.

"Thanks. Inspiration does take a lot of thought, some time, and a little luck," Patty replied. "For example, in the last fifteen minutes, I've watched the water streak down the window in these channels. And, bam, it hits me. I'm going to make art out of the weather. I got this grand idea from the rain. I'm going to roll clay into long, narrow tubes, the size of straws. I'll lay the clay tubes all over the canvas to form rain. I'll paint it, maybe different colors. It's never been done that way before; at least I haven't seen it. What do you think?"

"I think it's brilliant, especially if you make it look like your sketch there," Stacey said.

"Is there a meaning behind it? Don't you need a theme for this weather art? Or, is it merely meaningful for its uniqueness and beauty?" Jeff asked, finally looking up from his tablet.

"I don't know yet," Patty replied, slowly. Her eyes were glued to the window and her mind deep in thought. "Weather is cyclical. It's falling and then rising. It's movement. Swaying, drifting, and swirling. It's power. Gravity, evaporation, and erosion. It's a potpourri of human emotion. Happiness, sadness, elation, and disappointment. I have to create a series of paintings that capture all of that in a unique way."

"It sounds like you found yourself a topic for your project," Jeff said, proudly. He put his arm around her. "See, if we hadn't been on this trip, you might not have thought of this."

"Keep telling yourself that, honey," Patty replied, sarcastically. "You're right, though, that's the luck part of creativity."

Hearing a door slam and footsteps on the stairs, everyone paused for a moment. Wendeline emerged from the stairway, her dyed, blue hair hung limply in wetness.

"Hi," Wendeline announced.

Everyone looked up and nodded. The conversation began to simmer.

"Who wants to go to Tipico tonight?" Wendeline asked, smiling. Though it was raining, she was dressed in a slinky skirt and strapless top.

"What is Tipico?" Jeff asked, eyeing Wendeline's provocative attire.

"It is sports bar. We can watch games and put money for teams to win. I not know English word for it," Wendeline said, holding up her hands in a questioning gesture.

"*Betting* is the word you're looking for," Jeff added.

"Ya. We can bet." Wendeline looked around the room. "Where is Reece?"

"He's in the den using the computer," Patty replied, smiling at Wende and then returning her gaze to her sketching.

Before going to see Reece, though, Wendeline stopped by the kitchen to talk with Anneliese. Giggling at times, they spoke in German for a few minutes.

After Wendeline walked back to the den, Stacey returned to the kitchen with Anneliese to finish the dishes.

"You guys won't believe this," Reece shouted, the words muffling in from the den. He strode into the room with Wendeline trailing behind. "I got an email from an official at the PGA Tour. The guy who got second place in last month's tournament was injured and can't play in next week's Monday Qualifier. They've invited *me* to play in his place. *I'm* going to play for a spot on the PGA Tour." The excitement shined in Reece's eyes.

"Wow, that's great," Stacey exclaimed. He quickly dried his hands, walked over, and pulled his brother into a big hug. "So, theoretically, if you won the Monday Qualifier, then you'd play in the real PGA tournament?"

"Exactly, bro. I'm going for a spot on the PGA Tour," Reece proclaimed, hands in the air.

"You put in long hours preparing your game. You definitely deserve this. I'm proud of you," Stacey declared, giving Reece another hug.

"Thanks. I owe you props. I couldn't have done it without you that day," Reece said, putting his hand on Stacey's shoulder.

"I think you're right. It was my caddying that put you over the top. You know, all of the good advice I gave you on club selection and putting lines," Stacey teased.

"I know you're joking, but that brings up a good point. Who's going to caddy for you?" Jeff asked, staring intently at Reece.

"Oh, I don't know. I guess I'll have to call the clubhouse and ask if Kevin, the other pro, will caddy for me," Reece answered. "I guess it'd be too much to ask for you or Stacey to fly home and caddy, huh?"

"No, I can't, but I'll be with you in spirit," Stacey said.

"Keep me in mind. You never know," Jeff replied, showing a wily grin. "When do you have to leave?"

"In three days. Wow, the things I have to do to prepare," Reece replied, looking as if the reality of what he needed to do had immediately struck him. "I barely have any time."

"Aren't you glad you bought the more expensive refundable tickets? Now you can change the ticket without a fee," Stacey gloated.

"Yes, oh wise one," Reece teased. Turning to Wendeline, he said, "I know what Wende and I will be doing the next couple of days."

"What will we do?" Wendeline cocked her head, inquisitively.

"Play a shitload of golf, of course," Reece stated.

"Not if it rains," Wendeline declared.

"Even better if it rains. Gives me more practice with difficult situations," Reece said.

"Oh, no! I just realized that this means you won't be coming to Italy with us," Stacey acknowledged, scowling.

"I know. You, Jeff, and Patty will have to go without me. It won't be as much fun, but you'll get along," Reece said, punching Stacey lightly on the arm.

Stacey turned to Jeff and shrugged. "I guess we'll carry on to Italy with the same plans, huh?"

"Maybe," Patty cut in, holding up her arms. "Let's talk about it in a couple of days. Okay?"

"Okay," Stacey agreed, feeling disheartened.

"Before we go out, I wanna go back on the internet to change my airline ticket. Hopefully, they have seats available," Reece said matter-of-factly. He led Wendeline down the hall to the den.

"I'm happy for you, Reece," Stacey shouted. Reece turned around and winked before disappearing into the den.

Stacey and Anneliese went back to washing dishes. Overcome with feelings of pride and happiness for his brother, yet filled with disillusionment about the rest of his trip, Stacey fumbled around the sink aimlessly.

CRASH! Stacey and Anneliese peered intently through the kitchen window after hearing glass breaking in the backyard.

"I think a window broke on the sunroom in the backyard. You help me check, ya?" Anneliese said, grabbing Stacey's arm.

"Let's go," Stacey said.

"Do you need some help," Jeff asked, poised to get up from the couch.

"Nah, I'll come and get you if we need you," Stacey replied.

"All right. Let me know." Jeff relaxed and went back to his tablet.

Stacey and Anneliese put their jackets on, turned on the outside lights, and went out into the pouring rain.

Leading the way to the sunroom, Stacey inspected the wall of glass and immediately noticed the jagged edges of broken window panes accentuated in the light. Anneliese opened the door, and they both stepped inside. Stacey had been worried about getting his dirty, wet shoes on the carpet until he saw that the floors were tile. Carefully making his way across the room to where the broken panes had shattered, he came upon a busted flowerpot. Strewn on the floor lay dirt and chipped pieces of the pot. Rain fell through the hole in the broken panes.

"My mom hangs flowers from the tree. I think it fell off the branch and crashed through the window," Anneliese guessed. She bent down and moved the remainder of the flowerpot off the floor and onto a table. "What do we do with the window?"

"We need to cover the broken window so that rain can't get in." Stacey scanned the room for anything that might cover the hole.

"With what?" Anneliese asked, patiently waiting for a response.

"I'm not sure. Let me think for a moment." Stacey stared at the raindrops cascading down like confetti.

"Okay, I've got it," Stacey announced, hesitantly. "We'll put a tarp, or something, over the hole and then tape it so that water can't get in the room. That should keep the rain out tonight. Tomorrow, we'll call someone to fix the glass."

"I like the idea," Anneliese said, hugging Stacey. "What do you need?"

"I need a ladder, a small tarp, and thick tape," Stacey said.

"Okay, I go get it from the garage," Anneliese said.

Stacey watched her hurry out of the room, cross the backyard, and enter the garage. Meanwhile, Stacey tried his best to clean the dirt and pottery fragments with his hands and jacket sleeve. Anneliese returned carrying a light ladder, role of tape, towels, and large garbage bags.

"I not find the tarp, so I grab garbage bags. I hope it is good, ya?" Anneliese asked, holding out the bags.

"Sure, I can make it work." Stacey took the ladder outside.

With a concerned look on her face, Anneliese watched him climb the ladder and examine the hole. Despite raindrops stinging him in the face, he noted the size of the break and the window's slippery surface. He quickly realized that he wouldn't be able to fix the problem from the outside. Before going inside, though, he removed the two other flower pots hanging near the room.

After descending the ladder and bringing it in the sunroom, Stacey said, "The tape won't stick to the wet glass. I need to fix it from the inside."

"Okay. You fix the window. I will go get a bucket for cleaning the floor," Anneliese said. She ran back to the garage and returned with a bucket, some rags, and a broom. Broom in hand, she set to work cleaning the floor.

Stacey climbed the ladder, clutching the roll of tape and garbage bags. Holding the bag up to the hole, he taped the edges of the bag to the inside of the window.

Once he finished, he stood back and admired his handy-work.

"Hey, Stace," Reece yelled from the back door.

"We're out here," Stacey shouted, walking to the sunroom's door and poking his head outside.

"Jeff told me something broke out here. Did you fix it?" Reece called out over the battering rain.

"Yeah, everything's fine," Stacey answered.

"Good. Just wanted to let you know that Wende and I are headin' out for that bar. See you later, okay?" Reece called.

"Okay. Have fun," Stacey yelled in return. He watched Reece turn and closed the door.

"Are you sure you don't want to go out with Wende?" Stacey asked.

"Ya. I like to go out sometimes, but not tonight. I play hard in the day and rest at night," Anneliese replied. She finished scrubbing the floor and put the rags in the bucket next to the door. "Wende likes to be with many people. She not likes to miss . . . what you say . . . *the action* in town."

"I think Reece and Wende have that in common. They'll have a good time tonight," Stacey said, collecting the dirty rags and putting them in the bucket.

Stacey glanced around the sunroom. There was a long couch alongside the back wall. Placed in front of the wall of windows, the artist's table looked out into the backyard.

"Where's this picture from?" Stacey pointed to a large photograph hanging above the couch.

"It is the ballroom in Herrenchiemsee, a castle built by King Ludwig. It is near here and is beautiful. You can imagine," Anneliese said. She took off her jacket and hung it on the door handle. Stacey followed her example, thinking they might stay a while in the room.

"When I was young, I dream of dancing with prince in palace. We would waltz around statues and paintings in candlelight. So, when my parents build this room, my mom buys this picture and the chandelier so I will have fairy tale," Anneliese explained, pointing to the intricate light fixture hanging above the couch.

With a coy smile, Stacey strolled over to Anneliese. Wrapping his left arm snuggly around Anneliese's waist, his right hand clasped hers, and he pulled her close to his side. They started with a slow shuffle, but when Anneliese began to hum a melody, their steps slid into a glide.

Stacey kissed her lightly on the neck, moving slowly onto her cheek, across her forehead, and down the other side. They held each other, swaying gently to the melody.

"You are wonderful dancer," Anneliese whispered, resting her head on Stacey's chest.

"Thanks. I've had a little practice," Stacey replied, moving his hand from her torso to the roundness of her backside.

"Dancing with a prince was a good dream. But holding you near is real," Anneliese declared.

Stacey brought her towards him. He looked straight into her eyes and kissed her, seductively sliding his lips on hers. He put his hand under her wet shirt, feeling the warmth and smoothness of her torso and breasts.

Anneliese pushed his hands away and took a step backward.

"I not want you to think I do this with men I first know," Anneliese said, a worried expression on her face.

"I don't think that at all," Stacey said, softly.

"I like you. The moment is right, ya?" Anneliese whispered. She turned off the light and returned to Stacey.

With their eyes closed and minds blank, their bodies felt the raw, sensory emotion as they made love on the couch. It seemed as if Stacey and Anneliese were about to melt into one another's souls under the shroud of the rain.

CHAPTER 7

Relationships balance
Heaven rising from earth
Hell bleeding from sky

"Be still, sad heart, and cease repining;
Behind the clouds is the sun still shining;
Thy fate is the common fate of all,
Into each life some rain must fall,"
— Henry Wadsworth Longfellow, "The Rainy Day"

THE RAIN CLOUDS HOVERED low in the sky as Stacey, Anneliese, and Jeff biked into the mountains near Berchtesgaden, Germany. Joy filled Stacey as he rode in the Kehlstein area of the Alps where *The Sound of Music* was filmed. His mom had loved the movie dearly; he felt that she was with him as he pedaled.

They rode along a rocky trail next to a steep ledge. Sloping up the mountainside above, stretches of wildflowers highlighted a meadow of luxuriant grasses. Their vividness gleamed in the fresh rain. As beautiful as it was, Stacey felt a slight disappointment because he couldn't see through the thick rain clouds down into the Bavarian countryside or over the greenish waters of the Königssee.

Their rain gear was slick with a layer of moisture from the rain that persisted all the way up the climb. The ride was difficult, but the trail was still manageable.

When Stacey, Anneliese, and Jeff reached the pinnacle of the park, they found a small, vacant hiking hut that offered protection from the downpour. The hut was about ten by fifteen feet. Quickly scanning the hut, Stacey noticed a bunk bed and a set of chairs around a well-used table. Shelves spanning two walls held a mishmash of books, first-aid supplies, canned food, pots, and cups.

Stacey pulled their lunches from his backpack, while Anneliese and Jeff cleared the table of discarded magazines. As they sat down to eat, they heard the rain pinging on the metal roof.

"I am sorry for the weather," Anneliese said, resting her hand on Stacey's leg.

"It's not great for us mountain bikers, but it's given Patty a reason to stay inside and work on her art," Jeff said, taking a sip of water. He leaned back in his chair.

"Is that why she does not come today?" Anneliese took a bite of her sandwich.

"Yeah, she likes to be alone when she's creating." Jeff sighed. "She's not much of a mountain biker, anyway."

"I not know you very well, but I see you care much for each other. You hold hands and snuggle on couch and cook together," Anneliese said, biting into an apple. "But, Patty seems not happy here. Is it the rain, or something else?"

"You're right. I think she's frustrated about certain aspects of the trip," Jeff replied. Noticing a cringe appear on Anneliese's face, Jeff added, "It's nothing of your doing, though. We are thankful to be staying with you. In fact, Patty and I were saying this morning how wonderful you've been to take our whole group in. You've made us feel right at home."

"I am happy you like it here," Anneliese said. She reached across the table and squeezed Jeff's hand. "So why is Patty not happy on the trip?"

"The timing wasn't right for her," Jeff said, putting a handful of trail mix into his mouth.

"Patty said she not want to come here at first. She wanted to finish school, ya?" Anneliese asked.

"Yeah, that's exactly it," Jeff said. "We weren't going to come, but Patty changed her mind. She talked to her advisor at the university, and he allowed her to leave school for these three weeks as long as she worked on her art portfolio and researched the art in the museums."

"I think we all pressured her to change her mind and come to Europe," Stacey admitted, finishing a banana.

"I can honestly say that I didn't pressure Patty at all. It was her decision," Jeff said, sternly. "The thing about our relationship is that we've always tried to make each other happy, even if one of us has had to give up something in return. It's like a rite of passage, or something. I think we're unique."

"I think that's one of the reasons why I couldn't keep dating her. I couldn't compromise," Stacey theorized.

"I know it," Anneliese exclaimed. She stopped eating and leaned away from Stacey. "I see with my eyes you like her."

"That happened years ago. I still adore her, but I'm not in love with her," Stacey said firmly, embarrassingly aware of Jeff's presence. "She's a sweet girl who's made Jeff happy. I always thought she exemplified, or represented, the type of woman for me, but I blew it years ago."

"What happened? How did you lose Patty?" Anneliese asked, in a more serious tone.

"I was only fifteen, young and immature, when we dated," Stacey began. "Patty wasn't, though. She had her life mapped out; she wanted to fall in love, go to college, marry, and have kids.

"I was a typical teenage guy; interested in partying and hanging out with my friends. Before long, I stopped paying attention to her . . . and I lost her. I was too young to realize that I should fight to get her back. I thought I'd meet more girls similar to her, especially in college. My expectations were wrong. And now she's going to marry Jeff."

Anneliese shifted her attention back to Jeff.

"When do you marry her?" Anneliese asked, waiting to hear the answer before taking a sip of water.

"That's a good question. I think we're all waiting to find that out," Stacey teased. "When *are* you going to propose?"

"Despite what Stacey thinks, Patty and I have discussed it, and she wants to wait until she gets her master's degree to get married," Jeff answered, displaying a slight smirk.

"Don't worry too much about Jeff and Patty, though. They've had a lot of ups and downs over the past years, but they always work it out," Stacey assured Anneliese. "You should really worry about Wende and Reece."

"Oh yeah. I would warn Wende about Reece," Jeff added.

"Why? What do you think happens in the future with Wende and Reece?" Anneliese asked.

"I don't know, but I'd be worried about Wende because Reece and girls never last more than a month. He likes to have fun with them for a while, and then he moves on," Stacey explained, taking the final bite of his sandwich and opening a bag of carrots.

"I worry for Reece. Wende never gives her heart to men. She makes them think they are close but always keeps space between them. Many boys say she has a cold heart," Anneliese explained. "I have a secret. I like to watch what happens with her and men."

"It will be interesting to see who lasts the longest in their relationship," Stacey observed.

"Ya, I agree." Anneliese pulled out a bag of chocolates and passed them around to Stacey and Jeff. They took a few pieces of candy and thanked Anneliese.

"One last question," Anneliese said, glancing between Jeff and Stacey. "What is one worry or fear you have for a relationship?"

"I'll answer first," Jeff called out. "My worry is not with Patty. I know we'll always love and trust each other. I worry that I'll lose my friends. I could spend all day, every day with Patty. I lose myself in her. That's why I wanted to come on this trip. I want to maintain my friendship with Stacey and Reece."

"That is big worry. I can imagine," Anneliese said. "My mom has a problem like that when I was in school. She forced herself to join groups and make friends because all she knew was her family."

"I see myself heading down that road, especially since you're not going to be around the next few months," Jeff said, addressing Stacey's absence.

"We've talked about this before we left for Europe," Stacey interjected. "If he spends too much time with Patty, then he's instructed Reece to kidnap him, get him drunk, and dance with ten women."

"You try to be funny, ya?" Anneliese seemed insulted by Stacey's humor.

"Yes, I was joking. But, we have had that conversation before, and I'm sure Reece will make sure Jeff is out and about while I'm gone," Stacey said.

"What is your worry, Stacey?" Anneliese asked.

Not wanting to be too honest too soon in the relationship, Stacey answered with a half-truth. "Okay . . . I fear that women won't like the fact that I don't make a lot of money as a teacher."

It did bother him that he wasn't making enough money for his standard of living, but it wasn't a fear he had for a relationship. In fact, most women admired his job because it gave them a sense of confidence in his fatherhood skills.

"Men not have to worry much about money. Today, a woman can make more money in a relationship," Anneliese teased.

"That's true," Stacey said. "Why do you ask? What's *your* fear in a relationship?"

"I wonder this since we talk about problems with Jeff and Patty," Anneliese replied. "I worry about a man telling me the truth of his real feelings. I know I will be honest, but I worry that men will not."

"I see," Stacey mumbled. His cheeks burned because he sensed that she knew he wasn't quite telling the truth. Stacey was relieved when Anneliese and Jeff began putting their lunch bags into their packs.

By the time they got back on their bikes, the rain had made the trail muddy and slippery. They took their time weaving around slick rocks and puddles. Unlike earlier in the day, the rain had become a nuisance, especially when it landed like little darts on their face or trickled into their eyes.

Less than two miles from their car, Stacey lost control of his bike. He applied the brakes and slid into a rock, catapulting him over his bike. Landing awkwardly on his wrist, the pain shot up his arm as if it had suddenly caught fire.

"Fuck," Stacey yelled in agony. Clutching his wrist, Stacey muddled his way into a sitting position.

"That looked bad. Are you okay?" Jeff asked, stopping his bike near Stacey.

"Shit. My wrist hurts like hell," Stacey said, cringing in pain.

"Do you think it's broken? Can you move it?" Jeff got off his bike and let it fall in the mud.

Stacey gingerly rolled his wrist. "Ah, fuck! I don't know. I've never broken a bone before."

Anneliese, who was riding cautiously a few legs back, approached the scene and tumbled off her bike.

"I saw you fall. Are you okay?" Anneliese asked, kneeling down with Stacey in the muck.

"My wrist hurts like a mother fucker," Stacey held out his arm so that Anneliese could look.

"It is okay if the pain is in wrist only. I can fix it enough to get you to the car," Anneliese said.

Anneliese held Stacey's arm in one hand and carefully manipulated his wrist with her other hand, asking him questions about his pain level as she performed the tests. Her consensus was that he had probably broken his wrist. She went on to add that no matter whether his wrist was broken or sprained, she'd treat it the same way.

After asking Jeff to sit with Stacey, Anneliese jumped up from the sludge and quickly improvised to mend Stacey's wrist. Knowing she needed an object for a splint, she searched the area for a few minutes and found a short, wide stick. She took off her backpack and pulled out a long sleeve shirt. Clutching the stick and shirt in her hands, Anneliese sat next to Stacey again. She secured the stick to his wrist by wrapping it with the shirt. Stacey was impressed with Anneliese's composure and resourcefulness.

Before continuing the ride with his bandaged wrist, Stacey took a few practice runs on the trail to test his wrist. The pain was tremendous, especially as he gripped the handlebars tightly for braking or during heavy rattling and bumping. He could either walk or ride, but he had to get down the mountain to the car. He decided to descend by traversing the trails slowly.

Stacey followed Jeff's careful line down the trail. Jeff weaved back and forth so that Stacey wouldn't have to use his brakes so often. A few times, it was necessary for Stacey to walk his bike over the rocky or steep terrain.

Once they made it back to the car, they cleaned themselves off the best they could and drove to the hospital in Rosenheim. As they rode in the car, Stacey used the ice packs from their lunches on his wrist to cut down the swelling. Stacey didn't want to go to the hospital, but Anneliese insisted that he have x-rays.

Anneliese dropped Jeff off at the house before taking Stacey to the hospital. After haggling with the office staff about health insurance coverage, Stacey saw the doctor and x-rays were taken. As they waited in the lobby's hard plastic chairs for the results, Stacey felt guilty about not telling Anneliese the truth earlier.

Turning toward Anneliese, Stacey said, "I wasn't completely honest with you when you asked about what fears I have in relationships."

Anneliese shot him a look of concern.

"I said that I was worried that I didn't make enough money to date some women. That wasn't exactly true. I want to make more money, but I don't worry what women think about it," Stacey admitted. "The real truth is that I worry about getting bored with the women I date. I rarely get to that next step."

"Thank you for telling me and to be honest. That is a good step," Anneliese pointed out. "Why do you not tell me earlier?"

"I didn't want you to know my relationship problems. But, knowing your fear is honesty, I felt I better tell you the truth from the beginning," Stacey said.

"I not think bad of you." Anneliese kissed him on the cheek. "See, you will not get bored with me. I take you biking down mountain in rainstorm."

They laughed.

Leaving the hospital with the diagnosis of a sprained wrist and wearing a brace, Stacey and Anneliese wondered how the other members of their group had fared with their day. Reece and Wendeline spent the day golfing at a local course, while Patty remained at Anneliese's house brushing up on her art.

When Stacey arrived home, Reece, Wendeline, and Patty were eagerly waiting for him. He told the story of their muddy ride, lunch at the hiking hut, the fall, and the recovery. He praised Anneliese for her calmness and her wherewithal to engineer a splint out of a stick and shirt.

Unfortunately, the rest of the group didn't have a good day, either. Wendeline didn't enjoy being on a golf course in a downpour, and Reece was disappointed because he felt the golf he played that day was a poor prelude to next week's tournament. Patty couldn't find the creativity that had struck her so passionately the night before. About the only good thing to come of the day was that the two broken window panes were fixed.

The evening seemed to settle the demons of the day. Jeff and Patty played a rousing game of cribbage and talked of their plans to visit Vienna the next day. Wendeline and Reece spent the entire night in his room. Stacey and Anneliese sat on the covered deck, drinking hot tea, recounting the day's adventures, and eagerly awaiting an exciting day of sightseeing in southern Bavaria.

As he fell asleep, Stacey felt a heavy burden of guilt for sidetracking the trip to Rosenheim and for the rough opening day of their short stay. He worried his brother and friends would resent him, and he prayed that everyone would have a better day tomorrow.

CHAPTER 8

The integration of relationships
Changes structure,
Not substance

"My true love hath my heart, and I have his,
By just exchange one for another given:
I hold his dear, and mine he cannot miss,
There never was a better bargain driven:
My true love hath my heart, and I have his"

— Sir Phillip Sidney, "The Bargain"

T HE NEXT DAY, Reece and Wendeline, both beer connoisseurs, looked forward to spending the day tasting a variety of beers at the Herbstfest in Rosenheim. Jeff and Patty had chosen to travel to Vienna to see Gustav Klimt paintings and historical sights. They awoke early to catch the sunrise train. And, Stacey and Anneliese planned to visit the Alpine resort town of Garmisch-Partenkirchen.

Their first adventure was to the highest point in Germany, Mt. Zugspitze. However, once they arrived at the entrance to the cable car, they decided that the views and experience wouldn't be worth the high cost of the trip. The stormy weather had reduced the visibility significantly.

Instead, Stacey and Anneliese donned their raincoats and hiked up a short, steep hill to visit one of her favorite churches, St. Anton. Along the way, they passed small altars nailed to the trees, crosses rising from the ground, and bells hanging from arches. Stacey, not being religious, felt his spirit rise in the presence of such publicly expressed faith and devotion.

The part of the experience that brought him to tears, though, was the hundreds of plaques for the fallen soldiers displayed on the outside walls of the church. While inside the church, Stacey whispered prayers for his mom and dad, Reece's upcoming golf tournament, his teaching position, continued success in his relationship with Anneliese, and for Jeff and Patty to have a good end to their trip.

Next, they climbed into the Partnachklamm, a steep gorge caused by the powerful water of the Partnach River. Stacey and Anneliese found it thrilling to trek along the narrow wooden trails, tunnels, and bridges that carried visitors alongside the deafening, whitewater ripping through the gorge. After ascending out of the gorge, they strolled around the 1936 Olympic Winter Games Stadium. They passed through the stadium gates and partially up a hill that still housed the original ski jump from the Winter Olympics of the Third Reich. Stacey found the experience disturbing. He wanted to appreciate the beauty of the area, but he couldn't separate the history of the Nazi era from the ruins.

Stacey and Anneliese ended their tour of the area by driving about sixty kilometers west to King Ludwig's castle, Neuschwanstein. After arriving in the small town, they walked a short distance up a paved pathway to the entrance of the castle. Taking a guided tour, they were fascinated that King Ludwig slept during the day and stayed awake at night. They also found it interesting that the castle, built in the 1800's, had running water and a system of telephones.

After returning from their southern Bavarian tour, they showered and were lying in bed when Stacey received a text from Jeff addressed to both Stacey and Reece.

Can all of you meet Patty and me for dinner at Stockhammer's around six? Our treat. We have a couple of things to share.

Stacey read the text to Anneliese. She shot a puzzled look at him as if wondering what the announcement could be.

"They were supposed to be in Vienna until late tonight. I wonder why they're back so soon." Stacey placed his phone back on the nightstand. "I'd like to meet up with them. Will you go, too?"

"Ya, Stockhammer is much money. If they pay, I will go," Anneliese replied, chuckling.

"Okay, I'll text him back," Stacey said.

He reached for his phone and texted back. *Yes, see you at six.*

Moments later, he received a text from Reece. *Wende and I will be there, too. We're already downtown at the beer festival. We have an announcement, too.*

Great. See you soon, Jeff texted.

Stacey slid off the bed, careful not to bump his sprained wrist. Wearing only his boxers, he said "I better put on more appropriate attire for an evening downtown."

Anneliese, who was also wearing only panties, rolled across the bed and climbed out.

"What do you think they're going to tell us?" Stacey asked, buttoning his shirt.

"I not know what to guess. Maybe they got engaged?" Anneliese pulled a dress from her closet.

"That's what I'm wondering, but Jeff would've told me if he was going to propose," Stacey said.

"Maybe you not know him as good as you think. People have secrets they share with only their partner," Anneliese replied.

"You might be right. We'll find out in an hour," Stacey said.

* * *

STACEY AND ANNELIESE TOOK A TAXI to the Gasthaus zum Stockhammer. Along the way, they crossed a bridge over the murky waters of the Inn River, passed shops and restaurants on the Innstrasse, and parked at the crowded Ludwigplatz. They hurried through the rain and down the remaining few blocks, umbrellas in hand.

Stockhammer's was located in a four-story, pink building on the pedestrian-free Max-Josefs-Platz. The large, maroon umbrellas that covered the patio seating stood out against the white cobblestones of the square. When Stacey and Anneliese entered, Jeff waved at them from a table near the back of the restaurant. Reece and Wendeline sat to his right.

Stacey glanced around as he walked to the table. Dark wood paneling lined the walls about seven feet high, leading up to an arched ceiling of white stone. The pine tables were partially draped with white and green table clothes.

Stacey pulled a chair for Anneliese to sit next to Wendeline. They immediately began conversing in German. Before sitting down at the circular table, Stacey reached over and shook hands with Jeff and Reece.

"Thanks for coming," Jeff said, holding up a glass of wine.

"Yeah, thanks for the invite. We're happy to be here," Stacey said. "Anneliese was telling me how good the food is. Very Bavarian."

"The beer is even better," Reece chimed in, holding his pint of dark ale up in the air.

"I can see that. How many beers have you had today, bro?" Stacey asked.

"I don't exactly know. We tasted a shitload, though. I was a little drunk in the afternoon, but Wende sobered me up with a delicious German punch called *Bowle*." Reece winked at Wendeline and put his arm around her.

"So, what's the big news?" Stacey prodded. "Anneliese and I have wagers going. We've got five different guesses."

"And I'm curious about Reece's announcement," Jeff said. "Let's wait until Patty returns. She's in the back talking on the phone."

"Tell her to get her ass in here. I can't wait to lay all of our cards on the table," Reece declared.

Jeff gazed down the hallway where Patty had disappeared. Reece and Wendeline whispered to each other. Anneliese stroked her fingers on Stacey's thigh.

"She should be back soon. Meanwhile, look at the menus and decide what you want. The white menus are in English," Jeff offered.

Stacey and Anneliese perused the menu. They discussed the choices and decided what they wanted. The waitress, wearing a revealing dress called a *dirndl* and high white socks, arrived to take their orders.

Jeff ordered the crispy potato pancakes, dumplings, and salads as appetizers for everyone to enjoy. He chose a vegetable risotto to share with Patty. Reece ordered Stockhammer's Klassiker Schweinebraten; Wendeline ordered the goulash, and Stacey ordered a combination plate of Munchner WeissWurste and Wiener Wurstl to share with Anneliese. A few minutes later, the waitress brought Stacey and Anneliese their beers.

"Why are you and Patty back so soon? I thought you were spending the day in Vienna?" Stacey asked, sipping his beer.

"That was the plan," Jeff said. "We were going to visit a couple of museums with Gustav Klimt's art. But—"

"Because of the storm, our train was delayed about three hours in Salzburg," Patty interrupted, standing behind Jeff and putting her hands on top of his shoulders. "Something about a fallen tree on the train tracks between Salzburg and Vienna. We ended up in Salzburg for the day. I couldn't have picked a better city to be stranded in."

"Salzburg is a favorite city," Anneliese remarked. "I like the history and the music. There are many tourists. I like to watch them. It makes me dream of traveling."

"I'm glad you got to see Salzburg since that was high on your list," Stacey added. "But, you must have been disappointed about missing the Gustav Klimt paintings."

"Yes, I was." Patty pulled out a chair and sat down next to Jeff. "But, the memories Jeff and I made in Salzburg are dearer to my heart than a painting." Patty leaned over and kissed Jeff's cheek.

"Now you have to tell us your secret," Anneliese declared.

"I think I'll let Reece and Wende share their news first. You two don't mind, do you?" Patty flashed her contagious smile.

Before Reece could speak, the waitress brought a large plate of the potato pancakes and fritters. She passed out plates, and one by one, they all took a handful of pancakes, fritters, and a small cup of dipping sauce. Another waitress followed with the salads.

Jeff tried the potato pancakes and fritters. "God, these are great," he said. Everyone nodded in agreement.

"All right, Patty, I'll begin the festivities," Reece said, standing up to add drama to his announcement. "Wende's coming to California with me. We already bought the ticket. She'll only be there for a week, but it's enough time do some touristy things and to support me at the golf tournament."

"Wow, Reece. That's great," Stacey exclaimed, standing up and shaking hands with Reece. He bent down to hug Wendeline.

"So cool, you two," Jeff exalted.

"*Danke*," Reece and Wendeline said simultaneously. With a laugh, he blew her a kiss.

After the commotion settled, Patty asked Wendeline, "Don't take this the wrong way. I know Reece is a great guy, but are your parents okay with you flying to America with a guy you just met?"

"No, they do not like the idea, but I am twenty-two and they cannot say what I do," Wendeline said, swirling the beer around in her mug. "They meet Reece for the last two days and they see him as a nice man. Also, I have cousin at university near San Francisco. My parents warn me if anything bad happens I can call my cousin and go there."

"That's good. I'd hate for you to have a fight with your parents about this," Patty said.

"No fight. We had big discussion, though," Wendeline said.

"Whoa, that's a last minute ticket. That's gotta be expensive," Stacey declared.

"We're splitting the cost." Reece looked directly at Stacey.

Stacey frowned.

"I know you're thinking she should come later in the year, like at Christmas, to save money on the ticket. But, we wanna find out if we're right for each other," Reece said, hoping his response wouldn't elicit any further scrutiny. "No sense in spending time talking on the phone for three or four months and then finding out that we don't get along in-person."

"You're right. Sorry," Stacey replied.

"Wende, I must say that I admire you for being so spontaneous and instinctive. You know? Free and spur of the moment," Patty said, tasting the fritters for the first time. "Wow, these are incredible."

"My parents tell me I have been this way since I was a child," Wendeline admitted. "I have been looking at the rain fall today. I think my life is like a raindrop. Sometimes I go straight down where I fall. But sometimes, outside forces take me places I not know to go. They move me in life, and I feel I do not have control to stop it. So, I go for my heart."

"That is beautiful. Well said," Patty stated, holding her beer up in acknowledgment.

Anneliese was the only one that hadn't said anything. She stared incredulously at Wendeline.

Stacey knew that this would be a great shock to Anneliese. She and Wende had been friends since they were six years old. As if they were sisters, they didn't keep secrets, and they'd hardly been apart from each other.

Stacey put his hand on Anneliese's leg and glanced at her. He didn't know how she would react.

At the same time, though, Stacey knew this was a huge deal for Reece. He had never had a girl commit to him in such a bold way. Reece had had girlfriends, but never one so enamored with him that she'd fly around the world to be with him.

Everyone stopped talking for a moment. They took sips of their beer or nibbled on the fritters. As if in a trance, Stacey watched the raindrops splatter against the window and slide down the glass in skinny veins of water. Stacey contemplated what Wendeline had just said about her life being similar to a raindrop.

He watched the drops slide down the glass and hit the same area of the window. Most traveled down the same channels, but some cut their own paths, weaving away from the others. He wondered what made some drops of water change course when a revelation came to him. Some outcomes are chosen and some are destined.

A blast of thunder roared, awakening Stacey from his daydream.

"Well, I think I speak for everyone when I say that we wish you happy travels in California. I'm sure you and Reece will do very well together," Stacey toasted, raising his glass of beer. Reece took his seat next to Wendeline, and they raised their beers. Everyone clinked glasses in celebration.

Anneliese abruptly stood up with concern etched on her face and pulled Wendeline from her seat. They walked to the other side of the room and immediately began talking in German. Stacey could see Anneliese's face changing from concern to happiness. Wendeline's face continually epitomized joy with her huge smile and demonstrative speech.

As Wendeline and Anneliese talked by the window, a big grin crossed Reece's face and his arms opened as if to garner some accolades.

Jeff put his arm around Reece and said, "What can I say? That's great news. She seems like a great woman."

"She is. We're so in tune. I actually think I've met my soul mate." Reece gleamed with excitement. "I'd venture to say that if she lived in California, then we'd be a perfect match."

"So, if things go well this week, are you going to do a long distance relationship?" Jeff asked.

"That's the plan," Reece said, finishing the last of the potato pancakes. "I've been thinking about this for a couple of days and have decided that the LDR is awesome. There's the emotional part of getting to know each other . . . on the computer or phone. For the physical part, we see each other every couple of months. It's like the perfect set-up."

"LDR," Patty wondered. "What's that?"

"Long distance relationship," Reece replied. "We live so far apart so—"

"What happens if you find out that you really like her, and you want more of an intimate relationship?" Patty interrupted.

"I'm not thinking about that. I live in the moment," Reece reasoned.

"Let me know how that works out for you," Patty teased. She finished her beer and put it down, loudly, near Reece.

"I'll let you know. But these guys know exactly what I'm talking about. You can't rain on my parade," Reece said. He finished his beer and slammed it down near Patty. Smiling, they nodded at each other.

Patty suddenly stood up and waved at Anneliese and Wendeline.

"Okay, everyone, I'm going to make my announcement now," Patty shouted. She fidgeted with excitement.

Anneliese and Wendeline made their way back to their seats. They both looked happy.

"Before I make my announcement, I wanted to say something to Reece and Wende. And, I guess I'm saying it to Jeff, also," Patty began. "Jeff and I have been together for over six years. Though that might seem like a long time, it isn't. We're still learning about each other and are constantly making decisions that affect our happiness, which will continue forever, I imagine. The important thing is that we think as a team.

"If you can balance being able to remain an individual by speaking up for what you sincerely need, and at the same time being willing to sacrifice your wants for your partner's, then your relationship has a better chance of success. I wish you two all the best."

Patty held up her drink in a toast of happiness to the new couple. Then, she hesitated, appearing to be on the verge of tears.

"The reason we invited you to have dinner with us is that we have good news and not so good news to share with you," Patty began. A silence circled the table as everyone braced for the news. "I'll start with the good news . . . We're engaged!" Patty held up her left hand to show off her sparkling engagement ring. "Jeff proposed to me in Salzburg."

"Wow, that's fabulous. I'm so happy for you two," Stacey said. He turned to Anneliese, smiled, and patted her on the leg in acknowledgement of her correct guess. "Anneliese thought that your news might be an engagement."

"I know it in my heart," Anneliese said. "In German, we say that's *wunderbar*. You will make a beautiful bride and groom."

"Let's see the ring," Wendeline pleaded.

Wendeline stood up and hugged Patty; thus beginning a procession of friends standing up, walking around the table, and embracing both Patty and Jeff. The girls clamored over the ring, while the boys passed around high fives and words of admiration for Jeff. Once everyone sat down, Stacey toasted the newly engaged couple.

"Let's toast to Jeff and Patty. Their love and happiness for each other is a model for us all," Stacey said. They clinked glasses.

"I'd like to add something to the toast," Reece said, kissing Wendeline. "May the rest of us follow suit."

"Hopefully, it doesn't take you seven years to get here, though," Patty teased.

"It was a long time, but every moment built this relationship into a fortress. I wouldn't have done it any other way. I love you, Patty," Jeff professed.

"Now, tell us *how* the proposal happened," Stacey insisted.

"Well, we were supposed to go to Vienna today to see the landmarks and paintings of Gustav Klimt," Patty said. "But, because of the rain, we only made it to Salzburg. God bless the rain. If it hadn't rained, I don't think we'd be engaged.

"Anyway, we'd been strolling around the sights of Salzburg. It only sprinkled lightly for much of the morning. But suddenly, several loud claps of thunder and the light shower turned into a heavy downpour. We ran into the nearest store, a cozy antique shop. We were simply window-shopping, when I called Jeff over to look at a ring I'd discovered in a glass showcase.

"The saleswoman told us that the store had recently acquired the ring at an estate sale. It was the wedding ring of a ninety-six-year-old woman who had passed away last year. She fell in love with her husband in school, and they were married for sixty-five years before he passed away ten years ago. Jeff, you tell the rest of the story."

"Okay," Jeff agreed. "So, we had lunch at a restaurant right next door, and we chatted about the kind of love that lasts sixty-five years. As we discussed what makes love last, I realized that I was ready to propose to Patty. The entire time we're eating, I'm trying to think of how to get back to that shop to buy the ring.

"After lunch, we left the restaurant and walked around the corner. I told Patty that I forgot to leave a tip. I ran back to the antique store and bought the ring. The lady was ecstatic and gushed over the romance of it all. She asked me where I planned to propose. I told her that I hadn't thought that far ahead. She said that I *must* propose at the gardens of Mirabell Palace. I told her that it was our next destination."

"Wow, it sounds like serendipity," Stacey commented.

"It really was," Jeff said. "So, we walked to the palace under one umbrella. The entire time I'm trying to think of what I'm going to say. We toured the gardens and came across a large fountain surrounded by four large statues. These statues represented the four elements of the universe: fire, water, air, and earth. Off in the distance, obscured somewhat by the sheets of rain, was the castle, HohenSalzurg. God, the setting was exquisite.

"So, right there, in the midst of the rainstorm, I got down on my knee and took her hand. The words just poured out. I hope they were romantic because I can't even remember what I said. Anyway, I opened the ring box and asked her to marry me."

"And I immediately said yes," Patty blurted. "That's our engagement story."

"What a romantic story," Anneliese sighed.

"And all because the rain delayed our train," Patty replied.

"Have you told your parents yet?" Stacey asked.

"No. Not yet. I'll tell them tomorrow," Patty said.

Just then, three waitresses brought out the main dishes of food. The celebratory group began eating, commenting on their meal, and tasting each other's food. As they ate, they discussed wedding details and Wendeline's move.

Near the end of the meal, Patty interrupted everyone's conversations. "We do have one more thing to tell you." Jeff put his arm around Patty. "The bad news is that we decided to return home early — tomorrow."

"Wow, so soon. You're not going to wait until after Italy, huh?" Stacey asked, nodding his head and sighing.

"I know we'll be missing Italy, but Jeff and I agreed that if I go back now, I can begin my last semester of college. That's for the best," Patty shared. "Wende just spoke about how our lives are like raindrops. I feel surrounded by that rain, except I feel like a raindrop that has been thrust upward, against the natural pull of gravity.

"Anyway, I called my thesis advisor to let her know I'd be back early and that I hadn't completed all of the assignments. She said that it was okay, and she'd work with me to catch me up to speed. I went online to change our airline tickets. Like Reece, I'm glad we bought the refundable tickets. So, it's already a done deal. We're flying home tomorrow."

"I'm in shock," Stacey said. "Although, you didn't look like you were having a great time on this trip. I'm happy that you'll be able to go back home and finish up your degree."

"Thanks, Stace, for letting me come on this trip. You guys have always made me feel welcome. I've had a great time seeing the sights of Europe, especially the museums," Patty said, teary eyed. "I wanted to see Europe. But, I knew in my heart that it wasn't the right time.

"It seems that life is all about timing. Sometimes the timing is perfect for something you want, and the events come together perfectly. It's at those times when you think life couldn't get any better. Opportunities are presented to you, and you make the right decisions at the right times. You feel as if your life is gaining speed.

"Then suddenly, it seems that the universe changes. You've stepped out of the flow, or time has sped up or slowed down. You try to make things happen even though the timing is wrong, and it's like you're swimming upstream. That's what happened with me on this trip. Deciding to go home, I finally feel that I'm flowing in the right direction again."

"I think you are smart for going home. And now that you have a ring, you will be much happy," Anneliese said. Wendeline nodded in agreement.

"We could all see that you were totally turned around over here," Reece said. "But, why'd you come in the first place? I mean, first you guys weren't going to go and then you came. What changed your mind?"

"I thought I'd be able to do my art projects along the way and have a great time on the side," Patty replied. She looked deeply into Jeff's eyes and then back to Reece. "But, when I reexamined the situation, I realized the deeper reason I'd decided to come was that I wanted to make Jeff happy.

"Jeff and I had a long conversation about this. I told him that I changed my mind about coming because I wanted him to be happy. I didn't want him to feel disappointed or have regrets about not going with you guys. I should have been honest with him, and I'm sorry for that."

"I'm sorry, too, for pressuring you. I didn't realize how much missing your first few weeks meant to you," Jeff said.

"My dream is to get my master's degree. And that's what I'm going to do," Patty stated.

"And my dream has always been to make you happy," Jeff replied, lovingly. Patty melted into Jeff's arms, and they kissed.

"Before I forget, I wanted to thank Anneliese for letting us stay at her home. Even though I haven't been in such a good mood, I did enjoy staying there. Thanks," Patty said.

"I am happy you are here, also," Anneliese said. "You can stay with me any time you are here in Germany."

"Sorry we made some of the time here seem so tense," Jeff apologized.

"Oh, you guys were pretty cool. I mean, I wasn't *totally* uncomfortable," Reece joked. "It's okay. You demonstrated the power of love, and how a couple can make decisions that are win-win. It's awesome that each of you wants their other half to be happy."

"Damn, I am impressed. You're learning," Stacey exclaimed. He turned to Wendeline. "You are a lucky woman, Wende."

"That is why I like him," Wendeline said, proudly.

"Well, what are you gonna do now, Stace?" Reece asked. "I mean, are you still going to ride in Italy? Anneliese could join you."

Anneliese shook her head and said, "I not think I can go. I begin university in a few days."

"If I left the day after tomorrow, I'd still see a little bit of Italy, and maybe get a couple of rides in," Stacey thought aloud.

Anneliese pulled herself out of Stacey's grip and turned to give him a look of surprise.

"Italy is for lovers. I take you next holiday. It will be better. You can imagine," Anneliese offered.

"Yeah, it would be nice. But, you're going back to school, and I probably won't get a chance to ride in Italy again. The choice is so damn hard," Stacey said.

"Go to Italy alone now or wait to go with me. I am happy for you both ways," Anneliese said.

Stacey paused and turned to Reece. "She makes a good argument for going with her."

"Yeah, you got that right," Reece agreed. He and Stacey laughed.

"I don't mean to interrupt but we're leaving soon, and I wanted to know what flight you and Wende are taking tomorrow?" Patty asked Reece.

"We're taking a Lufthansa flight out of Munich at 11:00 in the morning," Reece replied. "What about you?"

"Perfect. That's the same one we're taking," Patty said.

This line of questioning sparked a conversation about airline flights and Wendeline's sightseeing plans in the U.S., which meant that Stacey and Anneliese were isolated for a moment.

Stacey turned toward Anneliese. He smiled, but didn't know exactly what to say. He stared past Anneliese to the window, trying to understand the ramifications of all that had recently occurred.

Until that moment, Stacey hadn't really thought about the future with Anneliese. He'd become so caught up in the moment that he'd forgotten that Anneliese's family would be back in a couple of days. What was he supposed to do? Go to Munich or stay with Anneliese and meet her parents? Neither he, nor Anneliese, had brought up what might happen next. He assumed their relationship was progressing and that he'd keep seeing her, romantically, in Munich, but he couldn't be certain what she was feeling unless he asked.

"What do you think about all that happened tonight?" Stacey asked.

"I am surprised Wende leaves," Anneliese replied. "I am also sad that she does not talk to me first. But, she seems happy with Reece. I hope she has good times in America."

"Isn't it funny that no one asked us what we were going to do?" Stacey remarked. "I guess they were all so focused on themselves that they didn't ask us if we had any plans."

"Ya, they all leave for America but not ask us," Anneliese said, sipping on a glass of water.

"Since they're leaving in a couple of days, can I stay with you until we need to go to Munich? Or, if it's going to be a problem with you or your parents, I can stay in Munich when we drop them off at the airport," Stacey proposed. Playing with a spoon on the table, he anxiously awaited her reply.

"Ya, I like you to stay with me," Anneliese said. She reached under the table to hold Stacey's hand. "I will show you around Rosenheim, and I have you meet my parents and friends. Then, we go to München in a few days. Do you like this idea?"

"Yes, that sounds great. I am looking forward to meeting your family and the rest of your friends," Stacey said.

Stacey noticed that everyone was preparing to leave. He helped Anneliese out of her chair and assisted her as she put on her coat. The friends exited the restaurant and hopped into two waiting cabs.

As they left, a fear seeped into Stacey's soul. The inevitability of saying goodbye to his brother and friends panicked him. Having them along on the first leg of his journey, he felt safe in their solidarity. Now that they were leaving, Stacey began to dread the passing of time because the moment of departure was unyielding and would advance until it snatched away the people he loved. He felt that time was an assassin that couldn't be stopped.

CHAPTER 9

Dusk
Night sky darkens
Pondering life's past integrations
Reflection

"Nothing makes the earth seem so spacious as to have friends at a distance; they make the latitudes and longitudes."

– Henry David Thoreau

T HE NEXT MORNING everyone took the train to the Munich Airport. Having found last-minute seats on the same flight, Jeff and Patty would be traveling with Reece and Wendeline.

Stacey and Anneliese accompanied their friends to the airport to see them off. Stacey stared in silence and exhaustion as the Bavarian countryside passed across his vision. He hadn't slept well the night before, dreading the moment when his brother would depart without him.

When they arrived at the security gates, Stacey sensed that an entire era of his life was ending. Holding tightly to Anneliese's hand, Stacey occasionally reached out to put his other arm around Reece or high-five Jeff.

The time finally came when the travelers had to leave for their gate. The entire group clung together outside the security gates. Stacey and

Anneliese hugged Jeff and Patty. Both sets of couples wished each other well in the weeks to come.

After Jeff and Patty strolled away to their gate, Stacey took Reece aside. "I want you to know that the only regret I have about the teaching exchange is that we'll be apart."

"Bro, it's okay. I'm twenty-two," Reece said. "We've always been around each other, so it'll be nice to be alone for a bit. Plus, I'll have Wende to keep me company for the first week."

"I know it will be good for you, but I have such mixed feelings about this whole teaching abroad program," Stacey said. "I know we'll both thrive. You'll kick ass in the golf tournament and have a wonderful time with Wende. I'll have my hands full with teaching and, hopefully, spending time with Anneliese."

"So, everything's okay," Reece said.

"No, because I feel like I'm abandoning you," Stacey admitted. "I wouldn't leave you if I didn't feel I'd be back again soon. But, if you don't want me to do this, tell me now, okay?"

"I'm happy for you," Reece said quickly. Realizing his brother wanted to hold a conversation, he set his luggage down. "I really am. The teacher exchange is a great opportunity for you, and, you're only going to be gone a short time. Three or four months is a breeze. There's nothing to feel sorry about. If you decide to stay the whole year, then you'll need to apologize profusely." He paused and they both smiled. "Plus, Anneliese is a great girl. You have to find out what's going to happen between you two."

"That's exactly how I feel," Stacey said, resting his arm on Reece's shoulder. "It's like I'm being pushed into this decision by fate, or destiny, or some fucking power. If I don't do this, then I'll regret it for the rest of my life. I know it. It's one of those times to let the experience play out. I steered myself into this situation, and now I have to guide my way through it."

"We'll all miss you. But, like you said, I'll be busy, and if I need anything you're only gonna be a phone call away, or an email, or something," Reece said.

"Do you think Mom and Dad would have approved of teaching abroad?" Stacey asked.

"Stace, are you kidding me? They would have loved it. Mom, especially, was such a traveler. She would have told you one of her favorite phrases, especially when you started to spend time with the girls. Remember?" Reece asked, smiling.

Simultaneously, Stacey and Reece said, "Family is the air you breathe that keeps you alive. Girls just make it smell nice."

They both smiled as they remembered their mom.

Reece picked up his luggage and took a few steps toward Wendeline.

"Thanks, Reece, for everything. I mean it. You're a great brother." Stacey reached for Reece, and they hugged. Stacey felt one hundred percent sure that they would both manage to get along without the other for a few months.

Stacey gave Reece one last, long hug but didn't shed a tear.

The outcome transpired differently when Stacey hugged Wendeline and gave her a kiss on the cheek. She wouldn't let go of the hug and whispered in his ear, "I hope you like your first week of teaching in München and life is good for you and Anneliese. I will miss you, but I see you in a week."

Wendeline's caring words startled Stacey. Suddenly, the departure became real. Tears came to his eyes, but he fought the emotions and tried to hold back the tears. Stacey never felt comfortable crying in front of people. He believed he needed to exhibit a strong demeanor so that he could comfort others. He couldn't allow himself to appear weak when others were in need of someone strong. Consequently, Stacey was so disciplined that only one tear trickled down his cheek.

When Wendeline said goodbye to Anneliese, he noticed that neither one of the girls had trouble displaying their emotions. They spoke giddily in German through their tears of joy. He succumbed to a feeling of jealousy because they were so free with their feelings and emotions.

Stacey then saw Reece taking a few hesitant steps toward Wendeline. He thought that Reece must be wondering what to do and how to do it. If he waited any longer to pry Wendeline away from Anneliese, he'd miss his flight.

Stacey decided it was up to him to take the initiative. He walked confidently up to Anneliese. He put his arm around her shoulder and whispered into her ear, "We have to let them go. She'll be back in a week, or maybe two. If they don't leave now, they'll miss their flight. Give Wende one last hug."

Anneliese reached out for Wendeline. They hugged and spoke some final words in German. Reece looked at Stacey, gave him a thumbs-up sign, and mouthed *thanks*.

Reece grabbed Wendeline's bags, as well as his. He nudged Wendeline toward the security gates. After they made their way through the metal detectors, they both turned around to wave bye. They slowly faded into the mass of people moving through the maze of corridors.

Stacey and Anneliese found a window that had a partial view of an air strip. They watched a handful of Lufthansa jets scream down the long runway. The last thing they saw was a jet blasting through the thick cloud cover only a couple of hundred feet above the ground.

It rained as Stacey and Anneliese left the airport, boarded the train to downtown Munich and waited for the train to Rosenheim. Stacey mindlessly bought something to eat and drink. He paced back and forth along the platform. Flipping through a magazine, he watched passengers loiter. He went to the bathroom. Trying to avoid the sudden onset of anxiety, that familiar numbness overcame him.

Gazing up into the gray sky, Stacey watched the raindrops fall in lines. He thought about how the rain connects the sky with the earth. Invisible forces of evaporation and gravity bring water back and forth between those two entities. He realized that human relationships also depended upon invisible powers that tethered individuals together through memories, thoughts, words and gestures.

Finally, Anneliese nudged Stacey and said, "Hey, I am speaking to you. Why do you not speak to me back? I am also much sad."

Stacey straightened his posture, took a deep breath, and looked at Anneliese for the first time in an hour. He then replied, "I'm sorry. This is how I get when I'm sad. I go deep into my head, and I don't talk much. I become oblivious to everyone and everything."

Anneliese wrinkled her forehead and scrunched her face in a questioning look. "What does oblivious mean?"

"It means that you don't notice anything for the moment. You're not aware of anything," Stacey answered. "I don't want to have to think when I'm in this mood."

"Oh, I know now," Anneliese said, nodding. "It is good to be oblivious when you sit alone. But now you are with me. I think it is good for us to talk. It will make us enjoy the moment."

Anneliese tickled Stacey around the sides of his waist. They laughed and kissed. Stacey took Anneliese's hand in his, holding it tightly. He realized that, as of now, Anneliese was all he had here in Germany. Until he began teaching, she would be his sole friend, his only date on a Friday night, his companion on mountain bike rides, and his translator in a land of a strange language. She was his life in Germany.

"I hate good-byes," Stacey admitted. "I've never been able to say it easily. I remember being a kid, and we'd have relatives over for a week. I'd play with my cousins and have so much fun. We'd fill up those days with so many things that it seemed as if it would go on forever. But in the back of my mind, I'd dread the day when they'd have to leave. It loomed in the distance.

"No matter how much I tried to stop it, the last day always came, and I'd be sad for a couple of days. That's how I feel right now."

"I am sorry," Anneliese said.

"Thanks," Stacey replied. He paused and then continued, "It's funny, though, because I only feel this sad when someone leaves me. I never felt sad when we'd be the ones leaving from my cousin's house after a week. I guess that's because we were the ones doing something and going somewhere."

"Now we are together," Anneliese said, enthusiastically. "When you were a child, you not have me. But now we are both here, and we miss people together. We put them behind and we walk forward."

"All right," Stacey said with a smile on his face. "I'm already feeling better. Thanks. You're right. Our future is ahead of us here in Germany."

They kissed as the rain fell around them on the platform, suspending them on a mystical island. Within seconds, the train arrived. Anneliese and Stacey ran through the rain to board. Minutes later, the train pulled away from the station. As it left, Stacey and Anneliese took the nearest seats.

They fell into a deep discussion of the next steps that Stacey needed to take now that he lived in Germany. Sitting with Anneliese, her legs draped over his, Stacey experienced peace within himself, his decision, and his life at that moment.

Neil Young's song, *Heart of Gold*, suddenly clicked on in his head. A line in the song that Stacey kept singing to himself seeped within the crevices of his mind.

That's kind of what I've done, he thought. I've crossed the ocean and found a heart of gold.

CHAPTER 10

Dawn
Sun warms the land
Life serenely wakens to new beginnings
Hope

"It's life that matters, nothing but life- the process of discovering, the everlasting and perpetual process, not the discovery itself, at all."

— Fyodor Dostoevsky, *The Idiot*

THE RAIN CONTINUED to fall sporadically; sometimes raining for hours in deep deluges and at other times only intermittent showers. But, at all times, the clouds hovered like huge, dark buzzards. The wind could not budge them, nor could the sun shrink them.

A new era in Stacey's life dawned that first week in Germany. It was as if a different world had opened; a world he was ready to explore. Each glorious morning, Stacey awoke to the warmth, comfort, and guiding light of Anneliese's soul. Her presence brought rays of hope that lit up his being. Each day was a new experience that he fully embraced.

Stacey understood that, similar to the rainy days ahead, new beginnings aren't always sunny. They came with uncertainty and challenges. Subsequently, he tentatively moved forward with his actions and emotions. He anticipated difficulties with the language, the people, and the process of reconfiguring his life.

Stacey completed many of the organizational tasks outlined in the directions from the teacher exchange program. He went to the local immigration center at the police station, registered as living in Germany for longer than 30 days, and applied for a visa. Next, Stacey exchanged his money into Euros and attempted to open an initial checking/savings account at the Sparkasse Bank. He soon found that he'd have to wait until his visa finalized to actually use the checking account.

Anneliese's parents arrived at the end of the week. She had informed them ahead of time that Stacey would be there when they arrived, so they were prepared to meet him.

It was surprising to Stacey that her parents spoke and understood English fairly well. Anneliese had told him that she didn't think they knew very many words. Stacey chuckled when they told him that they learned English from listening to American music when they were young.

Stacey liked Anneliese's dad, Jan, immediately after he introduced himself. Slightly balding and dressed in a blazer and turtleneck, he reminded Stacey of a wise professor. He put Stacey at ease with his soft-spoken English and his stories about his adventures in Europe and Asia. He was charismatic, opinionated, and well-traveled. Stacey saw a bit of himself in Jan.

Anneliese's mom, Charlotte, was petite and donned a short, stylish haircut. Based upon a first impression of her small stature, Stacey thought Charlotte would be the quiet, grandmotherly type. But right from the initial introduction, Charlotte surprised Stacey. She bubbled over with hospitality, charm, and outright concern for those around her, including Stacey.

Two nights after they arrived, they invited Anneliese's sister, Eva, and her boyfriend, Mika, to join them for dinner. Eva was an English teacher of intermediate schoolchildren. Stacey hoped that they would have a lot to talk about. But, as it turned out, Eva was more interested in her boyfriend all evening.

After introductions, Anneliese's family and Stacey sat around the dining room table talking and sipping on generously-filled glasses of Chianti. Charlotte stood in the adjacent kitchen preparing dinner. Since the kitchen opened to the dining room and family room, Charlotte was still a part of the conversation. The wind fired the pinging rain into the windows like a shooting gallery. Flashes of light and rumbling thunder periodically interrupted the evening.

"What was favorite place for travel in Europe?" Charlotte asked, rolling meatballs and placing them on a pan.

"Germany, of course," Stacey blurted, beaming. The others chuckled, lightly. "Anneliese showed me around Bavaria. We saw Neuschwanstein and Garmisch Partenkirchen, and we rode bikes near Berchestgaden. Beautiful country."

"Not so beautiful. You broke your wrist and it rains too much," Anneliese uttered, sipping her Chianti and stealing sly glances of approval from her sister.

"I could have broken my wrist anywhere. It's not Germany's fault," Stacey replied. "I agree with you about the rain, though. I would like to see the sun shine on the Alps."

"I am happy she shows you those places. But, you need to visit the car museum in Amerang," Jan added, pointing to a model car that was sitting on an armoire. "You see history of German autos."

"Yes, you see what words BMW really are," Mika said, cracking a smile.

"Isn't it Bavarian Motor Works?" Stacey asked.

"In Germany, BMW means Bavarian Manure Works," Mika teased, chuckling.

"In America, BMW is popular. It's a status symbol for wealth," Stacey remarked. "If you don't like BMW's, then what is Germany's popular car?"

"Mercedes and Porsche. They are best cars German auto companies make," Jan replied. "Come, I show you some more models in den."

Jan persuaded everyone to get up and follow him to the den where he showed off his collection of model Porsche and Mercedes racing cars. Stacey and Mika were impressed, but Jan's wife and daughters seemed bored and embarrassed that a grown man would treasure a set of model cars so much. After several minutes, Charlotte excused herself back to the kitchen to finish preparing dinner.

"Do you like to play darts?" Jan asked, holding out a set of three darts for Stacey.

Stacey took the darts. "Sure, I've played before. I'm better at pool than at darts, but I'll give it a go."

"I want so much to put pool table in den, but it not fit. So, dartboard it was," Jan said, pointing to the dartboard hanging on the wall.

"Any game is fun after a glass of Chianti," Stacey joked, finishing his first glass.

"Stacey throws first. Mika you play next. The girls play last. They beat each of us. I taught them," Jan said, smiling. "The way to score is add three darts. But, I always play the dart closest to bull's eye is winner. Is that okay?"

Everyone nodded in agreement. Jan left momentarily, returning with a bottle of Chianti and pouring Stacey another glass. Mika moved to one side of the room. Anneliese and Eva sat on the couch, looking unimpressed.

As they began playing darts, Charlotte and Jan asked Stacey more personal questions. He answered with charm and politeness.

"Why are you a teacher?" Charlotte called out from the kitchen as she cooked dinner.

"My mom was a teacher. Before she died, she told me that she thought I would make a wonderful teacher," Stacey explained, sipping on his second glass of Chianti. "After I graduated from college, I tried a couple of occupations which I didn't enjoy. I always had teaching in the back of my mind, so I went back to school. I've been teaching for a few years and love it."

"It is great job to be a father. Do you think you have child?" Anneliese's mom asked, poking her head into the den.

"I would like kids, eventually," Stacey replied.

"Do you think you can live in Germany, or you only live in America?" Charlotte implored.

"*Mutti, wir wissen was Du moechtest. Hoer bitte auf,*" Anneliese asserted, glaring at her mom.

"It's okay. I know what she is inferring," Stacey said, motioning to Anneliese to calm down. He turned back to Charlotte. "Since my parents died, I've been very protective of my brother. But, this job in Germany should allow me to break free of that obligation. So, yes, I do think I could live in Germany."

Charlotte went back to cooking in the kitchen.

"How is your brother in America?" Jan asked, pausing between throws for Stacey's answer.

"He is doing well at not missing me, but not so well at playing golf," Stacey explained, twirling the darts around in his hand. "He's trying to qualify to play in a professional tournament. We talked a couple hours ago and he had just played the first 18 holes of the 36-hole tournament. Of 24 competitors, Reece was 17th. He was disappointed in his performance and embarrassed that Wende was there to watch it."

"Tell my dad what you tell Reece. He likes to play golf, too," Anneliese stated.

"I told my brother not to play to win. Play to enjoy the experience," Stacey said. "I also told him to keep taking risks and big swings, but also be patient. The game fluctuates between finesse and power. His game has always been successful when he gets into that rhythm between cranking it and a soft touch."

"I think it great advice. I think you caddy for me," Jan joked.

"That's exactly what my brother said," Stacey said. He threw a dart and hit the bull's eye.

"Great throw," Jan exclaimed. "Will your brother play more days in tournament?"

"One more day, unless he wins, and in that case he would play two more," Stacey replied.

"Do you hear from Wende? How is she in America?" Eva asked.

"*Ja, sie ist gut. Sie verbringt viel Zeit mit Stacey Bruder auf dem Golfplatz. Aber. . .*" Anneliese paused after realizing she was speaking in German. "Sorry, it is easy to return to German."

"No, you shouldn't be sorry," Stacey acknowledged. "I am in your home country. I'm the one who is embarrassed that I haven't mastered German, yet."

"We both try better," Anneliese said, smiling. She turned back to her sister. "Wende goes with Reece and his friend, Jeff, to practice golf in Napa, California. Wende likes driving cart and to be in sunny, wonderful place of golf course."

Stacey turned to Jan and said, "My brother chose our good friend, Jeff, to be his caddy for the tournament. Jeff is a golf expert, and they both played together on the high school golf team. They're both playing out a dream at this tournament."

"I hope they play better tomorrow," Jan said.

"Wende does more than golf, ya?" Eva asked. She gave her boyfriend a glare. "There is more in life than sport."

"Ya. Reece took Wende to taste different wines of Napa," Anneliese began. "They ride on a special train for wine and food. She saw beautiful sights and tried good wine. Yesterday, she went with Jeff's girlfriend, Patty, to the river and ocean. They take boats around river. She said she saw seals play in the water."

"Is Patty woman who went back home for university?" Charlotte asked, coming into the den bringing a plate of fried meatballs and a dish of sauce.

"Yes, that's Patty," Stacey answered, taking a meatball off the plate and tasting it. "Delicious."

"Thank you," Charlotte said with pride. "Did the university allow her back in?"

"Yes. They allowed her to begin classes late," Stacey said, finishing the rest of the meatball. "She's already attended her classes, and she mentioned that she didn't have any problems transitioning after missing a few classes. She presented the idea for her final art project to her advisor. It was accepted, and she began to work on her art portfolio."

"That is good. I not like when large places make it difficult for small people," Charlotte responded. "What is difficult for you since you live in Germany?"

"The language has been the biggest problem for me. I should have been more prepared," Stacey admitted.

A beeper went off in the kitchen and Charlotte excused herself to finish getting dinner ready. While Charlotte was gone, everyone polished off the plate of meatballs in between games of darts.

"You not need to speak German for teaching?" Eva asked.

Eva's finally interested in something that concerns me, thought Stacey.

"No, not necessarily," Stacey replied. "I will be teaching the students in English, but I'm sure there will be many instances when I'll need to speak German."

"I think that right," Eva said, sharply.

"It's been difficult with Anneliese's friends, too," Stacey said. "We went out with her friends around the city. Greta and Bianka don't speak English, nor did they show any interest in speaking it with me. I sat next to her friends and pretended I knew what they were saying in German."

"Anneliese say sentences in English for you, ya?" Jan asked.

"Yes, she translated some things for me, but she couldn't do it all," Stacey said. "Making friends in another language is hard work. I miss the ease of speaking freely and the humor. I don't think I've laughed once when we've hung out with Anneliese's friends."

"You need to find your own friend that is not Anneliese's friends," Eva said.

"I have, sort of," Stacey said. "Anneliese introduced me to her friend, Erik. He's super nice, speaks English, and we have the same interests in sports. Plus, Erik attends the university in Munich, so I'm hoping I can see him during the school year."

"That is good," Jan said.

"Dinner is ready," Charlotte called out.

For dinner, Anneliese's mom served a mixed salad of lettuce, carrots, celery, beets, and cheese with an Italian dressing. Next, she dished out a traditional German sausage meal over wild rice with a baguette on the side. Stacey had two full plates.

Stacey was enthralled with the mealtime conversation. It began with their observations of American politics and its influence in the world. They were critical of American power in the region. They asked Stacey if he was religious. He told them he didn't belong to an organized religion, but that he was spiritual. Jan spoke of his interest in Buddhism initiated by his recent trip to Thailand. Anneliese and Jan translated the major ideas into English for Stacey and sometimes translated Stacey's speech into German for everyone else. The group would nod in agreement, scrunch up their faces in disapproval, or lightly laugh.

When dinner was over, they all went to the living room where they drank shots of port wine and conversed for another hour. Lightning flashed in the sky and claps of thunder were reminiscent of being drunk in a nightclub. When Stacey, Anneliese, and her family were too tired to talk, they stood up and said their good-byes for the night. Eva and Mika went back to her apartment. And, for the first time in a week or more, Stacey slept alone in Eva's old bedroom. He didn't mind, though, because he was too drunk to care.

* * *

TWO DAYS LATER, Stacey and Anneliese said goodbye to her family and left for Munich. They drove a Volkswagen hatchback filled with boxes and bags, and two mountain bikes were perched across a rack on the top of the car.

The rain had stopped, and the sun occasionally shined from behind the huge cumulus clouds. Like huge warships slowly changing course on choppy, blue waters, the clouds seemed to follow them on their northward path.

As they left Rosenheim, the sun warmed Stacey's soul. Eagerness about his new life flushed through him. He felt as if everything that lay ahead of him was golden. Tossing and turning with anticipation, he had spent much of the previous night envisioning positive experiences with the new staff, the program director, and his apartment. He was also looking forward to a phone call from Reece. He hoped for good news about Reece's last day at the tournament.

"You are not talking. You are sad, ya?" Anneliese asked, glancing over her shoulder as she changed lanes on the autobahn.

"No. I'm actually happy yet a little nervous about what awaits me in Munich," Stacey answered, checking to make sure the lane was empty before Anneliese merged.

"What makes you nervous?" Anneliese asked.

"For one, I'm anxious about teaching at this new school. I hope I get along with the other teachers," Stacey replied. "Also, I want to see where my apartment is in the city and what it looks like. I feel like an entitled American, but I'm used to living in a fairly comfortable house in a nice neighborhood, so I'm worried that the apartment won't have the same appeal."

"It will not be the same as house, but we buy pictures and chairs to make apartment more comfortable," Anneliese remarked, smiling. "I am glad you are okay. I think you might not enjoy last three days with my family. I was worried you not like my family because they ask many questions."

"Oh no, I had a wonderful time with your family," Stacey said, reassuringly resting his hand on her thigh. "Sometimes I am sad after I see your family, but it's not your family's fault. Being around them makes me remember my family before my parents died. I mean, in a way, I love feeling like I'm part of a whole family again. And, in another way, I miss my own parents when I see you with your parents."

"Oh, I am much sorry," Anneliese said, comforting Stacey by reaching down and holding his hand. "I not think of your parents when we see my family. I try to be aware of your feelings. I am happy you tell me the truth and not make your feelings secret."

"This feeling is unusual for me," Stacey recalled. "I've met the families of a few women that I've dated, but your family is the first one to make me reminisce and long for my parents."

"Is that good or bad?" Anneliese shot him a worried look.

"I think it's good. It means your family resembles mine," Stacey said. "They seemed to care about how I was going to do in Munich, my feelings for you, and my future intentions. I was part of the family for a couple of days. I haven't felt like that for a long time."

"Thank you for telling me how you feel," Anneliese said.

They drove the next ten minutes in silence. Anneliese zipped in and out of lanes. Stacey fiddled with the radio, trying to find music that he liked.

"Look, there is golf course," Anneliese stated, pointing to a swab of green grass through a wooded area. "When do you get call from Reece, morning or late noon?"

"He should call late tonight," Stacey said. "I hope it's good news. He sounded so dejected yesterday."

"He and Jeff have practiced so much. I know they do good today," Anneliese said.

"I'm glad Reece made Jeff his caddy. Jeff will take care of him today," Stacey said.

"And Wende will give him good luck," Anneliese said.

By the time they arrived, the sun had disappeared. The clouds towered above the city like a wave. They crashed down with rain across the green farmlands that surrounded the suburban boundaries of the city for miles upon miles. It smothered the view of the Bavarian Alps, which rose up on the horizon to the south. Their high, ragged, granite peaks sat hidden only a short distance away.

Anneliese drove and pointed out the different landmarks and sights of Munich. The car slowed down, and Anneliese parallel parked on the side of a busy street.

"We are here," she announced, happily.

"Which building is it," Stacey asked, scanning the multi-story buildings that lined the street on both sides.

Anneliese pointed to a six story, brick building about 200 feet away. She yawned and popped open the hatchback from a lever on the driver side floor. Reaching back, she grabbed the hood on her coat and pulled it over her head.

It's an appealing neighborhood, Stacey thought as he pulled his hood up and zipped his jacket.

Anneliese opened the door and quickly jumped out of the car, shrieking as the rain struck her dry skin. She grabbed a couple of bags from the back and dashed to a set of glass doors.

Once Stacey saw exactly where he'd be going, he climbed out of the car, ran to the doors while trying to avoid the slicing rain.

"Let me get those for you," Stacey offered. He lifted the bags from Anneliese's arms. Pain immediately shot through his arm.

"Mother fucker," Stacey exclaimed. He swiftly set the bags down.

"What is wrong?" Anneliese asked.

"I forgot about my wrist," Stacey said, holding his arm.

"Sorry. I forget, also," Anneliese said, putting down her remaining bag. "I take one bag, if you can take other?"

"Yeah, I can carry one in my good hand," Stacey said. He picked up one bag.

Anneliese unlocked the door, picked up the bags, and carefully arranged the luggage in her arms as they entered the lobby.

There were five rows of mailboxes against the right wall. On the left were a public phone and two, giant bulletin boards. Each board held a collage of advertisements, notices, and business cards. The fact that everything was written in German and that he could barely understand the messages filled him with an unexpected frustration.

Why did I waste my time with the *Rosetta Stone* program? I don't recognize a damn word, Stacey thought.

They rode the elevator to the third floor. Halfway down the hallway, Anneliese stopped in front of a door, unlocked it, and they walked in.

Shit. The living room is smaller than Anneliese described, Stacey thought.

A tan couch faced the television across the room. Stacey stepped near the windows and saw the beautiful English Gardens Park.

Anneliese took the bags from Stacey and brought them to her room. Stacey toured more of the apartment. He walked by some tall bookshelves, giving the books a quick once-over.

"All German titles," Stacey muttered.

"What did you say?" Anneliese called out from the bedroom.

"Nothing, just looking at your books," Stacey responded.

Glancing in Anneliese's bedroom, Stacey saw that the bed, draped in a red and gold bedcover, took up most of the space. A print of Van Gogh's *Sunflowers* hung over the bed. Candles lined shelves and the windowsills.

Not much room for two people, Stacey thought.

"Come, I show you kitchen," Anneliese said.

The kitchen seemed no bigger than a standard bathroom in America, yet it housed a small sink, two wall cabinets, a short amount of counter space on either side of the sink, a tiny microwave, and barely enough space for a shorter than usual refrigerator.

My fantasy of cooking meals together is shot, Stacey complained to himself. The necessities leave no room for any of the conveniences of life. No dishwasher or oven.

"Where do you eat?" Stacey glanced around for tables and chairs.

"Much of the time I eat on the table by the couch. I put it away when I not use it," Anneliese said. She pointed toward a table against the wall; its legs folded. "Sometimes I eat with friend at restaurant. We can do both, ya?"

"You're really smart to design your apartment this way, especially since it's so small," Stacey remarked.

"You like my apartment?" Anneliese asked, intently watching Stacey for a sign of approval.

"Yeah, it's perfect," Stacey said. He kissed her on the cheek.

"I feel it is perfect, too," Anneliese said, smiling.

"I hope my apartment is as nice as yours," Stacey said.

"You are ready to find new school and apartment, ya?" Anneliese asked.

"Yes. Let's do this," Stacey gave Anneliese a hug and then zipped his jacket.

Anneliese put on her jacket and grabbed her car keys. "Okay, I am ready."

They ran in the rain to Anneliese's car. Once in and under cover, Stacey turned to Anneliese and looked her in the eye. "You're stunning."

* * *

FAMILIAR WITH THE PHORMS BILINGUAL SCHOOL, Anneliese knew exactly how to get there. Stacey sat in the passenger seat, still relishing in Anneliese's beauty.

Stacey was content as Anneliese pulled into the parking lot of the school. He had seen pictures of it, but in person, it seemed more impressive and formidable. It was a multi-story, brick building surrounded by green gardens.

Curiosity took hold of Stacey, and he hopped out of the car. He and Anneliese walked, hand in hand, into the large arched doors of the office.

"*Kann ich Dir helfen?*" the office assistant asked, looking up from the computer on her desk.

Anneliese glanced at Stacey to see if he wanted her to translate.

Understanding the question because of his rudimentary German online course, Stacey replied, "Hi, my name is Stacey Shepherd, and this is my friend, Anneliese. I'm one of the new English teachers on exchange from California."

"Oh, *wunderbar*," exclaimed the woman. She had a light German accent. "My name is Ester. I work in the office. Nice to meet you."

Stacey was relieved that she spoke English.

"Nice to meet you, too. I'm looking for the director, Mr. Haas," Stacey said.

"Let me show you the way," Ester said. She led Stacey and Anneliese through the office to a door at the back of the room. "Please ask if you need anything or have any questions. Mr. Haas likes teachers to ask the office first before contacting him."

"That's how it is at my school, too. The office staff often knows more about what's going on than the principal," Stacey commented.

Soon after entering the director's office, Ester gestured for Stacey to come in. He and Anneliese met Mr. Haas, who stood up from his desk and shook their hands. He was short and stocky, so Stacey couldn't help but stare down at his thinning hair and bushy mustache.

"Have you had an opportunity to travel or explore München?" Mr. Haas asked, sitting back down in his chair and twirling a pen in his hand. His office was well organized and neat.

"Yes. My brother and friends were here for a couple of weeks. We biked in France and Switzerland. After they left, Anneliese and I took a few trips around the Bavarian region," Stacey replied, fidgeting because he wasn't sure if he should stay standing or sit down in one of the chairs. "But, I haven't had an opportunity to explore much of Munich. I'm looking forward to getting to know the city in the next few months."

"It is a wonderful city, and a great location to visit other places in Europe," Mr. Hass said. He turned his attention to Anneliese. "How about you? Another teacher? Girlfriend?"

Anneliese smiled brightly. "No, I am university student at Ludwig Maximillian."

"Ah, then you'll be able to show Stacey around München," Mr. Hass said.

Mr. Hass then gave a rousing talk about the school, which left Stacey's head spinning. Mr. Hass started with the school's layout, and quickly brushed over the variety of students they had, the teaching philosophy and curriculum each teacher was supposed to adhere to. He mentioned the names of relevant members of the staff, rules and the consequences for breaking them, and ended with the best local restaurants.

Stacey tried to take everything in, but as he let one subject of the conversation sink in, Mr. Hass would move on to another one. He remembered only scattered tidbits of information. He wasn't too worried, though, because he *knew* teaching. It was ingrained in his soul. As long as he had kids to teach, all else was white noise.

Changing the topic of conversation, Mr. Hass asked, "As I recall, you have a number of boxes in your classroom. Would you like me to show you to your class?"

"Yes, that would be great," Stacey said, trying to hold in his eagerness. "I need to pick up a few of those boxes for my apartment. And, I'm curious about the room."

"I'm sure you are. Follow me," Mr. Hass ordered, rising from his chair.

Mr. Haas led Stacey and Anneliese down a brightly lit corridor filled with student work and up a flight of stairs to the second floor. The director stopped at the third door from the right and opened it.

"Okay, young man, this is the key to your new classroom. This other key will get you into the hallways here and a staff room on the first floor." Mr. Hass handed Stacey two keys.

"Thank you so much. I am looking forward to this opportunity. I will do a great job for you." Stacey reached out and shook the director's hand.

"I know you will," Mr. Hass said. He ushered Stacey and Anneliese into the room. "Only a few more things. The two other exchange teachers from California will be in tomorrow, in case you wanted to meet them.

"We'll have a staff meeting the day after tomorrow. You'll get to know the rest of the staff, especially the other teachers in your grade level team. If there's anything you need, let me or the office know. Stop by my office on the way out. I'll have the information packet and key to your apartment on my desk.

"It's only a studio in a student housing building for the university. I apologize because we had you in a larger apartment, but the recent rain damaged the rooms."

"No problem. I'm sure it will be fine. Thanks for everything," Stacey said, trying to hide his disappointment.

Mr. Haas shook Stacey and Anneliese's hand one last time, wished them well, and walked out the door.

Once the director left, Stacey examined the classroom. Similar to American classrooms, white boards, posters, and bulletin boards lined the walls. Stacey found subtle differences, too. For example, the German flag flew next to the window. The tables and chairs were wood, instead of plastic and metal, and the floors were marble. The technology in the class astounded Stacey. There was a station of six computers along the wall, a wide-screen television, and a ceiling projector.

Exhilaration swept through Stacey because the school year at Phorms was about to start. He couldn't wait to get his classroom set up. Being aware of his sprained wrist, he asked Anneliese to help him move desks. He pulled out several items from his box marked for the classroom. They set out nametags on the desks and ended their work by hanging a few posters on the walls.

Realizing they had much more to do, Stacey and Anneliese carried his boxes of personal items out to her car, doing their best to keep the boxes dry by covering them with garbage bags they found in the school. Back in the office, he received the keys and directions to his new apartment. They thanked Ester and Mr. Haas once more and then drove off to find his apartment building.

Anneliese used the GPS system on her cell phone to find Stacey's building. It was located in an industrialized area south of the university and her apartment.

God, this thing looks like a block of concrete built in the Cold War era, Stacey thought. His feelings of elation sunk to that now-familiar anxiety.

After driving around twice, they found street parking near the building. They scurried out of the car, trying to dodge raindrops as they ran to the building.

Once inside, they found the elevator in the bleak entrance hall. They took the elevator up to the fifth floor. Getting off the elevator, Stacey found the corridor was long, dim, and cold. He felt like he was in a prison.

A communal kitchen area was halfway down the hall. One young man was cooking. Stacey said hello and moved on.

Shit, he thought. I'll have to cook my meals with college kids. Fuck, this is going to take a major adjustment in attitude to survive in this environment. His anxiety flared into a fire-like sensation in his chest.

Opening the door to his apartment, Stacey was pleasantly surprised at the size of the studio room. There was a living area with a couch, chair, and coffee table. Next to the couch was a small dining table with two chairs. Off to the right, a queen size bed was partitioned off for privacy with a large dresser. The window, though overlooking a narrow street, had a large sill for sitting, which he found pleasant. Stacey was disappointed, though, when he noticed the concrete flooring, no kitchen, and an open shower that emptied into a drain on the bathroom floor.

After touring the apartment and the rest of the building, Stacey and Anneliese went back to the car for Stacey's things. It took them two trips to lug the boxes, bags, and backpacks up to his apartment. They took a few items out of boxes and placed them around the apartment, but it was done with much less fervor than earlier in the day when they unpacked his classroom.

Anneliese offered to take Stacey out for dinner and to spend the night at her place. Stacey accepted, concluding that the only consolation about staying in that apartment was that he would probably end up spending many nights at Anneliese's place.

After celebrating such a whirlwind of a day with dinner at a restaurant, Stacey and Anneliese spent the rest of the evening relaxing in her apartment.

* * *

AS STACEY AND ANNELIESE PREPARED for bed, they received a phone call from Reece. Stacey set down his toothbrush and answered the phone.

"Hey, Reece. How was the last day of the tournament?" Stacey asked, cringing in anticipation of bad news.

"I shot a 67, 5 shots under par," Reece exclaimed.

Stacey could hear the enthusiasm in Reece's voice. Stacey gave Anneliese a quick thumbs-up sign.

"That's great, bro," Stacey said, sitting down on the corner of the bed. "I knew you could do it. Sounds like you improved vastly over yesterday's game. What place did you come in?"

"Ninth place for the two-day tournament," Reece answered. "Not good enough for the actual PGA Tour, but still fuckin' awesome. If I would've shot a 70 on the first day, I would be playing in the tournament on Thursday."

"Not bad for being in 17th place yesterday," Stacey said. "What do you attribute your success to?"

"I putted better, especially on the par 3's and 4's," Reece answered. "I also trusted Jeff's judgment more and took his advice on club selection and shot distances."

"I'm proud of you. I wish I could've seen it. Mom and Dad are somewhere beaming with pride," Stacey said. Tears of joy filled his eyes.

Anneliese walked over and nudged Stacey, raising her arms in the air in a questioning fashion. Stacey leaned over to Anneliese and whispered what place Reece ended the tournament and his scores. She wanted to talk, so Stacey handed her the phone.

"*Grüß gott*, Reece. I am happy for you," Anneliese told him. "Wende say to me how good you play golf, but now I know it is for real."

"Thanks," Reece said. "Wende has been wonderful. She's gone to the golf course so many times on *her* vacation. I owe her. She'll get to do whatever she wants on her last two days."

"Yes, she should," Anneliese agreed. She hinted at what else Reece could do. "They have much popular European tour for golf. You could play here."

"You and Wende seem to think alike, or you just talk a lot," Reece chuckled. "Do you wanna talk to her?"

"No, tell her we talk tomorrow. Congratulations, again," Anneliese said. She handed the phone back to Stacey. After a few laughs with Reece, he hung up.

Stacey reached for Anneliese's hands, gently leading her to sit next to him.

"I want you to know that I am happy," Stacey said. "I feel content here with you, like this is where I'm supposed to be."

"I am happy. There is a sentence we say in German for when we are happy. *Geteilte freude ist doppelte freude.* I said that two of us together makes happiness double," Anneliese explained.

"So much of happiness depends upon who you're with. I'm so grateful that I found you to share this joy," Stacey said. He pulled Anneliese to him, and they embraced.

Everything wasn't perfect, Stacey thought, but all was well in the lives of everyone he knew and that was the best he could have hoped for.

Time and space belonged only to them on their first night living together. It seemed as if the Earth had disappeared and they now floated in the star-studded peace of the universe.

The rain slamming against the window was a witness as Stacey forged a new life in a foreign country.

PART 3

SNOW

Snow is God's body
Cocooned in serenity
Omnipotent still

"There is nothing in the world more beautiful than the forest clothed to its very hollows in snow. It is the still ecstasy of nature, wherein every spray, every blade of grass, every spire of reed, every intricacy of twig, is clad with radiance."

— William Sharp

ORIGINATING FROM THE NORTH, frigid winds solidified water droplets into snowflakes over southern Germany. The flurries drifted silently over the Bavarian sky in rhythmical sweeping patterns. City lights captured the snow parachuting down like confetti from the clouds.

Arriving by the trillions, the snowfall covered the ground, trees, bushes, and plants. Piling up on the streets, cars, houses, and other buildings of Bavaria, snow encased the entire landscape in a snowy den for the hibernation of winter.

Ice permeated the surfaces underneath the snow. Rainwater remaining in puddles or shallow brooks froze into flat, slick plates of ice. Hanging from rooftops, water droplets froze into long icicles. Enclosed in thick layers of ice, leaves and branches drooped under the weight of winter.

Overnight, the world turned serene. The rustling of leaves stilled under the weight of the ice and snow on their branches. Replacing the loud splatter of the rain, a mild breeze swooshed the falling snow through the air. The colorful mountain scenery over southern Germany had changed to one of almost pure white. It was as if the world were completely consumed with the tranquil, yet inhospitable, space of the universe. Inhabiting a small place in that expanse, Stacey was grateful for the peaceful scene of the snowfall.

CHAPTER 11

Love's omnipotence
Hopeful expectations, shared moments and future

"A person does not hear sound only through the ears; he hears sound through every pore of his body. It permeates the entire being, and according to its particular influence either slows or quickens the rhythm of the blood circulation; it either wakens or soothes the nervous system. It arouses a person to greater passions or it calms him by bringing him peace."

— Hazrat Inayat Khan, *The Mysticism of Sound*

A S THE SUN ROSE on a morning in late December, the snow fell and sat silently six inches deep over Munich. Piling up around window sills and doorways, the snow entrenched itself on the roof of Anneliese's apartment building.

By midmorning, the lights in the apartment set off a subtle glow in Anneliese's window. Soon, the curtains in the living room and the shutters in the kitchen window were opened. Stacey sipped a cup of coffee and peered out the large living room windows to the snow-covered cityscape.

Wow, this is beautiful, Stacey thought.

Besides visiting the snow in the mountains of California or the occasional dusting of snow in his hometown, this was the first time he'd ever experienced such a heavy snowstorm.

"Hey Anneliese, come here," Stacey yelled. Even though Stacey took German classes twice per week, he and Anneliese still spoke in English. Anneliese had a better grasp of the English language than Stacey had of German, so for convenience, they conversed in Stacey's native tongue.

"Ya, I come," Anneliese replied. She stood in her bedroom doorway, stretched, rubbed her eyes, and then crossed the room with a lazy shuffle. The combination red pajama bottoms and white sweatshirt added to her adorable, messy hair.

"Look, honey," Stacey exclaimed, pointing out the window. "Look how much it's snowing. Can you believe it?"

"Ya, I imagine it," Anneliese said. "It snows much for winter."

"The way the snowflakes float like tiny feathers—there's an elegance to it. I could watch for hours," Stacey said, holding hands with Anneliese. "It's hypnotic. It reminds me of the feelings I get when I stand on the beach, watching the waves. I'm mesmerized by the power, the vastness, and the mysteries of nature. There's definitely something holy or divine about it. I wonder if it's the same feeling people get when they enter a church."

"I know the feeling," Anneliese said, yawning. "But, for me, it looks like much big place for play. I want to dive and slide in the snow. We make—how do you say—*schnee-engel*?" She made a flapping motion with her out-stretched arms. "You know, in the snow."

"Snow angel?" Stacey guessed, not bothering to hide his amusement.

"Ya. We make snow angels," Anneliese said.

"What else do you enjoy doing in the snow? Do you like to ski or snowboard?" Stacey asked, taking a sip of coffee.

"Ya, I like to ski down the mountain," Anneliese replied. "I am not fast. I ski slowly so I can see beautiful things like the trees and lake. I not like snowboarding; I fall much. We will ski soon for the winter holiday. Ya?"

"I'd love to go skiing with you," Stacey replied. "How 'bout we go sledding now?"

"Ya. I go sled with you. I have a sled here in the apartment. We sled today before my family comes," Anneliese suggested. She eyed his cup of coffee. "But first, you make me coffee, ya?"

"Sure. One cup coming up," Stacey said. They walked into the kitchen. Stacey put more water in the coffee pot. "Why don't you take a shower now? Then, we'll go sledding, and afterwards I'll go shopping for the food we need for tonight's dinner with your family. Is that okay?"

"Ya, it is good," Anneliese agreed. She reached in the cupboard and grabbed a cup.

"I know this is a normal winter day for you, but it's quite unusual for me," Stacey explained. "The snow is elusive where I live and *never* like this. I want to immerse myself in it. I imagine playing in the snow with a beautiful woman would be romantic."

Stacey leaned over and kissed Anneliese.

"Ya. It is romantic to look at snow falling while sitting next to a warm fire," Anneliese's smile beamed and sparkled like the snow in the morning light. "I am happy about the snow because it is our Advent gift today, and it is here for Christmas next week."

Anneliese reached down and grabbed a lighter next to the Advent Wreath. She lit four candles inside the wreath.

"I love *adventskranz*, but I not wait to have Christmas with you," Anneliese said, putting her arm around Stacey.

"Yeah, I can't wait for Christmas," Stacey said, sighing.

"You are not happy to stay here in Germany for Christmas?" Anneliese asked, her smile fading.

"I'm totally excited to spend the holiday with you and your family," Stacey reassured her, massaging Anneliese's shoulders. "I'm conflicted, that's all. It'll be the first Christmas without Reece. It's not a big deal. We're adults now and that's what happens. But, I still feel a little guilty about staying."

Stacey prepared Anneliese's coffee and handed her the cup. Anneliese poured milk and put a spoonful of sugar into her coffee.

"I understand how you feel to be sad and happy at the same time," Anneliese stated, taking a sip of the coffee. "Last Christmas, my sister went on holiday with the family of her boyfriend. It was difficult for my family. But, we did different things and had fun."

"We'll have fun, too. I guarantee it," Stacey said, stealing a sip from Anneliese's cup. "I'm not too worried about Reece, either. He'll spend Christmas with our aunt and cousins. Plus, he's got Wende there right now, and it sounds like they're having a great time."

"Ya. Wende says she had a wonderful day in San Francisco," Anneliese said, taking back the cup. "I am happy she flies over for the week. But, I think she wants Reece to come here for the next time."

"If things keep progressing between the two of them, then I'm sure she'll teach him to be better at compromising," Stacey said with a smile.

"One of us needs to compromise soon, too," Anneliese said, putting down her cup and looking at Stacey with a serious expression on her face. "We need to talk what we do after Christmas. You leave in two weeks to go back to California, and we have not talked about it. We pretend it is not happening."

"I have some ideas, but we should talk about it later," Stacey said, the smile slipping between his lips.

"Always later," Anneliese said with a pout.

The truth was that Stacey had received an email earlier in the week from the director of the teacher exchange program. The German teacher who had taken Stacey's position at his school in California wanted to continue teaching there, which meant that it was up to

Stacey to decide not only his own fate but that of the German teacher, as well.

He hadn't told Anneliese about the email because he wanted a few days to think about the pros and cons of the decision. Up to this point, he hadn't made a decision, but he leaned heavily towards staying in Germany for the next semester.

"You never want to talk about it, and you think it is funny. I will miss you," Anneliese said, reaching for his hand.

"I'll miss you, too." He kissed Anneliese, tenderly touching her face. "We'll talk after we sled. I promise." Then, he took her by the waist, pulled her close, and slowly began lifting her sweatshirt up.

"No, not now," Anneliese said, pulling her sweatshirt down and escaping Stacey's grip. "I will shower and get ready. We go before it is too late."

"Okay, sounds good," Stacey replied.

After watching Anneliese walk to her room, Stacey sat down in the living room next to the stereo. He needed a moment to consider if staying in Germany was what he *really* wanted to do. He turned on the radio and quickly perused the stations. Gustav Holst's "Jupiter" caught his ear. He left the radio on the classical station.

Holst's music swirled through Stacey's mind like a brush gliding across an artist's canvas. The melody took hold of his soul and spiraled down into it. His spirit felt like a snowflake dancing with the wind.

Stacey's heart began to beat in time with the allegro pace of the music. The string of notes aroused reflection and thoughts of those who were significant in his life: Anneliese, his brother, his friends, his parents, and his students. The melody strengthened his pride and devotion to each of those people.

The piece was followed by Beethoven's "Moonlight Sonata". The melody cascaded down into the depths of Stacey's heart and fanned his sense of emptiness. He remembered moments from his childhood when his parents were still alive: vacations to Oregon and Hawaii, joyous holidays spent with relatives, and sporting events he attended with his dad. During the next wave of arpeggio notes, he relived the emotional pain and anguish of his parent's death. He reverted back to when the police arrived at the house, the funeral, and the difficult times that followed.

Einaudi's "Two Sunsets" was the last piece of music. The swooping song heightened Stacey's emotions. The melody swept him away from the apartment. He and Anneliese faded into a dry sea. The images came in waves. The first wave rolled the two lovers onto a secluded beach. They swam, caressed, kissed, and made love. The second wave lapped them onto a boat where they shared laughs with their children. Another vision placed him in a home on the beach with his newly-formed family. He saw holidays being shared with Anneliese, his children, and Reece. He felt satisfied with the way his life transpired in his mind. He felt a deep sense of happiness surge through his body.

At that moment, he knew exactly what he wanted to do. He'd continue teaching in Germany, thereby deepening his relationship with Anneliese. It seemed rash, bold, and exhilarating. It was love.

He didn't know the exact details of what he needed to do next, and he knew there would be ramifications for what ensued. A sudden nervousness overtook him as he thought of the fallout on his life back in California. What would the consequences be with his job, his students, his friends, and especially with Reece? But, as much as the apprehension had strung a rope around his stomach, he felt absolutely petrified of losing his relationship with Anneliese.

I *have* to be with this girl, Stacey thought.

Anneliese came out of the bedroom fully clothed for a wintery day and announced, "I am ready to sled. Let's go before it is too late."

"Yes, let's go 'cause I've got a surprise for you later," Stacey teased, inadvertently putting his hand in his pocket to feel the printout of the email from the director.

"What is the surprise?" Anneliese asked, smiling coyly.

"I can't tell you. It's a secret," Stacey said.

"I have surprise to tell you, too," Anneliese said, patting Stacey on his bottom.

"What is it?" Stacey asked.

"I not tell you now. I tell you tonight after my family leave from dinner," Anneliese replied. "I only tell you now that it is something you have forever."

"I'll have it forever, huh," Stacey repeated. He thought for a few moments and then made a guess. "I know. It's some sort of jewelry. A necklace or watch?"

"No, not close," Anneliese stated. "We go now. I tell you later."

They grabbed their jackets. Stacey lifted the sleds from the large wall hooks and followed Anneliese out of the apartment. As they strolled through the hallways of the building, Stacey continued to guess what Anneliese's surprise might be.

Stacey opened the building's main door, and he and Anneliese were instantly struck with a blast of icy winter air. The coldness encased their faces and hands in a mask of frozen air. It slapped their cheeks, pricked their lips, dried their eyes, and squeezed their ears. Stacey tried warming his hands by bringing his hands to his mouth and breathing warm air into them. But once he took his hands away from his mouth, the moisture remaining on his hands and lips froze instantaneously, and he felt even colder.

Stacey and Anneliese crunched over the newly-fallen snow and ice. Enjoying the idea of forging new tracks, he purposely took them on a path down the snowy sidewalk where no one had previously made tracks. For a brief moment, he imagined himself trudging alone through the mountains on his way to someplace far away.

They walked huddled close to each other down sidewalks and across intersections as quickly as they could without slipping. Finally, they came to the entrance to the park near their apartment. Usually, the park was a green haven for nature lovers, dog walkers, beer drinkers, and sun soakers. Now, though, it emerged as a white retreat for solitude seekers and frolicking kids.

Scouting out possible sledding areas as they walked and talked, Stacey and Anneliese entered the park and followed the trail as it weaved throughout the small, rolling hills.

Anneliese asked, "You have many changes this last year, but the changes are for the better, ya?"

"Yes, of course. I've fallen in love with you," Stacey answered, quickly.

"That is good. I know we love each other," Anneliese said. "What about other parts of your life? What about your job?"

"The job has been great. I've really enjoyed my students and the other teachers at Phorms. So, that's been good," Stacey explained, kicking and spraying snow as he walked. "But, I've only taught a couple of subjects in English. If I could speak German better, they'd allow me to teach more subjects."

"You can take a German class," Anneliese hinted, squeezing his hand. "Not talking of language, do you begin to feel Germany as your home?"

"Germany is home," Stacey said. "My life here is similar to my life in California. I have a job, a couple of friends, and things we do every week."

"What things do you like best?" Anneliese asked.

"Walking around the Christmas markets has been cool," Stacey replied. Feeling the weight of the sleds in his arms, he dropped them and began pulling them with the rope. "We have small craft fairs, but nothing like the street party in Germany. Listening to music while sitting in the *platz* on a cold evening with a warm *platzchen* and a glass of *gluhwein* in my hands is my most recent best memory."

"Do you want anything that will help you to stay in Germany?" Anneliese asked, gazing at Stacey and waiting intently for his answer.

"I guess I'd want to establish some of my old teaching routines and feel that living in Germany is my normal life," Stacey announced.

"I think normal is not what you look for, Stacey. That is why you are here in Germany," Anneliese said.

"That might be so, but I'd still feel more secure having my two feet on the ground first, and then I can get a little crazy in Germany," Stacey said.

"Talk of crazy, Wende and Reece do well, ya?" Anneliese asked.

"They're doing great," Stacey exclaimed. "Reece isn't golfing in the winter, so they've had a lot of time together to do fun things. What I think is crazy is that she's picked up line dancing at the local country bar."

"I know. Wende loves dancing. In primary school, she danced on way to classes," Anneliese chuckled.

"It's too bad Reece didn't want to come for Christmas. He's going to be away from both me and Wende," Stacey remarked.

"Ya, I know it is sad for you and Wende," Anneliese said. "You miss Jeff and Patty, also?"

"I'm glad that they are doing much better than they were when they were here a few months ago," Stacey said. He paused briefly to scoop snow into a ball. He threw the snowball at a nearby tree, missing it by inches. "I can't believe she's got her master's degree and will host her own art show. Reece told me a couple of days ago that they're planning a wedding for September. So, you'll have to fly out to California for that."

"I will be happy for their wedding," Anneliese said. She also stopped to make a snowball and fired it at the same tree. Striking the target, the snowball exploded into a wave of spray.

"I talk to them, email them, text them. All of that. But, I still feel homesick every time I hear from them. I feel jealous of all the things they're doing together," Stacey confessed. He stopped walking and turned to Anneliese. "Plus, it's still hard to live in a foreign country with unfamiliar people, even when you're with the person you love. I don't have any roots or history of my own here. A person needs their history around them to remember who they were and to remind them of where they're going. I'm worried about leaving my history and memories behind me."

"I understand. That is what makes life not easy," Anneliese said. "We make choices about life. You not worry about what happens over there. I hope you will stay. You make new history and memories here."

"I miss the people in my old life. But, the real tragedy would be to go through life without you by my side," Stacey said.

Stacey leaned over and hugged Anneliese. As they were hugging, Stacey looked up and saw the perfect sledding hill. Guiding Anneliese up the hill with one arm, he lugged the sled with his other arm. At the top, they could see kids sledding on an adjacent hill.

"Before we sled, I have something I wanted to tell you." Stacey rattled off a drum roll on the edge of one of the sleds. Then, he set the sled down and took a copy of the email that offered him a second semester in Germany. "I found out last week that one of the German exchange teachers wants to stay for another semester. It turns out that she met someone in California. That means that I could stay at Phorms, if I wanted."

Stacey waved the paper in the air.

"How come you did not tell me last week?" Anneliese asked, looking concerned.

"I needed to think about it on my own," Stacey replied. "It's a big decision, and I wanted to make sure that I had time to think it over by myself."

"What did you decide?" Anneliese asked.

"So, I weighed my options," Stacey explained. "If I stay, I get to continue our relationship and the ones I've made with the students and teachers at Phorms. But with that decision, I'll disappoint my students and teachers in California, Reece, Jeff, and Patty."

Stacey paused for suspense.

"What do you decide? You will stay, ya?" Anneliese exclaimed, playfully pushing Stacey in the chest.

"Yes, I've decided to stay for another semester," Stacey declared, joyously. He lifted Anneliese and spun her around. "We'll be able to spend all of the school year together, plus June, July, and part of August before I go back to California to prepare for the start of the next school year."

"I am much happy and relieved. I not know what to do if I lose you next week," Anneliese admitted. "I pray for this many nights. God brings me snow for Christmas and my boyfriend for the New Year. I can breathe and enjoy our time together."

"I don't know about God making all of this happen, but I know *I've* made the right decision because I am completely in love with you," Stacey said, embracing Anneliese.

"I love you, also. I not tell you this yet, but I not tell any men I love them. You are the first," Anneliese admitted.

"I think Oscar Wilde said something about women wanting to be a man's last love, but that men want to be a woman's first love," Stacey said, trying to recall the exact quote. "It feels incredible to be your first love. And hopefully, we'll be each other's last love."

"Ya, I hope," Anneliese said. "You talked to Reece about staying here, ya?"

"Reece doesn't mind," Stacey began. "He's too busy playing golf and being involved with Wende."

"And your job in California, they do not have an opinion?" Anneliese asked.

"I'm sure Brian would like me to come back," Stacey said. "But, when I talked to him a couple of weeks ago, he told me that Gretel, the German exchange teacher, was doing a great job. So, I don't think he'll miss me too much."

"When do you make decision?" Anneliese asked.

"While you were getting ready, Einaudi's "Two Sunsets" played on the radio," Stacey began. "The music touched the deepest parts of my heart. I mean, it really felt like the music wove through my soul. It was then that it hit me. I've got to take this chance at love with you. That's all there is to it."

Stacey took Anneliese's hand.

"When we're together, we create a special world," Stacey continued. "The chance to make our lives into one life is worth the sacrifice. I know that you'd do the same for me."

"I feel the same for you," Anneliese replied. "I think much about me going to America. If I am not in university for becoming a doctor, I would go with you."

As they hugged, Stacey thought of his parents and wished they were around to witness his happiness. His dad had always told him to take a chance and give a relationship his best. He hoped his parents would respect his decisions. Was meeting Anneliese simply a rare occurrence of two people crossing paths at random, or had destiny mysteriously sent her his way? Either way, he hoped that his parents would bless this union and guide Stacey as he embarked on this life with Anneliese.

"I go home and call Mom and Dad to tell the wonderful words that you stay. Then I call my sister and Wende. I have much to tell, you can imagine," Anneliese said, feverishly trying to get all the words out as quickly as possible. Her mind worked faster than her speech.

"Yeah, I can imagine. I need to call Reece, too," Stacey said.

"Let's go," Anneliese proposed.

"Before you call, do you think we could stay up here on this hill for a little while longer?" Stacey suggested, pointing at the sled. "I think you and I should enjoy this euphoric moment together. I brought this sled all the way up here, so why not use it a few times."

"Ya, I think we can sled. I am happy now to do anything with you," Anneliese said, snuggling around Stacey. "I will call my family when we are home."

For more than an hour Stacey and Anneliese slid down the hill. Most of the time, they slid down together with Stacey sitting in the back and holding onto Anneliese as she sat between his legs. Sometimes he would lean left or right in a playful manner to try to get them to fall into a tumble. A few times they went down the hill by themselves. On those occasions, they had a contest to see who could glide the furthest before stopping. Anneliese won because Stacey would push her at the top as she began her descent.

It had brought them so much enjoyment that they didn't want to leave. They told each other that they had four last runs because they knew they had to prepare dinner soon. Before their final run, they sat on the top of the hill to enjoy the moment.

The snow had stopped falling. The clouds were momentarily swept aside by the mighty wind. The rays of the setting sun reached out and touched them in warmth and brightness. They were quickly awash on a sea of pinkish snow. Their eyes followed the reddish rays into the horizon. Not ten minutes later, though, the sun had fallen behind a cloud, and the snow became gray.

"Is this not one of the best days in your life?" Stacey asked, rhetorically.

"Ya, and better tonight when you know my secret," Anneliese mused.

"This is such a great moment. Tell me now," Stacey pleaded. "The times we remember most are those we live completely in the moment.

So, if you *really* want it to be special; you should tell me now under this amazing sky."

"No, I not," Anneliese said. "I not want you to know before my family is here tonight. I tell you later."

"Oh, come on. I won't tell them. Come on, tell me," Stacey prodded, playfully.

"I tell you, yah, so you not ask more," Anneliese said, smiling brightly.

"Okay, you have my attention," Stacey stated, sitting up in the snow.

"The secret is . . . Close eyes first and I tell secret," Anneliese instructed.

"Fine, I'll close my eyes," Stacey huffed. He closed his eyes, reluctantly.

Once Stacey's eyes were closed, Anneliese adjusted herself on her sled and pushed herself down the hill. As she began sledding, she screamed, "If you want to know the secret, you catch me first. Or, I never tell."

Stacey hustled to get himself on his sled. He rushed down the hill and caught Anneliese at the bottom. Even so, Anneliese did not tell her secret. In response, Stacey tickled her until she laughed so long that she got the hiccups. She still didn't tell, so Stacey quickly gave up. As they were about to leave, it started snowing again. Stacey picked up the sleds with his right arm and held Anneliese's hand with his left hand.

They headed back to the apartment where their day had begun. There was one big difference. They could now safely envision a long term future together.

CHAPTER 12

Moments are uniquely designed
Like snowflakes
Yet shaped by emotion

"It was the best of times, it was the worst of times . . . it was the season of Light, it was the season of Darkness, it was the spring of hope, it was the winter of despair, we had everything before us, we had nothing before us."

— Charles Dickens, *A Tale of Two Cities*

A
S STACEY AND ANNELIESE triumphantly walked home, Stacey's phone sliced the serene moment with a loud ring. He leaned the sled against his leg, took off one glove, and pulled out his cell phone from his pocket. It was Reece, but he let it ring. He wanted to talk to him, but he'd rather do it later.

"You not answer phone? Who is it?" Anneliese wondered.

"It's Reece. I'll call him later," Stacey replied. Just as soon as the phone stopped ringing, it began again. Stacey ignored it one more time as he began putting his glove back on. The phone stopped ringing and immediately began, yet again.

Frustrated, Stacey took off his gloves and answered the phone.

"What's up?" Stacey asked. He immediately turned from Anneliese and walked away. That was the last thing Anneliese heard from Stacey for another ten minutes, except for soft whispers.

Anneliese stood next to the sled and watched him for any signs of a reaction whether it be good or bad.

When Stacey ended the call, he took a couple of moments to himself. Lost in thought and emotion, he let his head fall back and watched the falling snow. The snow seemed different, now. It was neither romantic nor playful, but rather a primordial, lifeless killer. Jack London's description of the bleak Alaskan wilderness in *White Fang* seeped into his thoughts. After a few deep breaths, he trudged back to Anneliese with his head hanging heavy. As soon as Anneliese saw him, she knew something was wrong.

"That was Reece," Stacey said, on the verge of crying. "He called because he was in a serious accident, along with Jeff and Patty's brother, Brian."

"What happened? Is everyone okay?" Anneliese asked, a worried expression on her face.

Stacey paused before answering because he could feel the tears coming. If he began speaking again, he would cry. Stacey composed himself by taking some deep breaths.

"No, they aren't okay," Stacey said, solemnly. "Reece is in the hospital. He broke his back, but he's expected to have a full recovery.

"Jeff broke his neck and is in and out of consciousness. The doctors are worried he's going to have some paralysis. Patty's brother, Brian, died at the scene. He was my principal and friend. I can't believe it."

Stacey stared at the snow-ravaged ground. The tears finally streamed down his cheek. Anneliese quickly put her arms around Stacey in a comforting hug.

The penetrating silence magnified his sudden sense of loneliness and isolation. He felt helpless knowing Reece and his friends were dealing with this tragedy without him.

"I'm sorry. I can't imagine." Anneliese broke into tears. "How did this happen?"

"Something to do with skiing," Stacey muttered. While he and Anneliese were having such a wonderful time in the snow, Reece and Jeff lay in the hospital. Tentacles of guilt wrapped around his neck. "I couldn't understand Reece very well. He was distraught on the phone, so—"

"Is Wende okay?" Anneliese interrupted.

"She's fine," Stacey said, distracted. "Neither she nor Patty were hurt."

"I have to get back home," Stacey said, feeling the pressure weigh down on him. "I know this means we'll probably miss our first Christmas together, but I need to be there. I feel helpless and out of control." Stacey ended those last words in an intense, angry tone. His rage was toward himself for not being able to help his friends.

Anneliese stared at him with a concerned look on her face.

"I'm sorry. I'm not mad at you," Stacey said, trying to put her at ease. "I'm frustrated and mad because I'm so far away. Even if I can get a flight out tomorrow morning, I won't get to California until tomorrow night. That's a long time to wait to see people who are hurt, especially my brother, you know?"

"Ya, I can imagine," Anneliese replied. She paused for a moment and then took Stacey's hands. "I will come to California with you. I go for you. You want that, ya?"

"Really? You'd come with me?" Stacey said, surprised.

Anneliese nodded her head.

"I would love it if you came with me, but what about Christmas? You'd be away from your family," Stacey asked.

"No, it is okay," Anneliese began. "I come to California, but I stay for only three or four days. I be with you and your brother. Then I come to Germany for Christmas with my family, and you stay in California with Reece and friends."

"Oh God, I would really appreciate that," Stacey said, relieved that she understood.

"I do not think you go to California alone. I stand with you. That is love," Anneliese expressed, holding Stacey's hand. "What city in California do we fly into?"

"We'll be flying in and out of San Francisco," Stacey answered. "Maybe on your last day, since we are flying out of there anyway, we could go into the city since you haven't been to the States before."

"Ya, I would enjoy to see San Francisco and the golden bridge. Oh, I would like to see the ocean, also," Anneliese said. The excitement of the trip quickly faded as she became aware again of the real reason why they were going. She sensed that Stacey felt this, too, so she quickly added, "But, we see the city only if you do not need to be with friends for the day. To be with your brother and friends is more important."

"You're right. I can't promise that we'll go to the city or to the ocean, especially since we'll be at the hospital in Truckee, which is in the mountains about three hours away from the city. But, I'll try to get us there," Stacey offered.

"Where do we stay?" Anneliese asked. "I can try to find a room while you get the plane tickets."

"Thanks, but Reece and I have an aunt that has a second home up there. That's where the group of them were staying when the accident happened. Reece said we can stay there," Stacey explained. He picked up the sleds. "Let's get going, okay? I have to go online to check the flights that are available."

"Okay. I will get our bags ready for travel so you not have to worry," Anneliese said.

"Thanks for helping. You're more than anything I could have ever asked for. I love you." Stacey reached out and hugged Anneliese.

"I love you," Anneliese replied.

The snow fell steadily as Stacey and Anneliese walked back to the apartment. Anneliese called her parents and told them the situation. Then, Stacey and Anneliese readied themselves for their last minute trip across the ocean. Stacey worked at his computer for over an hour trying to get the airline flight with the best times and prices. Meanwhile, Anneliese packed their suitcases.

Later in the evening, Stacey told Anneliese that they would be leaving the next morning at 10:45 a.m. and that they would get to San Francisco by 2:00 p.m. the following day. He also mentioned that he booked her return to Munich on Friday morning, just in enough time for Christmas on Saturday. She agreed with the arrangements.

Anneliese showed Stacey what she had packed thus far. Stacey's bag was only partially packed because most of his belongings were at his apartment, and he didn't want to go there to get them. Any extra clothing, he'd find at his home in California or buy at a store. Once packed, they climbed into bed. Anneliese fell right to sleep, but Stacey laid awake struggling with his emotions. Peering out the opened blinds, he watched the sky fall to pieces.

The next morning Stacey and Anneliese lugged their suitcases out of the apartment. The gray snow had been shoveled off the sidewalk, so they easily rolled their bags to the taxi waiting at the curb.

The taxi slowly made its way to the airport. As Stacey and Anneliese rode silently in the backseat, they stared blindly out of their windows at the blanketed world that whizzed by them.

Stacey thought how life will forever be different in his small, bubbled world in California. What painful information will he find out that he didn't already know? What awful revelations will he be told? How would he cope with all the tragedy and emotional turmoil he'd soon be embroiled in?

CHAPTER 13

Tragedy
Emotional yearn for family is strong
Gravity

"Take heart. Suffering, when it climbs highest, lasts but a little time."
— Aeschylus

T HE CLOUDS AND COLD AIR SETTLED IN over Truckee, a small city northwest of Lake Tahoe in California's Sierra Nevada Mountains. Snow fell in avalanches from the clouds. It buried roads, cars, trees, granite boulders, and entire mountains. The sheer vastness of the snow's territory stretched from the Oregon border down to Southern California.

Stacey and Anneliese rented a car and drove from San Francisco to Truckee as soon as they had landed. The flight, alone, took 13 hours. It was the six-hour drive that made the two pull out their hair in frustration. Normally the drive from San Francisco to Truckee took about three hours. On this occasion, however, the white-out conditions forced a chain installment, two-hour highway closure, and then a 15 mile per hour speed limit.

By the time they finally reached the hospital, Stacey and Anneliese were exhausted. The curtain of snow draped the hospital in gloom and near vanishment. Parked in the hospital lot, Stacey closed his tired eyes and massaged them until they watered and were webbed in red. He took large sips of water as if it was coffee to keep him alert.

Anneliese stretched, arching her back as she sat in the seat. She pulled down the passenger mirror and fiddled with her hair, applied a trace amount of lipstick, and then took a sip of water.

"Well, are we ready?" Stacey said as if he were asking himself. "Are you sure you don't want to go to the house and rest for a while before we go into the hospital?"

"No, I am good," Anneliese responded. "We are here now. I know it is important for you to see your brother and friends much quickly."

"Okay," Stacey said, sighing.

Stacey and Anneliese opened their doors, but only slightly. They hesitated to leave the comfort of the car for the shock of emotions that were about to besiege them. After a few moments of looking at each other to see who would make the first move, Anneliese shoved the door wide open and thrust herself out of her seat. Standing outside of the car, she slammed the door shut and jogged through the swathe of snow and the stinging cold to the safety of the hospital's entrance. Stacey watched this all through the window and then the rearview mirror. He took a deep breath in. As he exhaled, he pushed the door open and began his run to the entrance.

The snowflakes stuck to Stacey and Anneliese as they ran. Though they brushed themselves off once they reached the hospital, the snowflakes fell into open pockets, slipped down other clothing crevices, and became entangled in their hair. Once stowed away on Stacey and Anneliese, the snow quickly melted and disappeared from sight.

"Reece is on the second floor of the hospital, and Jeff is in intensive care on the first floor," Stacey explained. "But, we can't see Jeff today. So, we're only visiting Reece."

"I go where you are," Anneliese said. "Wende is here, ya?"

"Reece said that she'd probably be here. She was in his room when I called from the airport," Stacey answered.

Sensing Stacey's apprehension, Anneliese sought Stacey's hand. They found the elevator and rode to the second floor in silence. Stacey pondered ways to broach the subject of the accident with his brother. He knew Anneliese was just as nervous to see them.

The elevator stopped and the doors opened. They walked out into the long hallways that stretched off in both directions. Stacey looked at the placard on the wall. Reece's room was to the left.

"I can't stand being in hospitals. They're so damn white and sterile," Stacey complained. "I'm nervous about what I'll see in here. I admire you, Anneliese, for wanting to be a doctor. I really do."

"I cannot be a teacher of small children. Our jobs have much challenges, but we do much good for people," Anneliese said.

They dragged their feet past door after door, nurses at their stations, patients and visitors stretching their legs, and doctors on the move. At last, Stacey and Anneliese reached room 239. Stacey opened the door and Anneliese entered first. As she walked into the room, Stacey paused behind the door. He took a deep breath. He didn't want to do this.

I have to get through these initial moments, Stacey thought. Time will eventually carry us onward to happier moments.

He heard Reece exclaim, "Hey Anneliese."

Stacey urged himself forward. Reece adjusted his bed so that he sat upright and reached out his arms and motioned for Anneliese to come towards him. Anneliese slid over to the edge of his bed and carefully gave him a series of kisses on both cheeks and a hug.

In the meantime, Stacey had only taken a few steps into the room. He watched Reece and Anneliese greet each other. Feeling uncomfortable looking at Reece, he scanned the room. Next to Reece, a machine kept track of his vital signs, and a bag dripped pain killer into his body. Four vases of flowers were on the table and one more on the window sill. Through the window, Stacey watched the snow drifting across the sky. In the corner, a rerun of Law & Order played on the TV. A small nursing station, with a table and cabinets, was off to the side. Behind Stacey, another patient laid mostly hidden by a white curtain.

"How do you feel?" Anneliese asked.

"I'm doin' all right. Better than most." Reece responded with a half-smile. Still unable to move closer, Stacey peered at Anneliese and Reece from the doorway.

"You have much pain?" Anneliese asked.

"No, not really," Reece answered. "I'm hooked up to this morphine drip. It gives me the right amount all of the time, and if I need any extra, I can press this button and it doles out more."

"I am relieved you do well in the hospital," Anneliese said.

"I'm doin' okay, but I still have some pretty high hurdles to get over," Reece said. He turned his head slightly and saw Stacey standing near the door. "Hey, Stace."

Anneliese moved aside so that Stacey had room enough to get near Reece's bed. Stacey shuffled over to Reece, and the two brothers shook hands in their unique style of grabbing forearms which quickly broke into a hug.

"Hey, I missed you, bro," Stacey greeted him, softly and hesitantly. "So, how are you *really* doing?"

"Well, they say I have a fractured spine," Reece answered. "It sounds bad, but it's just a broken back. They have me in this back brace until my surgery."

"Surgery?" Stacey asked. "Why? Anneliese and I looked it up on the internet and it said that broken backs will heal on their own."

"Some of them do. But, I have compression fractures in a couple of vertebrae. With that kind of fracture, they do a special spinal fusion surgery," Reece explained.

"When do you have surgery?" Anneliese asked, sitting down in a chair against the wall.

"The day before Christmas. That's my Christmas present. Merry Christmas and Happy New Year to me," Reece said, sarcastically. "I told them I wanted to wait until you were here to do the surgery. It's not life threatening or anything, only painful."

"How long is the recovery?" Stacey asked, assessing Reece's situation carefully. He noted the cut above his eye, the cumbersome brace around his torso, and the IV stuck in his forearm.

"It's not that bad," Reece replied. "I'll be in the hospital for a few more days after the surgery. Then, I can go back to Santa Rosa for rehab. It'll be about a week to learn how to work the back muscles again. I can go home after that, but I have to wear this back brace. I'll have weeks of physical therapy.

"They want me to stay house bound for four to six fuckin' weeks after I come home from rehab. I can get up and walk around, but the majority of the time I should be letting my back heal. All this means that I won't be able to work for a couple of months. Shit, they're gonna love that."

"Well, don't worry about work. They'll handle that. You have to deal with this," Stacey told him. "How about golf? Did you ask about how this will affect your game?"

"Yeah, I did ask him," Reece began. "He said that I should be able to play at the same caliber, but that it depends on a lot of variables, like the extent of my injury and the rehabilitation process. He mentioned how Tiger Woods's back injury altered his game, and his wasn't even major."

"At least you don't have to stay in the hospital for long. It's great that you can go home and recoup," Stacey said, pulling a chair from the table, sliding it next to the bed, and sitting down next to Reece.

"Yeah, it's great," Reece agreed. "But, it's different for Jeff. He'll probably be here in Truckee's hospital for a few weeks and then back in Santa Rosa's hospital for more time. Then, he'll probably have months of rehab. And, when he gets out, who knows if he'll be able to work. And what about Brian? All of those kids at the school are gonna be heartbroken."

Reece's eyes suddenly became glassy, his face drooped, and he stared at the bedspread. He pulled the sheet over his face and cried. The weeping turned into heaving sobs that lasted only minutes.

Eyes filled with tears, Stacey placed his hands on Reece's shoulder. Anneliese arose and hovered near the end of the bed, touching his foot.

Reece's crying dissipated. He sniffled many times and kept apologizing by saying, "Sorry guys. I hadn't really cried yet. I've been trying to be strong for Wende and Patty. I feel horrible about what happened, Stace. It was all my fault. It was me. I did this."

Stacey tried to comfort Reece by saying, "It wasn't your fault. It was an accident. You guys were in the snow. Dangerous things happen when you're out in nature. Jeff and Brian knew this and so did you. It was an accident."

"I know," Reece said. "I keep replaying it in my head and wondering what we could have done differently. It happened so fast. You know how people say that when something bad is about to happen, it feels like slow motion and their life flashes in front of them? Well, the only thing I remember thinking is how to stop from falling. There was no thinking of you, Mom, Dad, or Wende. No regrets or thoughts about what I'd missed doing in my life. It was pure survival."

"How'd it happen? What were you guys doing?" Stacey asked, hesitantly. He said the words cautiously and gently as to not cause Reece to think the question implied fault.

"We were skiing up at Sugar Bowl the day of the accident," Reece began. "It was snowing pretty consistently the whole morning, and the powder was unbelievable. All five of us were having a great time."

"I know. You have to take advantage of that virgin snow," Stacey said.

"Exactly," Reece agreed. "So, keeping that in my mind, we were at the top of Mt. Lincoln, and I suggested to the guys that we make our own trail through the fresh powder of the Palisades. You know, like we used to do when we'd cut through the trees."

"I remember. Finding untouched territory was the fun of skiing," Stacey remarked. "But the Palisades isn't just skiing through trees. It's steep cliffs."

"I know. But the plan was to ski above and parallel to the cliff line," Reece said.

"Did the girls want to do this, too?" Anneliese asked.

"No. We had told Patty and Wende to go down one of the black diamond runs off of Mt. Lincoln, and we'd meet them at the bottom lift," Reece answered.

"Beth wasn't there with Brian?" Stacey asked.

"No, she had to work, so Brian came by himself," Reece explained. "Once the girls left, we skied down to the Palisades. We stopped at the edge of one of the cliffs and discussed which way we should go down. We all agreed that we shouldn't try to snake down through the canyons. I suggested we just ski above the cliff line until we got to the end or to a safer canyon. They agreed, but it was my fucking idea."

"Don't do that," Stacey interrupted. "You're all adults. You all knew the risks."

"Regardless, I went first. Brian and Jeff both hesitated before following me," Reece continued. "Everything was great when we got to the next cliff. I even remember looking out over the ski area and thinking about how exhilarating it was to be up there.

"We all stopped for a break and to reevaluate. That's when the snow just gave way under our skis. The snow took us right over the cliff. I don't really know what happened after that, but one of the ski patrol guys who came to visit us said that witnesses watched us fall over the cliff. They said that I fell on an icy patch of snow. Jeff fell on his head near me. Brian, though, fell onto some exposed rocks. They said he was probably killed instantly."

"Shit . . . I can't imagine," Stacey said.

"I am so sorry for Patty's family," Anneliese said, returning to the chair by the wall.

Reece paused some moments before he continued, "I can't stop wondering why he had to hit that rock. Why? It was the only exposed rock on that whole bottom part of the cliff. They say he would've had some major injuries just hitting the snow, but he wouldn't have died. The rock killed him. One or two feet would have saved him. I can't stop thinking about how life comes down to seconds and inches. Mom and Dad's death came down to inches. A second and an inch has divided life from death so many times for me that I can't even count. I mean, how many times can the average person say that they would've died had it not been for a single second or an inch?"

"You can't think about that. You'll never know the answer," Stacey said.

"Once we started down the hill, I don't think we could have done anything differently," Reece acknowledged. "But, it was my idea to ski the Palisades, and I chose the path. If we had stayed on a legit trail, this wouldn't have happened. It was my fault."

Breaking down in tears, Reece became lost in complete and utter sadness.

"Listen Reece, I know you think it was your fault, but it wasn't. It was a tragic accident," Stacey said.

"I know in my mind that it wasn't really my fault. But I keep thinking of how it wouldn't have happened if just one thing had changed," Reece said. "If we would've gone down with the girls or if we would've skied down the canyon instead of staying above the cliffs."

"Well, I'm sure anyone would feel that way," Stacey said. "Shit, we felt that way about Mom and Dad. We wished we could go back in time and change one thing. But, the reality is that there's nothing you can do now.

"What you *can* do is change the future. You have people around you that care about you and will help you. When you get better, you can help Jeff and Patty."

Reece took a tissue from the tray next to his bed. He wiped his eyes and then blew his nose. "I'm glad you two are here. Thanks for coming."

"In a heartbeat," Stacey said, clasping his hand around Reece's shoulder. "Have you had many visitors?"

"Wende's been here every day to see me," Reece said. "As a matter of fact, you guys just missed her. She's been wonderful, although I think she's a little lost. Patty stops in a few times a day, but I don't really know what to say to her."

"I'll be here for you now," Stacey declared.

"How long are you guys stayin'?" Reece asked.

"Anneliese is only staying for a few days," Stacey said. "She has to get back to her family for Christmas. I'll be staying longer."

"Thanks for coming," Reece said, turning to Anneliese. "I know your family and school work are really important to you. It means a lot to me that you gave up some of your time for us."

"You are welcome. I am happy to be here to help you and your friends," Anneliese said, still sitting against the wall.

"I think Wende will be happier to see you than me," Reece sighed.

"Wende will be here soon, ya?" Anneliese asked, leaning forward in her chair.

"No, I think Wende is waiting for you at the house, or at least that's what she told me," Reece explained. "She didn't really know when you'd be here. She's been here a lot, so she said she'd wait at the house for you. You can go see her right now. I won't be offended if you go."

"I can ride in taxi, ya? I not have you drive," Anneliese told Stacey.

"Yeah, okay. I can call a taxi, and it'll take you to my aunt's house," Stacey said. He looked at his watch. "I'll be home around 7:30 or 8:00. I'm going to eat dinner here. So, maybe you and Wende can go out to dinner."

"Also, maybe you can talk to Wende about me," Reece suggested to Anneliese. "Everything was going really good between us since she's been here. I thought so, anyway. We've had a lot of fun together, but then this happened.

"Now she's acting totally different around me. She's still very nice and has been here a lot to visit. But she talks to me differently. She sits and looks around. I try to ask her things, but she only shrugs or gives me one word answers. I think she wants to leave."

Reece stopped talking. His hands fiddled with the sheets. Stacey noticed how visibly agitated Reece became after speaking about Wendeline. Stacey glanced out of the window instinctively trying to ignore another uncomfortable moment in his life. He felt that if he didn't acknowledge the bad things in his life, then they wouldn't be real.

"Do you think you could ask her about me, and what she's gonna do now?" Reece asked, sullenly.

"Ya, I ask Wende about you," Anneliese answered, standing up and moving next to his bed.

"Thanks. I really like her, and I'd hate to lose her because of this," Reece declared. "Oh, and tell her that I'm gonna be better in couple of months. I told her already, but I don't know if she really believes it."

"Ya, I will tell it to Wende," Anneliese assured Reece. "She tells me on phone all the time that she likes you much."

"All right, I'm going to call a taxi for Anneliese. No cell phones in the hospital. Can I use that phone?" Stacey asked, pointing to a phone lying on Reece's bed by his arm.

"Sure. I think there's a phone book in the drawer," Reece said.

Stacey leaned over to the nightstand and took out the phonebook. He found the number for a taxi company. He picked up the phone, dialed the number, and ordered one for Anneliese.

"The taxi will be out front in about ten minutes," Stacey said. "We'd better get some of your things out of the car so you can have them when you get to the house."

"Thanks again for comin' out here. I wish your first trip to the U.S. was under better circumstances," Reece said.

"I hope you and friends do better soon. I see you next day," Anneliese replied. She leaned over and kissed Reece on the cheek.

Stacey said to Reece, "I'll be right back. I'm going to walk Anneliese to the cab."

"I'm not goin' anywhere," Reece joked.

Stacey took Anneliese's hand and led her out of the room. They walked out of the hospital towards the taxi. It had stopped snowing, but the ice and fallen snow covered the parking lot. Holding Anneliese by the hand so she wouldn't slip, Stacey guided her along the sidewalk.

At the taxi, Stacey opened the back door for Anneliese and helped her in. Then, he ran over to the rental car, opened the trunk, withdrew Anneliese's suitcase, and carried it over to the taxi where he deposited it into the trunk. He rushed around to Anneliese, said his goodbyes, and gave the taxi driver the address and directions to the house.

"Before you leave, I wanted to say thank you for being here with me. It means so much that you came," Stacey whispered.

"I do it a thousand times for you," Anneliese whispered back.

"One more thing, if Wende is gone, there's a key in the garage underneath the tool box on the counter. Okay?" Stacey said. Anneliese nodded. "If you need anything, call the hospital and ask for Reece Shepherd's room. Okay?"

"All I need is sleep," Anneliese confided. "I am wonderful. I love you."

"Love you, too. See you in a little bit," Stacey said. He handed her some cash for the ride, closed the door, and watched the taxi drive off.

When Stacey returned to Reece's hospital room, they watched television together. Television was always a good distraction for the two brothers. They used it as a crutch for the questions that they didn't want to ask and the answers they didn't want to give. At times, they turned to each other and held a short conversation, but the words that passed between them only connected them physically in the space.

After a couple of hours, Stacey and Reece said goodbye and hugged each other. They even told each other that they loved one another. He realized in that exact moment why he felt the strong need to be with his brother. The tragedy had connected them on an emotional level that went far deeper than they had each previously shared. Stacey couldn't remember the last time he'd told his brother that he loved him. He felt the gravity of brotherhood and of family. He cherished the feeling.

As he left, Stacey felt relieved about visiting with his brother. He knew Reece would eventually recover fully. At the same time, though, Stacey felt a wave of apprehension about seeing Jeff and Patty. Their situations were much worse than Reece. He dreaded the emotional reaction of seeing Jeff and Patty for the first time.

CHAPTER 14

Tragedy forces contemplation of
Pain, suffering, faith, healing

"Gone — flitted away,
Taken the stars from the night and the sun from the day!
Gone, and a cloud in my heart, and a storm in the air!"

— Alfred Tennyson, "Gone"

AS STACEY DROVE BACK to his aunt's house in the resort neighborhood of Tahoe-Donner, he took his time on the roads because of the darkness, snow, and icy conditions. When he parked at the house, he was surprised to see Patty's car in the driveway. He'd known that she wasn't at the hospital and had assumed that she would be with her family mourning her brother's death.

After parking the car, Stacey hesitated. Tired and emotionally drained from his visit with Reece, all he wanted was to take a hot shower and sleep. Summoning the energy and initiative, he stepped out of the car into the light flurry of snow. He went around to the rear of the car and pulled out his backpack and suitcase. He walked up the driveway and entered the dimly lit living room. A brighter light streamed in from the kitchen area in the back. He approached the kitchen.

"Is anyone here? Anneliese? Wende? Patty?" Stacey shouted.

From outside the glass doors at the rear of the house, he heard his name muttered. He walked to the backdoor, cupped his hands to the glass, and looked out across an expansive, wooden deck that overlooked a snow-covered golf course. Protected from the falling snow by an awning, Patty glowed in the illumination of the outside spotlight.

"Stacey!" Patty cried out. This time Stacey heard his name quite clearly. He opened the glass door. Patty bounced up off of the cushioned chair and lunged at him as if she'd never let go. He felt unprepared for this. As she gripped him, she continued to say one phrase, "Oh God, Stace. Oh God."

"I'm so sorry," Stacey said, repeatedly.

Patty closed her eyes and tears fell. Similar to Reece, Patty's emotions overwhelmed her when she spoke with Stacey for the first time. Reece's crying, though, arose from sadness and guilt. Patty's outburst originated from deeper in her soul. Her crying transpired as an act of pain, and Stacey could feel it. Her brother, who she adored, had suddenly died. Her fiancée had broken his neck and probably wouldn't walk again. Life would never be the same. Stacey was no stranger to this tremendous loss and the pain associated with it.

Patty slipped out of Stacey's arms and collapsed into the chair. She leaned over and put her head in her hands. Sobbing, she allowed herself to slowly slide from the chair to the deck. She knelt on her hands and knees and broke into a mournful wail. Crying he could endure, but the wailing ripped through him.

With tears blurring his vision, Stacey glanced inside and spotted a blanket. Patty had already turned on the outdoor patio heater, but he wanted a task that would momentarily give him a chance to regain his senses. He opened the sliding glass door, grabbed the blanket, and gently let it fall over Patty's back. Stacey knelt down beside her and rubbed circles on her back in a soothing manner.

Eventually, Patty tired herself out. With her energy, thoughts, and worries released and exasperated from the crying, she arose from her hands and knees and sat down in the chair, the blanket still wrapped around. Her hair lay matted and greasy. Her cheeks and eyes were red and puffy. Streaks of tears plunged down her face. Some drops still hung to the edge of her chin.

Patty wiped the tears, flipped her hair back from her face, and turned to Stacey.

"Sorry I lost control. I've been doing that a lot lately," Patty admitted. "It happens when I see someone for the first time. I broke down crying the first time I saw my parents, my grandma, Jeff, Anneliese, and now you."

"Where is Anneliese?" Stacey asked.

"She and Wende went to dinner. I told them about a place in downtown Truckee," Patty responded. Tears streamed down her face. "I just can't stop crying."

"No need to be sorry. If anything, it's totally natural. I'd be worried if you didn't cry," Stacey said. "Remember, I've been through it, too."

"Is this how you felt when your parents died?" Patty asked as she sniffled and continued wiping her tears.

"Well, kind of," Stacey answered. He took a seat in the chair next to Patty. "My breakdown didn't happen until way later. I kept myself so busy organizing everything and taking care of Reece that I didn't even give myself time to cry, not even at their funeral. I still feel bad about that. What son doesn't cry at his parent's funeral? I had the best parents ever, and I couldn't cry."

"I remember that," Patty said, as her face revealed what she saw in her mind. "I watched you at their funeral. I remember thinking it was odd that you weren't crying."

"Maybe I tried to protect Reece, or maybe it was a little bit of a macho thing." Stacey shrugged. "Whatever it was, my breakdown took a slow progression. It started with insomnia and if I *did* sleep, I'd have nightmares or anxiety dreams. Then came the edginess and mood changes. All of my anger and feelings were building up. I tried to push away my grief. I made it about seven or eight months."

"Eight months? That's a long time not to grieve," Patty commented. "What happened to make you break down?"

"Do you remember that playoff game where I got kicked out for fighting?" Stacey asked.

"Yeah, I remember," Patty replied. "Jeff and I had recently started dating, and he took me to that game."

"The fight started because one of the guys on the other team said I played like a mama's boy," Stacey explained. "That sent me over the edge. Nobody could calm me down. That's the day I began to grieve. From that point on, I felt emotionally vulnerable. I cried myself to sleep, cried in front of Reece, at movies, at restaurants . . . everywhere. I was no longer afraid of crying."

"How long did the grieving last?" Patty asked, intently waiting for the answer.

"It hasn't really stopped," Stacey said, bluntly. "After our parents died, my English teacher, Mrs. Morrison, gave me a copy of a letter Proust had written to a friend on the death of his friend's mother. I think it explains the pain of loss. I printed out a copy before we left Germany. Let me see if I can find it."

Stacey walked back into the house to search through his luggage for the letter. About five minutes later, he returned with a piece of paper that he handed to Patty. She took it and read it hesitantly.

The letter from Proust read, "Now there is one thing I can tell you: you will enjoy certain pleasures you would not fathom now. When you still had your mother you often thought of the days when you would have her no longer. Now you will often think of days past when you had her. When you are used to this horrible thing that they will forever cast into the past, then you will gently feel her revive, returning to take her place, her entire place beside you. At the present time, this is not yet possible. Let yourself be inert, wait 'til the incomprehensible power ... that has broken you, restores you a little, I say a little, for henceforth you will always keep something broken about you. Tell yourself this, too, for it is a kind of pleasure to know that you will never be consoled, that you will never love less, that you will constantly remember more and more."

Studying Patty's face and eyes, Stacey watched her read the letter. Tears came to her eyes and he knew that she neared the middle. She nodded in agreement to the letter as she read the end. Her tears flowed freely.

"Thanks. That was helpful. This letter reminds me of what I was thinking about earlier today," Patty explained. "Alone in the car, I suddenly got the urge to call Brian's cell phone. His voice spoke. It's haunting. Part of him is still here. I know he's dead, but in all other aspects he's still here. His Facebook page is running. His office is exactly how he left it. He has a bank account, car payment, and credit card bills. It's like he's on vacation."

"Slowly, though, all of those things will be taken away," Stacey said. "One of the saddest jobs after my parents died was finalizing all of their affairs. With each completed step, I felt as if Reece and I erased another part of them from our lives. But, it's a part of the process, and you grieve your way through it."

"When is it going to get easier?" Patty asked.

"The pain of losing my Mom and Dad will always be with me," Stacey began, solemnly. "It's a kind of pain that is hard to describe. It's like your soul is drowning. You're desperately trying to reach the air of comfort and the love of the thing that kept you alive. But, you can't grasp it, ever again. That gloom will shadow you for a long time. But, you'll find other sources of happiness that will bring you joy. I still cry sometimes when I'm trying to fall asleep. I miss them, especially on holidays. Even talking about them now, brings me back to the grief."

"I forgot about holidays," Patty cried. "His birthday is in two months. And Christmas . . ."

But, Patty never finished her sentence. Instead, she looked up at the snowy sky. Stacey followed Patty's gaze and saw the deck's lights illuminate the snow's slow, silent fall. Snow dusted the railings and floor of the deck.

"Hey, this might be a good time for a hot drink. Want me to make you one? Tea? Coffee? Hot chocolate?" Stacey asked, scooting out from his chair and standing up.

"That sounds nice. I'll have green tea," Patty replied. "Do you want some help?"

"No, I got this," Stacey said. "Do you want anything in your tea?"

"A little honey or sugar. Thanks," Patty said, wrapping the blanket tighter around her.

Stacey walked back into the house and made two cups of green tea. He brought out the steaming drinks and handed Patty a cup. Holding the cup in her lap with both hands, the heat of the cup warmed her.

"I'm sorry, Stace. You don't have to be here with me," Patty stated, sniffling her nose and wiping her eyes.

"Do you want me here?" Stacey asked. "If you'd rather be alone, it's okay, just tell me."

Patty didn't hesitate with her reply. "No, I need you here. But, if you have something else to do or someone to see, then I'd understand."

"*You're* what's important right now," Stacey said, sipping his tea and wishing he'd put more sugar in it. "This is the reason why we flew back, to be here with you, Jeff, and Reece."

Patty took a sip of her tea and said, "Perfect tea. Thanks."

"My pleasure. Could use a bit more sugar, though," Stacey said.

"Thank you so much, Stace. You've always been a great friend. Not the best boyfriend, but yes, a great friend," Patty stated, smiling.

"I'll take that as a compliment," Stacey said. "Although, I thought I happened to be a pretty good boyfriend, until the end."

"Yeah, that's true," Patty offered, smiling for but a second. "You were really nice to me. I guess the only difference between you and Jeff is that I can *trust* him."

"Ouch. Good one," Stacey said. "Listen, for your information, Anneliese and I are doing really well. I've matured a lot since you and I dated. Look at the difference between me and Reece. I used to be like him when we dated. Now, Anneliese can trust me, and I have no intention of leaving her or hurting her."

Patty paused before she spoke, "I know you're good to Anneliese. You've got a wonderful gift of making people feel better, and I'm sure Anneliese benefits from that."

Patty gazed back to the falling snow. Stacey joined her. The snow, gently gliding through the air, reminded him of a time sitting on a chairlift with his mom. He remembered being upset with his mom because she talked nonstop the entire way up the lift. He hadn't wanted to talk. He preferred losing himself in his own thoughts while watching the snow fall. Looking back on the moment, Stacey felt a tinge of guilt. He suddenly wished he could go back to his teenage self and have a pleasant conversation with his mom.

Stacey didn't want to ignore Patty like he had ignored his mom, so he impelled himself to ask, "How's Jeff doing? Reece mentioned surgery, but he didn't know much about his situation."

"Jeff is doing okay, considering the circumstances," Patty explained, sipping her tea. "He's been alert most of the time, but the pain medications are making him go in and out of consciousness. He keeps saying it's going to be all right, and he's going to be fine.

"He won't listen to the doctors, though. Two doctors have told him everything about his situation, but he still doesn't believe them."

"So, what do the doctors say? What's his prognosis?" Stacey asked, drinking his tea.

"I'll tell you what we know," Patty began. "First, he doesn't have any feeling or movement in his legs or feet. He had trouble breathing, but they didn't have to put him on a machine. They did an MRI on his spine. They told us that Jeff has a T-2 spinal fracture. What that means is that he broke his neck, and he'll probably be paralyzed from his waist down. The doctors recommended immediate surgery for repairing the fracture.

"So Jeff, his parents, and I all agreed, and he had the surgery a couple days ago. They replaced one of the broken disks and then fused the vertebrae together. The doctors told us that everything went well. He should be stabilized enough to move into a rehab center in about a week, or two. Right now he's recovering from the surgery. He has this huge halo around his head and neck."

"With the surgery, does that mean he might be able to walk again?" Stacey asked.

"No, unfortunately not." Patty sighed, taking a sip of tea and setting the cup on a small table next to her chair. "They performed the surgery to make sure the vertebrae in his spinal cord don't move, similar to a brace. Jeff's vertebrae broke higher up on his cord and those vertebrae are responsible for so much more movement than the lower ones. So, Jeff lost almost all movement and senses from the waist down. They said he probably wouldn't be able to walk again."

"When will they know for sure?" Stacey asked.

"Once he gets into rehab, we'll know a lot more about his condition and what he can and won't be able to do," Patty said. "The one good thing is that he does have some feeling in areas that are above the T-2 vertebrae. He might be able to do a lot more than the doctors think right now. But, who really knows."

"God, this is so fucked up," Stacey declared.

"I know it sounds bad, but I'm trying to stay positive because it could be a lot worse," Patty said. "If he'd fractured his cord a little higher, he would've lost the ability to breathe on his own. And higher still, he would have been paralyzed from the neck down, like Christopher Reeve."

Patty started sobbing again. Stacey reached out his hand and took her hand in his.

"I'm sorry." Stacey consoled Patty.

"Every time I think about it, I get overwrought. My soul feels like it's being crushed," Patty cried. "This is such a huge obstacle for Jeff and me to overcome. His whole life is going to change, and so is mine. Most of the outdoor things we did together, we won't be able to do anymore. Do you realize that he's not going be able to go mountain biking with you guys anymore?"

"I know," Stacey said, his mind wandering to how his life would change if he were confined to a wheelchair. He couldn't imagine a life without athleticism. He lived for riding bikes. It would devastate him to be immobile. Paralysis is a life sentence. "I can see how being confined to a wheelchair will take away his freedom."

It was at this moment that Stacey felt the crushing weight of the aftermath of Jeff's accident.

"I can't imagine Jeff not riding a bike. But . . . I mean . . . that's not even the worst. There's so much more," Patty began. "All the things I've been reading about say that we need to rearrange the entire house so that he can reach things from a wheelchair. We need to add ramps over the steps and get him a special van so that he can drive. Plus, he's going to have more health problems later in his life. Paraplegics have bladder and bowel problems. They're also prone to bed sores. Then there's the mobility problems he'll have. How's he going to get around stores and shop by himself? It's too much, too fast."

"I know it's a lot to take in on such a short time, but you and Jeff will be able to get through this, like thousands of other families of paraplegics," Stacey assured Patty. "My advice is to try not to think of everything that has to be done at once. If you do, then it does become too much. My mom used to say, 'All it takes is small steps.' I believe that. Just take it one day at a time. Make a list of things you have to do and do them as you can."

"It's a lot to do by myself," Patty declared, picking up her cup of tea and taking a drink.

"You're not going to do this all by yourself," Stacey said. "You have his parents and your parents. And, you'll have Reece and me to help."

"Yeah, I know we have help, but what about when it's only us?" Patty wondered, solemnly. "How will we be as a couple?"

"I don't know, Patty, but I hope it's similar to the way you were before the accident," Stacey answered. "The things you do together are going to be different, but the way you relate to one another should be the same, maybe stronger."

"I hope so," Patty said. "I know this sounds horrible, but I don't know if I can live that kind of life."

"What do you mean?" Stacey asked.

"I'm worried that this will be a huge compromise on how I had envisioned my future. How am I supposed to travel? How can he help with all of the household duties? What happens when . . . or if we can . . . have kids?" Patty asked, tears welling in her eyes.

Stacey knew that these were all valid concerns. Yet, he didn't have any answers to them. All he could think of doing was to reassure her that things would be worked out and arrangements made when the time came.

"Don't fear the future because nothing in the future is certain," Stacey said. "Try to focus on what needs to be done each day."

"It's hard not to think of all the difficulties waiting for us in the future," Patty confessed. "Oh, God. I'm disgusted with myself because I don't know if I can do it. That's why it's so nice to talk to you, Stace. I know you feel bad for Jeff, but you don't have that intimate connection to him. You're here for me and that makes me feel good."

"I'll be here for as long as you need me," Stacey said.

"How long is that?" Patty inquired.

"Anneliese is leaving in a few days," Stacey said. "I'll stay for another week. I start teaching again the second week of January. If you need me longer, then I can find a way to make it work. I know Anneliese would understand."

"So, you'd stay a little longer?" Patty asked.

"Yes, if you really needed me," Stacey replied.

"Jeff's going to be in this hospital for another couple of weeks, and then he'll go into rehab back in Santa Rosa for another month or two," Patty began. "I'd really, really love it if you could stay through that time. We could fix up the house and get things ready for when Jeff comes home. And, I'm sure Jeff and Reece would love having you around, too."

"Okay. I'll see what I can do," Stacey said, reluctantly. He hesitated for a moment, finishing his tea and placing the cup on the end table. "Don't say anything to Anneliese. I'll have to break the news to her gently."

"I won't," Patty agreed. She picked up her cup of tea, quickly finished it, and placed the cup on the table.

"Want another cup?" Stacey asked.

"No thanks," Patty said.

They both stopped talking. Stacey looked into the blackness of the backyard. The snow seemed to fall out of complete darkness. It would have been a memorable scene in days gone by. In this moment of grief and despair, though, not only did beauty feel irrelevant to Stacey, but with one friend dead and another seriously injured, the silent snow brought with it a desolation of spirit and a stark reminder of how the past had been filled with hopes and dreams. All of it gone.

"When's the service for Brian?" Stacey asked, hesitant about addressing the death of Patty's brother. Brian was Stacey's good friend since middle school, his boss, and had played an integral part in helping him when his parents had passed. Brian had also been the person who had encouraged him to get a teaching credential and hired him for his first job. Brian's beacon of light had now been darkened.

"It's going to be on the Friday after Christmas at the church off of Montgomery Drive," Patty answered, solemnly. She paused a few moments mindlessly chewing on her nails. "My parents, Brian's wife, and I are putting together the service. We have a priest and a choir. We're going to have his favorite poems read and some of his favorite music played. We invited some teachers and students to talk at the service, too. You can join them if you want."

"I'll definitely be at the service. I don't know about talking, though," Stacey said.

"I don't know if I can talk, either," Patty confessed.

"I'm so sorry about Brian." Stacey had trouble looking directly at Patty as he spoke. "He was that guy that everyone gravitated toward, especially me. I'm going to miss him so much." He and Patty grabbed onto one another as if they were saving each other from the terror of reality and began sobbing.

"Not only has this been gut-wrenching sadness, but the logistics of all this has been a fucking nightmare," Patty said, tugging on her hair. "Jeff, my fiancée, is up here in Truckee, but my parents are three hours away in Santa Rosa grieving for my brother. I've been back and forth almost every day. It's so incredibly stressful."

"I understand. It must be difficult to decide who needs you more. The distance doesn't make it easy," Stacey agreed.

"With all that's happened, I've been trying to pray, to feel God with me in some way . . . but I don't feel him," Patty said. "I don't feel anything except loneliness and sadness. I don't feel Jesus walking with me. 'Even though I walk through the valley of the shadow of death, I fear no evil; for thou art with me; Thy rod and thy staff, they comfort me,' so says the Bible. Aren't I in the valley of the shadow of death?"

"I would say this is that valley," Stacey answered.

"Well, I don't feel God, Jesus, or anyone with me," Patty admitted. "I've believed all of my life. But, I've never really needed them until now. And now that I need them, where the hell are they? I feel as if everything they taught me about God and Jesus is a lie."

Patty began sobbing. Stacey took her hands in his. He gently stroked her arms and hands in comfort.

"Talking to you right now is more real than any conversation I've tried to have with God or my brother," Patty said. "Talking to you has done more for me emotionally than my entire praying put together. I feel like I'm being heard, and that you'll help me survive this mess. Does that make sense?"

"Yeah, it does," Stacey concurred. "As a matter of fact, Anneliese and I have been talking about God and death because she's also religious."

"Well, what do you believe in? I know you're not religious, but you must have some faith in something," Patty asked.

"I believe in God, but it's not the religious God that you believe in," Stacey began. "I believe a power flows through every living thing, which is similar to what organized religions believe. But, I believe this power is unknowing of anything, totally without thought. It is a power that has no intentions, no plan, no conscience, no notion of good or evil, and no idea that we are even alive. It is what it is.

"It's like water flowing down a hill into a valley. The water has no way to control where it goes or what it does. It just flows, and it changes something in the world along the way. It's the same thing with my God. Anytime this mystical power is released, it causes change in the world. Based on the laws of physics within the universe, this power flows throughout our world. It fills everything with its energy. This energy or God has the power to cause change. That's what I believe."

"That's beautiful, but I don't know if I can believe that God is not consciously helping us," Patty said. "I want to believe God watches me, making sure all is well. I guess my mind is so ingrained with stories from the Bible."

"I don't have the faith enough for organized religions, so that's why I created my own beliefs," Stacey said. "I kept asking myself how God could watch all of the pain and suffering and not be inclined to do anything about it. If he can't interfere with life, then why can't God at least give people a sign to show us that the suffering will be worth it when we get to heaven?"

"I feel the same way," Patty said, quietly and hesitantly. "What do you think happens to people when they die? What do you think happened to your parents? If heaven doesn't exist, then where do people go?"

"Well, the easy answer is that I don't know," Stacey said. "I would love to think that the essence of who we are continues after we die. Maybe our soul moves on somehow, and eventually we are reborn. Or maybe, we get absorbed into god like a drop of water into the ocean.

"I think it's more believable than floating into the sky and entering heaven. I've looked up and I've never seen heaven the way religions describe it. But, I can tell you that I've looked around down here, and I've found many places that have appeared as if they could be heaven."

"It's a beautiful belief, but it's not as comforting as my thoughts on heaven," Patty said, her voice scratchy from the sobbing. "In your belief, I can't talk to God, I can't picture my brother in heaven, and I have no hope of meeting him after I die. If it were up to you, we would all be lost and jumbled up in this free fall through the universe. I can't handle that."

"Hey, I wasn't . . ." Stacey began and then stopped upon hearing the front door close shut and female voices rambling.

"I guess that's Anneliese and Wende," Patty commented. "Thanks for taking the time to talk with me. *I mean it*. Thanks! I'm so glad you're home."

"Yeah, this is where I need to be right now. I'm glad I could help. Listen, I didn't mean to preach to you or try to get you to switch religions or anything," Stacey apologized.

"No, I know. I asked you to tell me. It was nice to hear, though," Patty replied.

"Listen, I have one more thing to say," Stacey paused.

Patty stared into his eyes, waiting, as if Stacey were an oracle of sorts.

"Now that you have been touched by death, you're going to feel its presence all around you," Stacey explained. "What I mean is, you're going to feel your own mortality. You're going to realize that death can happen at any time to anyone. You might have thought you knew this, but now you've seen it with your brother, and it's going to scare you to your core. It did me.

"I was supposed to go on a backpacking trip the summer after my parents died. I didn't end up going because I suspected death awaited me. It took me a long time to get past the fear."

"How did you stop being fearful of death?" Patty asked.

"I didn't stop. I still think about it and fear it. I simply learned how to hide the fear deep down in my psyche. I have to live like I don't know it exists," Stacey explained.

"Thanks for all your help tonight, Stace. I'll never forget your kindness," Patty said.

Stacey reached out and touched Patty on the top of her thigh. He only meant it as a sympathetic gesture of mutual affection or comradeship between companions who've gone through the loss of a loved one. But as soon as Stacey laid his hand on Patty's thigh, Patty leaned into Stacey and gave him a short kiss on the lips. Stacey knew it was wrong. He knew Patty only kissed him because of her grief. Nonetheless, the kiss stirred his emotions because he'd always had an underlying attraction for Patty.

After Patty slowly slinked away from the kiss, she quickly blurted out, "I'm so, so sorry, Stace. Oh my God, I can't believe I just did that."

Patty hid her face in her hands out of shame, but Stacey reached out and lowered her hands down so that she looked at him, again.

"Listen, that's nothing to be ashamed about, okay. I know you didn't mean it that way. Why would you ever want to kiss me? Shit, you didn't want to kiss me in high school, why start now?" Stacey said. Then he chuckled and said, "Forget about it. It didn't happen."

Trying to change the subject, Stacey added, "I can't believe we're back here at my aunt's house. Remember that winter back in high school when we all came up here?"

"Yeah, I remember," Patty said. She looked off of the deck and into the snowy air. "We all cut school and drove up in the blizzard. Brian even came with us. Reece got us all sleds, and we went sledding down the golf course fairways."

"Those were the days," Stacey observed. He knew Patty was thinking of her brother. She had that look of being far away in the past.

As Stacey watched Patty, Anneliese pulled open the sliding glass door. Stacey whirled around to see Anneliese and Wendeline coming out onto the deck.

"Hey," Stacey said.

Stacey got up out of his chair and gave Wendeline a European kiss and a hug. Then he went up to Anneliese and gave her a short kiss on the lips.

"Wende, it's nice to see you again," Stacey told her. She nodded at him. "How was dinner?"

"Dinner was good. We talk about my trip," Wendeline answered. Stacey noticed that her English had improved since meeting Reece.

Patty slowly got up out of her chair. She made her way over to the group.

"If you don't mind," Patty said to Anneliese and Wendeline, "I'm going to go back to the hotel. The funny thing is that I'm exhausted, but I can't sleep because my mind won't shut off. I'll probably lay in bed thinking of my brother and Jeff."

"You can sleep here. There's plenty of room," Stacey announced.

"Thanks, but I'd rather be alone," Patty said.

"I wish you a good sleep. We will talk tomorrow," Anneliese said, sympathetically.

The group made their way into the kitchen. They said their goodbyes and Patty left for the night. Wendeline headed for bed twenty minutes later.

Stacey and Anneliese stayed up for another hour talking about their conversations with Reece, Wendeline, and Patty. Stacey learned that Wendeline loved Reece and thought the world of him. The accident, though, put those feelings up against another set of feelings — fear. When the accident occurred, Wendeline didn't have anyone to turn to. She was alone. She wanted to go home where people and things were comforting to her. If anyone could understand, it was Stacey.

Finally, Anneliese excused herself to get ready for bed. After she left, Stacey stayed outside. For some reason, he couldn't stop watching the snowflakes gliding softly down to the ground. It was like watching a campfire late at night; both inspired hours of philosophical musings.

One of the thoughts that flittered in and out of his mind was Patty's kiss. He couldn't stop thinking about it. He knew it didn't mean anything, especially to Patty. But for Stacey, the kiss acted like a lightning rod in his mind.

First, the kiss created a physical awakening. The thought of someone liking him stimulated his interest in the possibility of having sex with someone new, even if he was in a serious relationship. He found himself daydreaming about what that kiss could lead to. Although he repeatedly felt guilt about these thoughts, he realized it was purely his male hormones acting up.

Second, the kiss created an emotional attachment. It made Stacey feel closer to Patty, which is what he had always wanted since they broke up in high school. Regardless, Stacey understood the kiss would probably never lead to anything substantial between them because of their other attachments to Jeff and Anneliese. Consequently, he pushed his confused thoughts deep into the hidden realms of his mind.

Stacey ended the night with a spiraling fear haunting him. Visiting Jeff in the hospital tomorrow, he didn't know what to expect of Jeff's emotional reaction, let alone his own.

We can only go forward in life, Stacey mused. Similar to the snow falling through the sky, it can only fall downward. It can't go back into the clouds. That's the way he felt about seeing Jeff. Some power seemed to force him toward tomorrow when he'd finally have to face Jeff. He had to visit him. There was no option. He couldn't ignore him. The hidden forces that rule nature also rule human destinies.

CHAPTER 15

Healing
Put your trust in others,
Especially family and friends

"God grant me the serenity to accept the things I cannot change;
Courage to change the things I can;
And wisdom to know the difference."

— Reinhold Niebuhr, "Serenity Prayer"

"Without friends no one would choose to live."

— Aristotle, *Nichomachean Ethics*

T HE NEXT MORNING, Stacey, Anneliese, and Wendeline
shuffled out the door and made their way to the car. Being an
emotional day for everyone, they either looked straight ahead
to the car or down at the snowy ground.

Feeling nervous about his upcoming visit with Jeff and uneasy
about telling Anneliese his intentions to stay in California, Stacey was
filled with anxiety as they drove to the hospital. All of these worries
had made his stomach nauseous and his head pound.

At the hospital, they met Patty and she led them down the white
halls of the hospital. Wendeline said goodbye, entered an elevator, and
headed to Reece's room, upstairs.

It was a solemn walk to the intensive care unit. Before entering, Patty reminded Stacey that they could only stay with Jeff for a short visit. Then they turned down a long corridor and came upon Jeff's dad who leaned against the wall.

"Stacey, it's . . . great to see you," Mr. O'Dell uttered. Tears welled in his eyes as he greeted Stacey with a long hug. "Jeff's mom is in with him now. He's doing really well today. He's the most alert I've seen him since he's been here."

"That's good, Mr. O'Dell. I'm looking forward to seeing him," Stacey replied.

"Patty, do you want to go in and let my wife know that Stacey's here?" Mr. O'Dell said. "We'll go out for some coffee and give you guys some time to talk."

"Sure," Patty answered. She gave Jeff's dad a hug. "I'm glad he's doing better. I've been so worried about him."

Patty slowly opened the door and walked in.

"He hasn't had many visits from friends, so I'm sure he'll appreciate that you came home to see him," Mr. O'Dell said.

"I wish I could've been here sooner." Stacey said. Then he introduced Anneliese to Mr. O'Dell.

"Nice to meet you, Anneliese," Mr. O'Dell said, extending his hand. "Jeff and Stacey have been best friends since middle school."

"Nice to meet you, too." Anneliese shook his hand. "I am sorry for Jeff's accident."

"Thank you," Mr. O'Dell replied.

"How are you guys doing with all of this?" Stacey asked, cringing inwardly from the pain of asking the question.

"Not so well," Mr. O'Dell whispered, shaking his head and leaning back against the wall. "This has been a nightmare. The intensive care is a horrible place to see your child."

"Or your best friend," Stacey concurred.

"Is it still snowing outside?" Mr. O'Dell asked.

"Yes." Stacey took a step back.

"The problem with the snow is that it sticks to everything it touches," Mr. O'Dell said. "You can't get rid of it. Even when it melts away, the chill still clings to your bones."

Patty came out with Jeff's mom. Mrs. O'Dell gave a quick smile to Stacey, but turned away and sobbed quietly next to her husband.

"We'll let you guys see Jeff," Mr. O'Dell said, turning to his wife and leading her down the hall.

"Only two people are supposed to be in the room, so I'll let you and Anneliese go in first," Patty said.

Stacey reached for Anneliese's hand, and they hesitantly walked into the room. The first thing Stacey noticed was the halo brace that Jeff had attached to his head. It was bigger than Stacey had imagined it to be. Another brace surrounded his torso region and an extensive number of wires and tubes were attached to his body. Stacey realized that the medical devices were so much more complex and extensive than in Reece's room. Feeling the gravity of Jeff's situation, his soul fell open and his breathing became impaired.

"Come . . . I can't see you." Jeff rattled off the words in a raspy voice.

Stacey walked ahead of Anneliese over to the edge of the bed.

"Lean over," Jeff requested. "I can't move my head."

Stacey bent over the halo. Looking down at the shell of his friend, he saw tubes protruding from Jeff's nose, bandages that covered his neck and shoulders, and screws that held the halo to his skull. Finding his friend amongst the chaos was difficult at first, but Stacey quickly focused his attention on Jeff's dark-green eyes.

"Hi, Jeff." Stacey reached out his hand and touched Jeff's arm. Jeff moved his arm slightly but then remained still.

"Good of you . . . to come." Jeff labored with the words.

"Anneliese is here, too," Stacey said, gesturing for her to join him.

Anneliese knelt at Jeff's bedside and gently kissed his hand. She leaned over and said, "I am much sorry for you to be in hospital."

"Thank you," Jeff replied.

"This wasn't the way I expected our next visit to be," Stacey said. He tried to smile, but regretted the awkward joke.

"You can . . . thank Reece," Jeff shot back.

"I saw Reece yesterday," Stacey began. "He feels deeply saddened and guilty about the accident."

"He should," Jeff stammered. "I might not . . . walk again."

"That's not Reece's fault." Stacey put his hand on Jeff's arm again.

"Yes, it is." Jeff brushed Stacey's hand off of his arm.

"It was an accident," Stacey said. He felt awkward and defensive about the tone of the conversation. Patty had warned him, and now he witnessed this anger and frustration. "Listen, I'm feeling uncomfortable. I didn't want to upset you on my first visit here. Why don't we change the subject?"

"Okay," Jeff said, weakly.

"Tell us about Patty's art exhibition last week," Stacey inquired. "She hasn't told us about it, yet."

"Ya, I would like to hear about it," Anneliese said, rubbing Stacey's back, glad that Stacey had changed the subject.

"It was nice . . . but you would know . . . if you were there," Jeff jabbed, breathing quick and gasping for air.

Stacey's heart began pounding. The corner of his eye twitched in response to the edginess of the situation.

"What is this? Why are you attacking me?" Stacey asked.

After catching his breath, Jeff continued, "You weren't around . . . and now I'm gonna be . . . in a fucking wheelchair."

Jeff closed his eyes and brooded in silence.

Stacey suddenly realized that it had been a mistake in talking to Jeff like he had with Reece. He'd entered the situation thinking that, like Reece, Jeff needed consoling and someone to tell him that everything would be all right. But, Jeff's anger seemed pointed, so Stacey tried to come up with another tactic to comfort his friend.

Filled with frustration, Jeff slammed his eyes tight. Stacey took that moment to survey the situation. Jeff had become a pathetic sight compared to how he had left him in Europe. It was then that the reality sunk in. Jeff's life had been changed forever: his daily routines, time spent with friends and family, work situations. This was a life changing event, and nothing Stacey could do or say would make Jeff's journey any easier.

Anneliese suddenly said, "I think you two need to talk. I will go see Wende and Reece. I will return soon." She gently picked up his hand and kissed it.

"Bye," Jeff said.

Anneliese gave Stacey a kiss and left the room.

"Listen, Jeff, I'm so sorry," Stacey said with a very sympathetic tone. "I know you're pissed. I am too. I'm mad that this whole thing is happening, and I'm mad at myself for not being here."

"I can't . . . ride bikes," Jeff said, a tear streaming down his cheek.

"I know, but we'll all be here to help with that transition process," Stacey said.

"*You* won't be," Jeff said, sharply.

"Oh, that's such bullshit, and you know it," Stacey retorted. He felt sorry for Jeff, but he wasn't going to allow Jeff to patronize and ridicule him. "Listen, you don't need to test me. I'm always going to be your friend, even if you can't walk or ride again. That doesn't mean you can't do other things such as play wheelchair basketball or swim or take pictures. And who knows, maybe we can figure out some way for you to come with us on the trails. And if we can't, we'll all still go places and do things together. So, stop thinking I won't be there for you. If anything, this will hopefully bring us even closer. Okay?"

"Okay," Jeff whispered. Stacey could see him glancing aside as if he was pondering something. "But you'll still be . . . thousands of miles away . . . in Germany. You won't have to . . . deal with any of this shit."

"I don't know where I'll be. But, what I *do* know is that I'm going to stick around here for a while," Stacey assured him.

"*Really?* . . . How long?" Jeff asked, looking back at Stacey again.

"I don't know. I guess for however long you all need me to help you deal with this shit," Stacey replied.

"When did you decide? . . . After seeing me?" Jeff asked.

"No, last night while talking to Patty," Stacey said.

"What about your job . . . or Anneliese?" Jeff asked.

"Well, I don't know about my job in Germany. I guess it depends on how much time they're willing to let me take off. I might have to work back here," Stacey admitted. "With regards to Anneliese, I haven't told her that I'll probably be staying longer. She's leaving the day after tomorrow because of Christmas, and I am scheduled to leave around the New Year. I know she'll be pretty hurt that I won't be coming back on time. So, don't say anything to her, okay?"

"I won't . . . spill those beans," Jeff said, smirking.

"Thanks," Stacey said.

"You talked to Patty?" Jeff asked, staring intently at Stacey.

"We talked last night for a while, mostly about you and Brian," Stacey replied.

"Brian," Jeff hesitated. "To be honest . . . I haven't had time . . . to think about him."

"I know. Patty knows that, too," Stacey said.

"Patty and I haven't . . . talked about Brian," Jeff admitted. "I haven't had . . . much empathy . . . How is she?"

"She's all right," Stacey acknowledged. "She's worried about you, though. She doesn't think you want her around. She wants to help you. We all do. She loves you."

"I haven't been . . . very nice to her," Jeff said. "I'm scared she won't . . . marry me. Or, if she does marry me . . . it will be out of pity."

"That's a legitimate worry. It would scare me, too, but that's something you and Patty will have to talk about," Stacey admitted. "She really loves you and wants to show you. You need to let her. She's an adult, and if she wants out of the relationship because it's too much, she'll tell you. Right now, though, she wants to take care of you because she loves you. If you keep pushing her away and being an asshole to her, she *will* pull away. I can tell you Patty is the woman any man would want by their side if this happened to them. I know I would."

"I don't know . . . if she'll be happy . . . with me," Jeff said. Tears welled in his eyes and streamed down his cheek. "Shit . . . crying like a big wuss."

"You need to cry for what happened to you. And for what happened to Brian, to Reece, and for the new realities of life," Stacey said.

"That's all you get," Jeff said. He forced himself to hold back his emotions.

Just then, a nurse entered the room with a clipboard and a small box. Other than a quick smile to Stacey, the nurse went straight to work. Stacey watched her copy down numbers from the machines. She reached into the box and took out an IV bag and replaced the old drip with a new one.

"Do you need anything, hon?" the nurse asked Jeff.

"My back hurts," Jeff replied.

The nurse adjusted his IV, gave him a pat on the hand, and headed out of the room.

"I've been thinking a lot about sudden tragedies," Stacey said. "Most people live their lives the same ways day in and day out. Then a tragedy happens, and the next morning, you're starting a brand new life.

"I would hate to think that our lives are already mapped out for us. But, I can't help but think that some of these random tragedies might not be random. Even the simplest, mundane decisions are going to lead us down a path toward potential disaster."

"Maybe you're right," Jeff concurred. "If a decision is made . . . it can't be random. . . I decided to ride and . . . this is my destiny."

"Well, whatever our destinies, we still need to work at our lives no matter what the circumstances," Stacey said.

"We both have . . . jobs to do . . . when our . . . girlfriends get back," Jeff observed. "I'll talk to Patty . . . about helping me . . . I will listen to her more . . . You need to tell Anneliese . . . about staying here."

"Well, let's not get overly ambitious about me," Stacey said, coyly.

"You have . . . to tell her sometime . . . The sooner . . . the better," Jeff said.

"Okay, I'll tell her," Stacey agreed. "Honesty and communication; that's what it all about, huh? I've always admired that about you and Patty. I, on the other hand, have never been able to be whole-heartedly honest and devoted to a relationship with a woman. I'm learning with Anneliese, though. She's a great partner."

"She reminds me . . . of Patty," Jeff hinted. "That's why . . . you like her."

"Dude, shut up." Stacey laughed, but inside he was nervous because he knew that Jeff's statement was true.

Stacey felt more comfortable around Jeff now. He sat down on a chair by the edge of the bed, and they chatted for another 15 minutes. They talked about all the professional sports that Stacey missed hearing about in Germany, such as baseball, basketball, and football. They rehashed the specific details of exactly how Jeff proposed to Patty, her reaction, and the subsequent celebration. For that moment, Stacey and Jeff were just two friends catching up on each other's lives as if they were sipping beers in a bar downtown, until reality rang on the phone.

"Should I pick it up?" Stacey asked.

"*I* can't do it," Jeff said.

Stacey picked up the phone.

"Hey, Stace, glad you answered," Reece said, relief in his voice. "Wende and Anneliese went to meet Patty in the cafeteria." He paused. "Wende is going back to Germany, as scheduled. I feel overwhelmed with grief that she's leaving. I feel separated from things. Left out."

"I know," Stacey replied.

"I wanna speak with Jeff," Reece muttered. "You know, clear the air. What do you think? Can I join your conversation?"

"Just a sec." Stacey put the phone aside and asked Jeff, "Hey, it's Reece. He wants to join our conversation. Is that okay?"

"I don't mind," Jeff said. "I'd love to talk . . . to the guy . . . who did this to me."

Stacey switched the phone to speaker.

"Okay, you're on speaker," Stacey declared.

"Hi, Jeff. I just wanted to be part of the group and hang out," Reece said.

"What do you have . . . in mind? Go for a ride . . . or a walk?" Jeff asked. The sarcasm stung.

Jeff came out swinging at Reece, similar to what he had done with Stacey. Stacey knew he couldn't get in the middle of this talk. It wasn't his place. He had already discussed with Jeff how he should forgive and accept what had happened. Acceptance was easier said than done, Stacey realized.

Reece met Jeff's anger and sarcasm with a strategy of his own; an apology.

"I'm so sorry," Reece began. "I know it was my fault that we went down that trail. I haven't slept very much because of it. I feel guilty. I do. The accident is the first thought that comes to me when I wake up. All day I'm thinking about how I can make the situation better, but no solution ever comes. Then it's night, and I'm replaying the accident in my mind. I'm livin' a fucking nightmare.

"If I could change positions with you right now, I would in a heartbeat. I want you to know that I'll do anything for you, any help you need, anything."

Stacey stared at the floor in silence. Too painful to watch and almost too painful to listen, Stacey momentarily thought about leaving. He heard Reece sniffle and guessed that Reece was crying. Stacey glanced up at Jeff who still stared without expression. Stacey supposed that Jeff felt so overwhelmed with sadness, anger, and anxiety that he didn't really know what to say.

Jeff laid there in silence. This put Stacey in a very precarious position. He didn't want to break the trust he had re-established with his brother or his friend. He stared at Jeff, as if willing him into further talking.

"Jeff, I know you're really mad at me, but, I hope you can forgive me for the accident," Reece pleaded.

Stacey could hear the desperation in Reece's voice. He knew Reece would get down and beg for forgiveness if he thought that would help to get Jeff back in his graces.

Finally, after a couple more minutes of silence, Jeff reluctantly said, "Thanks for apologizing . . . But fuck you . . . I can't accept it and I can't forgive you . . . Hang up the phone, Stace."

Stacey swung around, grabbed the phone, and pushed the speaker button off.

Walking to the corner of the room and whispering into the receiver, Stacey told Reece, "Shit, I didn't see that coming. Sorry, bro. Don't take it personally, okay?"

"Hard not to, especially since I'm the one he blames. And, *damn*, I admit I'm guilty. Fuck him, too," Reece cried out.

"Just give him some time. He doesn't mean it," Stacey said.

"I know he's pissed off. He has every right. But, I can't live knowing he hates me. Talk to him, *okay*?" Reece begged.

"Okay. I'll talk with him, but don't expect anything soon," Stacey replied. "I'll be over to see you in a bit."

They said goodbye, and Stacey hung up the phone.

Just then, the door opened, and Patty poked her head into the room.

"Hey, you're back," Stacey said.

"Yeah, I had a coffee," Patty replied. She took a more concerned look and asked, "How did everything go in here?"

"Okay. Jeff and I had a good talk," Stacey answered. He stared down at the white, tile floor. "Reece just called to apologize, but Jeff wasn't ready to hear it, which seems reasonable given the situation."

Stacey raised his head, nodded it back and forth, and gestured a sign of caution to Patty with his hands.

"Okay. Well, I'm sorry to hear that," Patty said, glancing over at Jeff, and then letting her head droop.

"It's his fault I'm here," Jeff called out.

Patty hesitantly made her way over to Jeff's bed. She softly said, "Can I get you anything?"

"No . . . Leave me alone," Jeff said. His face turned red and his breaths were labored. "I don't need anything . . . and nobody should need anything from me."

"We just want to help," Patty said, taking his hand in hers. "Letting us care for you would be helping us."

"But look at me . . . I can't help you," Jeff stated. "You need someone . . . to help you get through . . . the pain of losing Brian."

At the mention of Brian, Patty fell apart. She sat staring at Jeff with watery eyes and her right hand held over her mouth. She ran her hand through Jeff's hair. She tried to ease her pain and suffering with a deep gaze into Jeff's eyes, but he had closed them.

So that Patty and Jeff could have some time alone, Stacey slipped out of the room without even saying goodbye.

Stacey went upstairs to visit with Reece, Wendeline, and Anneliese. When he walked into the room, Reece was telling stories from their childhood. Stacey hoped the stories would further endear Wendeline to Reece.

Once Stacey established himself into the conversation, he and Anneliese had the opportunity to talk about their lives in Germany. Anneliese told funny stories about Stacey learning the language and the difficult situations that he'd gotten into by hearing or saying the wrong things. She shared about her studies and what she had to look forward to when she got back home in a few days.

Finally, Patty knocked on Reece's hospital door, informing the group that she was ready to go. Everyone said their goodbyes.

Stacey held the door open as everyone left the room. He let the door shut and walked over to Reece.

"I just wanted to make sure you're okay with Jeff's reaction today," Stacey said, resting his hand on Reece's shoulder. "You know he's going to forgive you, eventually. It's just going to take time. Okay?"

"When you fuck up like I did, you wanna make things right as soon as you can," Reece explained. "I'll be okay, but I have that unsettling feeling that things aren't right and won't be for a long time. It's like in Star Wars when they say there's a disturbance of some kind in the Force."

"I understand." Stacey reached around Reece's head and gave him a gentle hug. "I'll see you tomorrow morning." They said goodbye, and Stacey left the room.

Stacey, Anneliese, Wendeline, and Patty fumbled down the hospital corridors and crunched through the icy snow of the parking lot to the car. The water was in a precarious state of flux. Already the top layer of the snow had hardened into thin sheets of ice. There were also slushy pools of water on the ground where people and cars had mashed the snow and ice into liquid.

Similarly, Stacey's life seemed to be in a state of uncertainty. The shell of his life in Germany was slowly dissolving as time elapsed, and soon his new life in California would be revealed to him. Stacey wondered if he could move in and out of both worlds as easily as the snow froze into ice or melted to water.

As they reached the car, Anneliese remarked, "Since I study to be a doctor, I feel Reece and Jeff will be okay. I pray a lot for them. I imagine them to be much better in weeks ahead."

"Ya, I feel Reece will be better, too," Wendeline said. She paused and then continued by saying, "I think to stay for Reece. I not know what I am going to do. I think to stay and help, and I think to go back home and come back next month. I not know what to do. But, I know I love him."

"He understands that it's Christmas, and you need to leave," Stacey said. "He'll have us to help him. You can always Skype or email. Maybe you'll come back in a couple of months, or maybe Reece will go over to Germany."

"Ya, I think you are right. Tonight I spend time thinking of what I do, and tomorrow I do something," Wendeline said.

"Time sure has a way of forcing a decision," Stacey philosophized, referring to Wendeline's dilemma. He realized it would also pertain to his upcoming discussion with Anneliese when he would have to tell her that he was staying in California longer. He dreaded the conversation, but it would come and pass, similar to all events in his life.

CHAPTER 16

Love is unity
Walking trustfully
Through the heart's shared passages

"Life is a series of natural and spontaneous changes. Don't resist them; that only creates sorrow. Let reality be reality. Let things flow naturally forward in whatever way they like."

— Lao Tzu

AWAKING EARLY, Stacey, Anneliese, and Wendeline drank their tea by the glow of a fire and discussed their plans for the day ahead. Wendeline informed them that she had decided to leave and changed her airline ticket last night for the same flight home as Anneliese. Both women were pleased to fly home together.

Since it was the women's last day in California, they all decided to spend the morning with Reece and Jeff. Wanting to spend the entire day with Reece, Wendeline had accepted Patty's offer to drive her to Stacey's house later in the afternoon on Patty's way to her parent's house.

Given that Wendeline was busy for the day, Stacey proposed that he and Anneliese spend the afternoon in San Francisco and go back to his house in Santa Rosa for the night. Then, he would drive her and

Wendeline to the airport on the morning of their flight. Everyone approved of the plans, so they began preparing to leave.

After arriving at the hospital, they had a quick visit with Reece, Jeff, and Patty. They spent the majority of time with Reece because Jeff did not want visitors. Teary-eyed, Anneliese said goodbye to each of them and wished them good health until she could visit again.

Leaving Wendeline behind at the hospital, Stacey and Anneliese drove at a turtle's pace along the snowy highway until they reached Sacramento. From there, they had a smooth drive to San Francisco. During the ride, they discussed what they were going to do in the city. She told him how she really wanted to walk on the Golden Gate Bridge and ride on the cable cars.

Although anxious to show Anneliese the sights, Stacey felt guilty about hanging out in the city for the day while Reece and Jeff were in the hospital. He didn't know if he could have a good time with Anneliese given the situation at the hospital, nor did he think that he should have one. But, he did feel that he owed it to Anneliese to provide her with an American experience. He decided that he'd do his best to pretend his way through a pleasurable day.

Though it was cold with intermittent rain, Stacey and Anneliese were outdoors most of the day. He took her on a walking tour of Ghirardelli Square, Pier 39, and Fisherman's Wharf. They took a cable car to Chinatown where they had lunch, walked over to Union Square to window shop, and finally perused the art at the Museum of Modern Art.

The famous Golden Gate Bridge was Stacey and Anneliese's last destination on their San Francisco tour. Stacey had planned this as their last stop because he knew from personal experience that the view of the city at night would be spectacular.

Stacey parked the car and proceeded to walk Anneliese over to a two-foot retaining wall. The wall barricaded people from the steep cliffs. Stacey hopped up onto the wall and helped Anneliese up by offering her his hand and pulling her up. Sitting together on Stacey's outlaid jacket, their legs dangled over the edge.

They sat facing one of the greatest views in the world. Spread out before them was the San Francisco Bay. Sizzling lights from the skyline sparkled off its body. The tall cliffs carried the sounds of crashing waves from the rocky shore below.

Putting his arm around Anneliese, Stacey pulled her tight against him. They cuddled for warmth on the frigid night.

As Stacey looked out over the water, he noticed that the waves seemed to be moving in all different directions. He wondered how this seemingly chaotic scene began and how it would resolve. The waves constantly crashed into each other and changed direction. But somewhere amongst all the turmoil, Stacey knew some sort of harmony existed. He realized he was witnessing something more profound in the water. The phrase *order out of chaos* came to his mind.

"San Francisco is much beautiful. I did not see it when we flew in because of the weather, but now I can imagine it," Anneliese declared. "I see it like a painting in museum."

The idea that Anneliese compared the city to a painting sent the neurons in Stacey's brain into a frenzy. Connections were being made deep inside. Suddenly, he felt compelled to talk. He didn't know exactly what to say, how to convey it, or the sequencing of his thoughts. He did know he wanted to tell Anneliese how he felt, and he had to tell her he was staying in California for a while longer than he originally planned. The words started spilling out of his mouth without a rehearsed strategy.

"It's a combination of paintings," Stacey began. "It's romantic because the lights lure you in, yet there's a darkness to the shadows that make it mysterious and abstract. The entire image intoxicates me when it's all lit up. I feel an urge to go into the city to feel the lights and the excitement.

"But, that's the illusion of it. Once I've been in the city for a while, the crowds and the traffic overwhelm me. The imperfections are so apparent up-close. The illusion of beauty works from a distance. That's romance. Romance is seeing something from a distance, but never really knowing it."

Stacey's thoughts seemed out of control. He felt he was rambling and took a moment to collect his thoughts. He realized how he could make sense of his previous remarks. He moved away from Anneliese a bit so that he could look into her eyes when he began to explain his next line of thoughts.

"I've always been afraid of unmasking the beauty of relationships," Stacey realized. "I never allowed myself to get too close to any of my girlfriends because I was afraid that I'd tarnish the romantic image that they had of me or that I'd had of them. Whenever I felt that that perfect image was fading, I would break up with them.

"But with you, that didn't happen. We've lived together for a few months, and I've gotten to know you as the real woman you are, not just some image in my mind.

"What I'm trying to say is that my romantic image of you has been replaced by this love I feel for who you are as a person. I love you for who you truly are, not some image I have of you."

Stacey leaned toward Anneliese and kissed her passionately. In this moment, his love for Anneliese hit full force. He wished that the kiss could fully convey this love. He kissed her slowly and gently, gradually feeling the intensity rise between them. They sat on the wall for a while, staring out over the dark water to the shimmering city.

A mist flickered through the illuminated night sky. Stunned by the beauty, Stacey suddenly felt a sense of urgency to tell Anneliese about his intentions to stay longer.

Stacey continued, "I said all of that earlier because I really wanted you to know how much I love you and how much I love the idea of us being a part of each other's lives. And, well, I—"

"I am very happy you say it," Anneliese interrupted. "I also love you very much. In future, life is good and happy for us."

"I think of a future with you every day," Stacey said.

"I think now is the best time to tell my secret to you," Anneliese stated.

Stacey didn't really have any idea of what Anneliese was about to say. The thought of her secret had been buried under the avalanche of sorrow that now surrounded them both.

"Stacey, I love you," Anneliese said.

Stacey listened, but also thought about how he was going to word his plan.

"I . . . Sorry, I am really nervous," Anneliese admitted.

"That's okay," Stacey reassured her. "Take all the time you need. It's such a wonderful evening. We can sit here until you're ready."

Why is she so nervous? Stacey wondered. An awful thought whizzed through his mind. His heart skipped a beat. *Maybe she's breaking up with me?* He pondered the possibility for a few minutes, while Anneliese readied herself for her reveal. His mind ran backward across the last few days.

Were there any signs that I missed? Stacey wondered. He couldn't think of any problems between them. Stacey reassured himself of Anneliese's love toward him.

"I am ready." Anneliese reached for Stacey's hand.

"Okay," Stacey replied, waiting.

"Stacey, I am pregnant," Anneliese said, smiling. She looked adoringly at Stacey. "We are going to have a baby together. It comes in seven months."

"Wow, Anneliese. That's . . . that's great. Congratulations," Stacey stuttered. "That's great, right?"

"Ya, a baby is good. I am much happy. You can imagine," Anneliese said, glowing in euphoria. Stacey could feel Anneliese gazing intently as if she were trying to decipher the emotion in his face.

"Yeah, I can imagine," Stacey said, slowly. "How did this happen? You're on birth control, and I used protection in the beginning."

"I not know. I take my pill every day," Anneliese replied. "We are the one percent miracle."

Stacey tried to understand how all of the intricacies of Anneliese's pregnancy would affect his plans. His mind, once again, raced in a new direction. He asked, "So, I guess you've thought about this, and you want to have the baby? I mean, you don't want to—"

"No . . . no!" Anneliese shouted, taking her hand away from Stacey's. Her face cringed. "You not want the baby?"

"No, Anneliese. That's not it at all. I would love to have this baby with you," Stacey assured her. Turning to face her, he realized this was no longer a casual conversation in a romantic spot. This had become real life, emotions, and decisions. Stacey took one of Anneliese's hands in his. "I do want this baby. It's just that I'm still in shock. I had no idea . . . I thought your surprise was something else. But this . . . this is big."

"Ya, I know you have a lot to think about," Anneliese said. "I am in much surprise when I learn we will have baby. I know this for two weeks, and I had time to think about it. You only know it now."

"So, you've known for two weeks, huh?" Stacey asked.

"Ya, I tried to tell you a few nights past in Germany when you had the call from Reece. I found out the week before that day," Anneliese explained.

"So, you've thought everything through? What are you going to do about finishing university and about becoming a doctor once you're a mother?" Stacey asked.

"I think a lot about this in the last two weeks," Anneliese replied. "We have much to talk about and plans to make. The baby will be born at the end of July. I have time to finish university in early July. Then, I will take one year away from university to be with the baby. I hope to go back to university in two years."

"Well, that sounds good," Stacey concurred. "I know how much you want to be a doctor, and I'd feel awful if you had to compromise your dream."

"I not know before, but I know now that I want very much to be a mother," Anneliese stated, proudly.

"What about marriage? Should we get married before the baby is born?" Stacey asked.

"Do you ask me to get married?" Anneliese smirked. "I not want you to ask me to get married because we have a baby. I want you to ask me because you love me."

"I love you. I do," Stacey said, kissing Anneliese on the cheek. "I've thought about marriage, but just not so soon."

"It is okay. I also think about marriage, but now is too soon," Anneliese admitted. "Having a baby and to be a mother and father is too much to think about."

"Wow, I'm going to be a father," Stacey exclaimed, still trying to absorb the momentous news. "I can't believe it. I'm going to be a dad. I'm going to have a child like my Dad did years ago. This is amazing."

Stacey bent over and let his head rest on Anneliese's stomach. They sat together, staring out into the drizzle surrounding San Francisco.

Stacey thought of his parents and how he wished they were here for all of this. The changes he has gone through in the past six months would have brought so much excitement to their lives. He remembered how involved they were as parents. They loved hearing about his and Reece's new love interests, school progress, friends, hobbies, and even about their problems. His mom would have loved being told that she would be a grandmother. Reminiscing brought a tear to Stacey's eyes.

Stacey sat up and said, "I need to talk to you about one more thing."

Anneliese nodded in recognition. Stacey cringed inside and focused on choosing the right words. The wrong wording would quickly escalate Anneliese's hurt feelings from bad to worse.

"Listen, I think I am going to stay here a little longer than a week," Stacey began. "Reece and Patty asked me if I could help out with things for a while, at least until Reece has his surgery and Jeff is in stable condition. So, I'm going to call the exchange coordinator and rescind my offer to work at Phorms next semester. I'm so sorry, Anneliese. I know it's not what you want to hear right now."

"You will not come back to Germany?" Anneliese asked, trying to clarify what she had heard.

"Probably not for a little while," Stacey explained. "I need to make sure Reece and Jeff are going to be okay, and I don't think the director at Phorms is going to let me take a month off. I'm thinking that they're probably going to make me teach back at my school here in California."

"When do you know this?" Anneliese asked. Stacey saw the tears welling in her eyes. These tears were, unfortunately, tears of sadness, not the tears of happiness which she had shed earlier.

"Reece and Patty asked me last night, and I told them that I'd do it," Stacey said. "It's not something that I want to do. It's something I *have* to do. I know you don't like it, but you understand, right?"

"Ya, you stay here in California," Anneliese said, laying her hands on Stacey's leg. "You help your brother, Jeff, and Patty. They need you more now. But, I will need you soon."

"I know. I'm already going over all of the possibilities of when and how I can return," Stacey said. "Maybe they'll let me continue the exchange sometime later in the semester. I don't know until I talk to the director. Regardless, I will make sure I come back to see you in the next couple of months, and I'll begin looking for a full time teaching job around the Munich area."

"What will you do with the airline ticket for next week?" Anneliese asked.

"I haven't thought of that, yet. But, I guess I'll call the airline and change the ticket," Stacey told Anneliese.

"What will you make the new date for on the ticket?" Anneliese asked.

"I don't really know. I guess I'll leave it open-ended," Stacey answered. He knew Anneliese would have a lot of questions, but without talking to the director of the exchange program, he couldn't answer them precisely.

"We will continue to talk, ya?" Anneliese probed.

"Yes, every day," Stacey replied. "We'll Skype and email. And, I'll write you letters every week. For some reason, I've been thinking that writing letters could be quite romantic."

Anneliese looked up at Stacey with sad eyes and said, "You think you come back to me in Germany, ya?"

"My family and friends need me," Stacey began. "I know you need me, too. But, I'll only be gone four or five months, at the most. I haven't had a chance to think this through yet, but I'll be back to begin our new family, I promise."

"You promise?" Anneliese asked, once again. Underneath her watery eyes was a dawning smile.

"I promise. I'll fly back, sweep you off your feet, and we'll have our baby together. I love you," Stacey said.

"I love you, too," Anneliese replied. She took his hand and cradled it in her lap.

Holding and kissing each other, they sat staring at the city. They both went inside their minds and reflected upon the momentous events that had recently occurred.

"I guess we should get out of here," Stacey said, as he felt the temperature drop more distinctly. "Plus, I'm sure you can't wait to tell Wende that you are pregnant."

"Ya, I tell Wende now, but I wait to tell my parents when I get back to Germany," Anneliese said.

"Okay, let's go," Stacey said. They stood up and walked toward the car.

The rain began to fall steadily on their 50-mile ride home north to Santa Rosa. They spoke incessantly and giddily of baby names for both boys and for girls. They discussed where they'd live with a baby. They figured that they'd need a larger apartment. They also wondered who would take care of the baby when they were both busy. Anneliese's mom didn't work, so they were curious if she'd be willing to help out on a regular schedule.

As they filled the car with talk, they each withheld from the other their apprehensive thoughts and questions that were an undercurrent of the conversation.

When Stacey and Anneliese arrived at the house, Patty and Wendeline were talking on the front porch.

"Hey Patty, I didn't expect you to still be here," Stacey remarked, walking up and giving her a hug.

"I'm just leaving. We picked up sandwiches in town, and Wende insisted that I have dinner with her," Patty explained, fidgeting with the keys in her hands.

"Can you stay for a just a few more minutes?" Stacey asked.

"If it's quick. I really need to see my parents at home," Patty said. "Why do you have that secret smile on your face?"

"First, let's go in the house. It's cold out here. Then I'll tell you," Stacey said, opening the door and entering the house. He and Anneliese removed their jackets and hung them on the wall rack. Patty and Wendeline entered, too, but Patty stood near the open door.

"I told Anneliese that I'd be staying longer than we'd anticipated. She's fine with it," Stacey announced. Patty and Wendeline both glanced at Anneliese to see her reaction. Anneliese offered a half-smile.

Patty hugged Stacey and said, "Thank you so much. That's very generous of both of you, especially in terms of your relationship and job."

"We are happy to help. I would like to be here, too, but I can't miss university," Anneliese said, giving Patty a kiss on the cheek.

"I understand," Patty replied, kissing her in return.

"I not know if it is right time. But, I have something to tell you," Anneliese said, puffing out her stomach and resting her hands on her belly.

"What is it?" Patty and Wendeline asked, simultaneously.

"I am pregnant," Anneliese announced. "Stacey and I will have a baby."

"Wow, this is *wunderbar*," Wendeline shouted. She hugged Anneliese, and the two of them began talking demonstrably in German like two giddy school girls.

Initially in a state of awe, Patty quickly shifted into one of a smirking sleuth who tried to find clues. As Wendeline and Anneliese giggled on one side of the room, Patty prodded Stacey about all of these quick changes in Stacey's life. Stacey took all of the questioning in good humor. He sensed Patty's gentle teasing about Anneliese's pregnancy was a jealous reaction to the news. After all, he experienced envy when she and Jeff got engaged.

Furthermore, the kiss between them was the elephant in the room, and it couldn't have come at a worse time. But, it wasn't something he felt he could address with Patty, just yet.

A short time later, Patty wished the couple her congratulations and said a tearful goodbye. Wendeline wanted to be alone, so she excused herself to her room.

Stacey and Anneliese spent their last night together curled up in bed and had a muffled conversation about how often they'd write, e-mail, and phone each other. The consensus was that they'd communicate daily via any means possible. They also discussed when

Stacey would actually know for sure of his date to go back to Germany. Finally, they put themselves to sleep by whispering to one another how much they loved each other and how much they'd miss the other one.

CHAPTER 17

For two united souls
Parting is sharing a heart through the ether

"May the road rise up to meet you, may the wind be ever at your back.
May the sun shine warm upon your face and the rain fall softly on your fields.
And until we meet again, may God hold you in the hollow of his hand."

— Irish Blessing (author unknown)

THE LOW CLOUDS CAST a flat gray across the sky, leaving a single, solemn light of a slanted winter's sun. The rain poured down as Stacey drove Anneliese and Wendeline from Santa Rosa to San Francisco. Once they arrived at the airport, Stacey parked the car in the short-term parking garage. They gathered their belongings and headed toward the airport terminal. Pulling their rolling suitcases behind them, they emerged from the garage and entered into the airport terminal.

A large structure with thick, sound-proof glass walls and roof, the terminal was similar to a massive, multimillion dollar aquarium without the water and fish. Magnifying the subtle intricacies of relationships in one moment of time, the airport's glass dome was a lens for looking in at human connections.

Most couples who traveled together held hands and helped each other. These couples seemed to have a symbiotic relationship. Some couples, though, were constantly bickering or not talking at all. Others were apathetic toward their traveling companion.

Put under the airport microscope, Stacey and Anneliese exhibited passion, thoughtfulness, caring, and love. Their relationship upheld the litmus test of the airport's zooming lens. Stacey helped Anneliese and Wendeline through the check-in process at the ticket counter and bought them an early lunch outside of the security area.

Before Anneliese disappeared into the inner sanctum of the airport terminals, Stacey reached for her, taking both of her hands in his. Wendeline stood a few feet away. The great passion and love he had for Anneliese, the deep sense of caring, and the overwhelming feeling of losing her overtook Stacey in that moment. He wanted to say so much, but each time he tried, no words came out. Tears filled his eyes when Anneliese leaned into Stacey.

After wiping away tears, Stacey found his words.

"I have something for you." Stacey pulled a long, narrow box out of his jacket pocket. He opened the box and took out two necklaces, each with a picture locket.

"This was my grandma and grandpas' promise necklaces. Before my grandpa went to war, he gave my grandma this necklace as a promise that he would come back and marry her," Stacey explained, opening the locket to show Anneliese the pictures inside. "I put our pictures over my grandparents' pictures. I want us to wear them, as a promise that we'll return to each other."

"I love it because it has much meaning. I wear it every day," Anneliese said. She held it up so that she could admire it. "You talk with Reece about the necklaces, ya?"

"Yes. Reece was happy that we would be wearing them," Stacey replied.

"I have more to tell and show my family when I come home," Anneliese said. She slipped it over her head and onto her neck.

"It's lovely on you," Stacey said.

"I will think of you much," Anneliese said, touching the locket. "You promise to come back to me, ya?"

"I have to return to you. I have to be near you," Stacey said. "My soul is drawn to you as it is to water. I've always had this strong longing to be near oceans and rivers. I'm attracted to you in the same way."

"I feel the same pull for you," Anneliese said. These last words caused Anneliese to reach for Stacey's comforting arms once again. They hugged, and their heads gently fell together.

Meanwhile, Wendeline stood at the entrance to the security gates listening to music on her phone. She glanced up at the clock on the wall and lost her patience.

Wendeline shouted something in German and then shouted, "Stacey, let her come. Talk your goodbyes and she must go. Anneliese we leave now."

"All right, all right. She's coming," Stacey shouted at Wendeline. He turned to Anneliese. This was the last real goodbye. Her plane departed soon and they still had to go through security. The tears immediately filled Stacey's eyes and slid down his cheek.

"I love you so much," Stacey muttered. "I'll miss you, but just know that I'll see you soon."

"I too love you, Stace," Anneliese cried. They hugged and kissed. Anneliese slowly backed away a couple of feet at a time.

"Call me when you get back to Germany," Stacey commanded.

"Ya, I call when we land," Anneliese acknowledged. She stepped back another few feet.

"I put your Christmas gifts in your bags last night," Stacey called out.

"I put gift for you under the tree," Anneliese replied.

Anneliese stood at the security gates with Wendeline. They walked unfettered through the maze of walkways to the guards. Placing their carry-on bags and purses onto the conveyor belt, they walked through the metal detectors.

Stacey watched Anneliese pass through the machine, collect her belongings, slip on her shoes, and walk toward the long corridor that led to her departing flight. Along the way, Anneliese spun around to wave at Stacey. She did it twice before time, distance, and mobs of people swallowed her up. She was gone.

Stacey breathed a sigh of relief that the goodbye was over. A sense of calm came over him. He wandered aimlessly through the airport. At times, he reached for a hand that wasn't there.

Finally, Stacey exited the airport and stood outside. He walked past the roof line and felt the rain fall on his face and arms. Taxis, shuttles, buses, and cars splashed along the narrow and crowded street. People moved in all directions around him, lugging suitcases while they tried to get to their destinations.

Depleted of energy and motivation, Stacey was an island of nothingness in this chaos. Distracted, he put one foot in front of the other, trudging over the street, and wading through puddles. With his mind 30,000 feet up in the air and wondering when he'd see Anneliese and his unborn child again, he somehow managed to locate his car and drive all the way back to Santa Rosa without even being fully aware of what he had just done.

PART 4
WATER

Water is God's soul
Linking the world
In a romance of life and death

"Water is a medium that links different aspects of humanity and the divinities into a coherent unit; it bridges paradoxes, transcends the human and divine realms, allows interaction with gods, and enables the divinities to intervene in humanity. Water is a medium for everything - it has human character because we are human, it is a social matter, but it is also a spiritual substance and divine manifestation with imminent powers. But still it belongs to the realm of nature - the hydrological cycle links all places and realms. Water transcends the common categories by which we conceptualize the world and cosmos."

— Terje Oestigaard, *Water, Christianity, and the Rise of Capitalism*

AMALMAGATING AMONG MILLIONS OF GALLONS of water, the recently fallen rain exhibited its cohesive nature by entering the various lakes and ponds of Northern California. The surface of Lake Mendocino lulled and swayed with occasional sounds of bubbles gurgling, waves lapping, or currents swishing. Creatures, large and small, drank from the edges of the serene water. Underneath the surface, however, the water churned as plants, animals, and insects lived and breathed in the water. The water teemed with activity and life before emptying into various creeks and rivers.

One of the largest rivers of the Sonoma County watershed, the Russian River meandered quietly around farmland on its way out of Lake Mendocino. As the river entered into Sonoma County, the water screamed down narrow canyons and romped around a gauntlet of large boulders and small cliffs near the town of Cloverdale.

The river slowed again when the water poured into wide pools next to the vineyards of the Alexander Valley. It slid leisurely in its channel between budding grapevines and fruit orchards. It crept around the town of Healdsburg. Bridges crossed the river at various points and roads often paralleled it. People took healing sanctuary in the water as they floated upon or walked along the river.

Far below the current of the Russian River, though, some of the water quietly percolated through the seemingly impenetrable ground to join the vast subterranean reservoirs. Pumped up to the surface in pipes, the purified water was distributed for consumption.

Nearing the end of its journey, the water of the Russian River veered west toward the ocean. As it did so, it entered back into an environment almost untouched by humans. The water's still surface reflected giant maples and oak trees towering over the river. Ivy plants crawled up the trunks of the trees, and blackberry bushes wrapped themselves around most of the living plants near the edges of the river, blockading most human foot traffic. A few trails wound their way through the thick brush and trees.

Nearing Guerneville, a small resort town, the river became shallow and slowed to the pace of an old couple's stroll. Even in its deepest sections, the water only reached depths of about eight feet. Traveling a great distance, the water became so murky that the bottom of the river wasn't visible.

Before long, the narrow landscape of the Russian River entered the expansive Pacific Ocean at the town of Jenner. The brackish water of the river seemed to slip gently out to the ocean underneath the crashing waves. It was here that Stacey, once again, crossed paths with the water.

CHAPTER 18

Romance is an illusion
Deceiving present life
With future love

"Oh my William! It is not in my power to tell thee how I have been affected by this dearest of all letters- it was so unexpected- so new a thing to see the breathing of thy inmost heart upon paper that I was quite overpowered, and now that I sit down to answer thee in the loneliness and depth of that love which unites us and which cannot be felt but by ourselves, I am so agitated and my eyes are so bedimmed that I scarcely know how to proceed."

— Mary Wordsworth

SITTING ALONE in the passenger seat of his car, Stacey took a sip of water and gazed out to the stormy sea. Dull, gray light filtered through thick clouds. Sheets of rain obscured his view. The only thing he could discern was the violent nature of the waves; white water spraying and rolling onto the beach. His heart felt as dreary as the landscape.

It was late afternoon on New Year's Eve, and Stacey didn't have anywhere to go or anything to do. He had visited Reece in the morning, but Reece was too tired to have Stacey come in the afternoon. Patty had gone to the hospital to be with Jeff, and Anneliese wasn't answering her phone.

Filling a backpack with a math textbook, a lesson-plan book, and paper, Stacey decided to drive to the beach where he hoped to find the inspiration to plan his first week of school, which started in two days. Although he was anxious to begin teaching again at his home school, Stacey couldn't focus on preparing the curriculum. His emotions concerning the accident and Anneliese's departure kept getting in the way. He needed to address these issues before tackling his school work.

He wished he could swim across the ocean to Anneliese. Instead, he took out a notebook and pen. Under the dim light of a miserable day, Stacey wrote his first letter to Anneliese.

I feel as if I'm about to go on an extraordinary journey, Stacey thought. This is a trip into my soul. If I'm going to keep Anneliese in love with me while we're apart, then I need to make her feel that my heart still beats with hers. I have to make our love stronger than the gap that divides us. My written words must become my soul that she holds when she reads the letter.

With the raindrops pummeling the car in an orchestra of loneliness, Stacey began writing his first love letter to Anneliese.

Dear Anneliese,

It's been raining since you left last week, and there's nothing in the forecast but rain. Water trickles down my window like the tears I have shed these past days. It's true. The clouds and my sadness commiserate. I miss you like the moisture in the clouds misses the water on Earth. Similar to those raindrops reuniting with the waters in the ocean, lakes, and rivers, we'll be in each other's arms once again.

They say that when someone loses an arm or leg, the person will often have a sensation that they can move their missing limb. Or, the person will have vivid dreams with the missing limb still intact. Anneliese, you are the lost part of my soul. I know distance separates us, but I live like you're right here with me. My mind has conjured a false reality of you and me together, similar to what the mind of an amputee will do.

I've imagined us going on walks, bike rides, late night dinners, and gelato runs. I daydream about spending time with your family, hanging out with friends, and having sparkling conversations. I envision times to come. I look forward to holding you, helping you through the pregnancy, and eventually rocking our baby to sleep at night in my arms. I can't wait to teach our child how to play basketball and ride a bike. I'm so excited to be a father!

Reece is still doing better after his surgery last week. They fused part of his spine. He is recovering well, except for the pain. In hopes of impressing his pretty nurse, he's not using the morphine. (Don't tell Wende about the nurse.) I drove him to a rehab center in Santa Rosa yesterday. He'll spend a couple of weeks there. He's excited to get out and come back home. He is still distraught about the accident and Jeff's refusal to talk to him. He saw a grief counselor yesterday to help him through his anxiety.

Jeff has his emotional ups and downs, but he's doing better physically. The doctors have been doing tests on him. Thus far, he seems to be paralyzed only from the waist down. I know that is still bad, but it could be much worse. He could have lost his ability to breathe or move his arms. Luckily, his upper body is fine. That's the positive news. The negative part is that he's going to have a couple more surgeries. One is to try to stabilize his vertebrae. The doctors said he'll be in the hospital in Truckee for another couple weeks until they're sure the vertebrae have healed. From there, they will take him by ambulance to a rehab center in Santa Rosa where he'll probably be for a couple of months. Jeff has a long road to recovery ahead of him.

Patty is all right, considering the circumstances. I seem to be the only one that she can talk to. Her parents are grieving, Jeff is in his own world, and her friends don't know what to say. So that leaves me, which is okay because helping her is one of the reasons why I came back. Until yesterday, our lives seemed to revolve around the hospital hours. I would take her to the hospital in the morning. I spent most of the time with Reece, and she spent her time with Jeff. We would see each other for lunch, and then we spend more time with Reece and Jeff. Finally, I'd take Patty out for dinner and then back home.

Now that I've come back home, I won't be able to help her as much. I hope it gets easier for her.

Patty still wonders if her relationship with Jeff will survive. She doesn't know if Jeff is willing to continue with it. He is still treating her as though he doesn't even want her around. He gets angry, and it's often directed at Patty. He forces her to leave the room for long periods of time.

She says she also has selfish feelings about leaving Jeff once he comes home. That's probably a normal reaction, and I told her so. I hope they can learn to adjust to the new situations. I really do. They are such a good couple.

Thanks for the phone calls, e-mail, and Skype. It's so sweet to get the daily updates about you and what you've been doing. Words and pictures are nice, but my heart aches to feel you next to me. I miss you so much, Anneliese. My soul feels empty without you by my side.

Voltaire said, "Paradise is where I am." Well, I'm here in California, but it's not paradise. Paradise is in Germany with you. The only thing that keeps my spirits up is the knowledge that I'll be with you again. Sometimes when I look at the beautiful watch you gave me for Christmas, I figure out what time it is back in Germany and wonder what you're doing at that exact moment. Are you happy or sad? Are you thinking of me at the same moment I'm thinking of you? That would be something special.

Hope to read a return letter from you soon.

Love Always,

Stacey

P.S.

I am so proud of how well you did on your exams last semester. You are the smartest and most talented person I know. I wish you good thoughts for your upcoming semester. As my dad used to say, "Give 'em hell."

Stacey folded the letter, slipped it into an envelope, and put it in his backpack. Feeling like the letter was closing the distance of two continents, a euphoric feeling rushed through him. He deemed the letter a necessary element to mend his loneliness. He knew that the catharsis would continue if he walked on the beach, heard the waves crashing, and felt the frigid waters engulfing his feet.

Putting on his jacket and grabbing the umbrella, Stacey opened the car door. He slipped his shoes off his feet and felt the grains of sand on his skin.

Climbing to the top of a dune, he paused before heading down to the water. Stacey marveled at the power of the waves—a never-ending series of white-water swells.

The ocean, vast and tumultuous, reminded Stacey of everything that separated him from Anneliese. The plight was like Saint Exupéry walking across the desert. It was James Ramsay trying to get to the lighthouse. It seemed so close, yet such an immense distance to cover.

Stacey walked down to the water. As he reached the ocean-drenched sand, he felt a stab on the bottom of his left foot. Lifting his foot, he saw a chunk of glass wedged into his heel. The moment he pulled it out, blood trickled from the wound.

Stacey realized he was a few feet away from one of the greatest healers in the world. Renowned for its curative properties, the ocean contained a plethora of therapeutic salt water. He hobbled to the water, waited for a wave to wash up high enough onto the beach, and stepped into the water. As he stood in the frigid waters, his feet numbed. He took in several deep breaths. After a few minutes, his foot felt better, the blood had nearly stopped, and his outlook on the separation from Anneliese improved. With suffering being temporary, a voyage across the ocean to see Anneliese seemed attainable.

* * *

A FEW WEEKS LATER, Stacey strolled underneath a canopy of large evergreen trees near the edge of the Russian River. Recent rains had swollen the river. Water surged over the plant line on the banks of the river, close to the path Stacey walked. He hummed the majestic, meandering melody of Smetana's "The Moldau".

Stacey came to an open, grassy meadow adjacent to the river. There sat a long, pillared gazebo with a steel roof. Entering the structure, Stacey saw an open-air classroom containing six large, empty tables and two tall, free-standing cabinets.

Having brought his students on a field trip to visit the local water agency, Stacey needed to prepare an experiment before they arrived at the gazebo. His class just finished a tour of one of the water pumping stations where drinking water was extracted from underground along the banks of the Russian River. The students were due to arrive at the gazebo in about 20 minutes.

Setting down his backpack on a table, Stacey pulled out the instructions on how to set up the experiment. Along with this was an unread letter from Anneliese.

Stacey's heart fluttered as he opened the envelope. He hoped the letter would contain Anneliese's quirky English phrases of love and passion. He needed to know that she missed him as much as he missed her. He wanted his feelings of love and hope reciprocated in Anneliese's letter. Figuring he had time before his students arrived, Stacey pulled out the letter and began reading.

Dear Stacey,

I also miss you much. I think of you many times in a day. The apartment is very lonely. You can imagine. But I see you in things beautiful like the snow, trees, and mountains. I hear you in bird songs, people speaking English, and when I listen to music. I feel you in bed under the warm blanket, on my tongue with sweet wine and chocolate, and in my legs hiking through the mountains.

I think to thank you for such a beautiful letter. Waiting for the letter and finally reading it is more magic than e-mail. It makes me think of old times when lovers are away and only reach each other with letters. I feel it in my hand and unfold it and see your writing. I smell you on the paper. My heart is warm when I read the words you write to me on a cold day. You can imagine.

I feel all the marks of ink come from your heart. I think you show how much you feel for me. I feel we are together if we are not.

I hope to see you quickly, but I think it is wonderful you care for your friends. I am happy to know Reece is good at rehab. I am also happy Jeff heals well from surgery. Please have Reece and Jeff know that I think about them much. I hope to see them soon. Also, I think about Patty. How is she feeling? I am happy you are in California to help her do better.

I ask you to think also of me. Please do not forget me.

Oh, I not think to write that. I am sorry.

Here in Germany I am good. I feel wonderful for my good marks on exams at university. You can imagine. I study many days and nights. I did not sleep much before the exam. I not think I have good marks on exams. But I was surprised when I have good marks. I am closer to finishing my university and to be a doctor.

My days are much busy. I go to classes at university and see friends and study. I go home two times to see family after you leave. They also visit me one time. I think they miss you also. My dad wants me to write that he and you will play tennis when you come to Germany. I see Wende much. She sleeps in the apartment sometimes when she visits München. She talks much about Reece. You tell Reece that she says she loves him every time we talk.

I am very happy to be pregnant. I feel good most days. Some mornings I am sick, but I feel better in two or three hours. I not yet see my stomach grow from the baby. I hope to see signs of the baby soon. My mom comes for a visit in two days. She comes to see my doctor with me. I hope we see a picture of the baby. I cannot wait. You can imagine. I send you in email and you see our baby boy or girl.

I must leave for class so I will end the letter. Write to me quickly. I like to have letters. I miss you. I love you. I think of you much. Tell Reece and friends I think of them. I hope to see you soon.

Love Always,

Anneliese

Stacey smiled after finishing the letter. Enamored, he read it a few more times. All in all, it was more than what he'd expected. He thought her lack of English might hinder the meaning or shorten the length of it, but instead, it made it more unique and special.

Believing that the letter confirmed her love, it aroused in Stacey an even deeper love for Anneliese. It sent his soul aloft like a bird soaring on a spring day.

"What are you doing? Shouldn't you be setting up the stations?" Patty asked, startling Stacey as she took a seat across from him.

"Yeah, I was about to get the supplies," Stacey muttered, folding up Anneliese's letter. "You're early. The class won't be here for ten more minutes, right? Why are you here before them?"

"I came ahead to give you a hand," Patty said, taking off her small pack and putting it on the table. "By the way, you have an excellent class. They're well behaved, smart, and excited to learn. Makes your job a lot easier, huh? Although, you do have that one student who blames everyone for his misfortunes."

"Drives me crazy. I've been working with him since I got back," Stacey remarked, chuckling.

"Having such a good class must have made your transition back to California easier," Patty speculated.

"Yeah. The students have been helpful since I took over," Stacey explained. "The first few days were rough. Gretel had her unique teaching style and management techniques, so I've had to do my best to use her methods, or slowly transition to mine. Other than that, it's like I never left."

"I'm glad the kids made it easy. I'm sure it's been hard without Brian," Patty said, leaning against a table.

"Fuck, that's an understatement. Brian's death left a massive hole in the school community. It's been tough for everyone," Stacey said. "I used to go to the office on my breaks just to bullshit with him about sports, movies—whatever. We'd play basketball in the gym after school. Shit, we used to watch March Madness games in my classroom at lunch, and sometimes even when the students were there. Can you believe that?"

"That's ridiculous," Patty commented, patting Stacey's leg. "Sounds like you two were good friends."

"Yeah, I guess we were," Stacey said. "I never thought of him as a close friend because we never hung out much outside of school. But, you're right, we were good friends. I still can't believe he's gone. Every time I walk past his office, I expect him to call me in."

Trying to be discreet, Stacey slid Anneliese's letter into the envelope and dropped it into the nearest open pocket of his backpack.

Glancing at the envelope, Patty asked, "Was that a letter from Anneliese?"

"Yes." Stacey smiled.

"Ooh! A love letter," Patty teased, mocking Stacey with a pretend kiss.

"It was in the mailbox this morning," Stacey explained, hiding the letter deeper in his backpack. "I couldn't wait to get home to read it. This felt like the perfect moment, so I read it."

"And?" Patty asked.

"And what?" Stacey said.

"Was it a good letter?" Patty asked, batting her eyes for effect.

"The best. Far better than an email," Stacey replied.

"You guys email and Skype every day, right?" Patty asked. Stacey nodded in agreement. "So, what's so great about writing letters as opposed to emails or Skype?"

"Easy," Stacey said. He took out the envelope again and held up Anneliese's letter in front of Patty's nose. "First, I can smell Anneliese on the letter. Smell her?"

Patty sniffed and said, "Yes, it smells like her perfume."

"Second, Anneliese's handwriting is like art," Stacey remarked, offering the letter to Patty. "Anyone can type the words she wrote, but only Anneliese could style her cursive letters so loopy and curvy. It's another thing I love about her."

"Letters as artistry. I can agree with that," Patty said, taking the letter and analyzing the cursive strokes.

"Plus, writing a letter is different than talking. I have time to formulate what I want to write," Stacey said, taking back the letter from Patty. "If we're going to remain in love, then I have to write out my feelings and thoughts as if we were together at that moment."

"That makes sense," Patty agreed. "Jeff and I have never been apart long enough to write letters to each other. Although, he's written sweet cards and love notes that I've saved."

"I would expect that much from him," Stacey said. "Speaking of art, are you drawing again?"

"No. Too much on my mind to create art," Patty stated.

"They say that art can be therapeutic," Stacey hinted.

"It is, but not now. It's just too soon." Patty picked up an empty water pitcher. "Hey, shouldn't we set up the experiment? The students should be here any minute."

"Yeah, probably a good idea," Stacey agreed. He read the instruction sheet. "I'm going to fill up the buckets with water and place them on the tables. Will you put these dowels and a roll of paper towels at each table?"

"Sure." Patty put the pitcher down and took a handful of dowels from the counter.

"They hang a paper towel in the bucket of water and watch the water climb up the paper towel," Stacey explained. "They learn that water can defy gravity with its capillary action."

Stacey filled the bucket with water from a faucet next to the gazebo. He precariously lifted the bucket up on the table. Meanwhile, Patty distributed the dowels and rolls of paper towels to each table.

"I wanted to thank you for inviting me to come on this field trip. I'm glad I just happened to be in town visiting my parents when you needed me. I've had a great time," Patty said, placing her hand on Stacey's shoulder as she walked past him.

"No problem. Like I said, it wasn't so much an invitation as it was a command." Stacey laughed and grabbed another empty bucket. "I was shorthanded on chaperones."

"I'm glad I could help," Patty replied. "Being out here has helped me more than you realize. It's given me a refreshing break from dealing with Brian and Jeff issues."

"With Brian's funeral last week, Jeff's paralysis, and the surgeries, you've had a hell of a new year," Stacey remarked.

"I sure have," Patty agreed. "Brian's death and his service were the worst. I don't know how I got through it. I honestly don't think my soul was even there. It seems like a dream."

"I thought the funeral was perfect, as far as funerals go," Stacey said, pausing his work to look at Patty. "There were so many people: families, former students, and teachers. He was a real leader in the community."

"I remember people filled the room," Patty said, leaning against a table. "So many people came up to me—I can't remember who, except for the school kids. I do remember them."

"They were one of the most memorable parts of the funeral for me," Stacey said. "Instant tears when the students stood up in their school colors and sang our school song. And that slideshow of Brian made me very emotional."

"Those kids spoke better than me," Patty said.

"No. You gave a moving eulogy. You really did." Stacey put the bucket down and gave Patty a hug. "Those two poems were poignant and touching. I looked them up on the internet when I got home. I've heard "Gone from My Sight" before. It brought tears to my eyes thinking of my parents existing somewhere over the horizon. "Do Not Stand at My Grave and Weep" made me think of Brian. I liked it and want it read at my funeral someday."

"I chose Van Dyke's, and my mom picked out Mary Elizabeth Frye's," Patty said. "I don't remember much from the service, but I will never forget my parents' emotions. My dad trying to speak, but unable to get the words to come. My mom telling such lovely stories about Brian. It was so intense when she wailed."

"That was painful to watch," Stacey said, reaching out for Patty's hand.

Just then, Stacey and Patty heard children's voices in the distance. The students were minutes from the gazebo. Stacey let go of Patty's hand.

"I wanted to talk to you about that kiss last month. I don't want any confusion or weird feelings between us," Patty said, staring down at her ring. "I'm sorry. I was obviously distraught."

"I know. That kind of loss will drive anyone to madness," Stacey said. "And we all know it takes madness for any woman to kiss me."

Patty laughed.

"I do have feelings for you. I think you're a great guy, but I still love Jeff," Patty said.

"I know you do," Stacey said, reaching for another bucket and filling it up with water. "How are things between you two?"

"For me, taking care of him has changed me," Patty began. "For the first couple of weeks, all I could think about was a future with a paraplegic. The whole time I've been with Jeff I've fantasized about the wedding, honeymoon travels, and eventually kids. The accident changed everything. I found myself worried about getting him dressed, his job, and if he could travel.

"But, once I began helping the nurses care for him, he wasn't just a paraplegic anymore. He was Jeff. I find that I love him even more."

"That's great. I'm happy something stronger has come out of this for you," Stacey said.

"Yes, that is nice. But, those are just *my* feelings," Patty said, picking up a bucket of water and placing it carefully on a table. "Jeff is still not receptive to me helping. He doesn't want hugs or for me to kiss him. I can't even hold his hand.

"I'm worried about the future. Even if things get better between Jeff and I, it's a different future than I imagined. But whose future is ever the same as they imagined?"

"Not mine," Stacey stated. "A month ago, I thought I would still be teaching in Germany and dating Anneliese. Totally unexpected."

"It reminds me of this experiment you'll be doing with the water," Patty stated, picking up one of the paper towels and dipping the corner into the water. She watched as the water rose up the towel. "The water does the opposite of what we think it will do, sort of like us when we defy our futures because our expectations are altered or don't turn out like we thought."

"Like we're going against our destiny or our fate," Stacey said.

"Exactly. Like the accident," Patty added.

"How is Jeff doing after this latest surgery?" Stacey asked.

"Jeff's doctors said the surgery to stabilize his vertebrae appears to be successful," Patty began. "Unfortunately, the doctors still believe that he won't be able to walk. He doesn't have any more surgeries scheduled, so his body will get a chance to strengthen for the next phase of treatment. Later this week, he's moving into the rehab center where they'll do physical therapy and slowly introduce him to life as a paraplegic. He'll probably be in the center for another month or two."

Patty's cell phone rang.

"Speak of the devil. It's Jeff," Patty said, walking to the meadow to talk in seclusion.

Stacey put the last bucket of water on a table. The experiment was ready.

A group of students, led by the water agency guide, emerged from the forested trail and walked across the meadow toward the gazebo. Each member of the group wore a light-weight poncho. The guide led them to the edge of the gazebo and had the students line up.

After a quick glance at the tables, the guide told Stacey, "Thanks for setting up the experiment. It looks great."

"No problem. It didn't take long," Stacey replied, handing the guide the instruction paper.

As he shoved the paper in his pack, the guide called the students to huddle around him. He began the experiment by asking the students what they knew about the flow of water.

As the guide spoke, Patty returned and pulled Stacey aside.

"Sorry, Stace, I have to go." Patty looked concerned. "That was Jeff's mom. The doctors are concerned because Jeff has some fluid in his lungs."

"What does that mean?" Stacey asked, taking Patty to the other side of the gazebo. "Is it serious?"

"It's not serious now, but if it gets worse, then it'll be serious," Patty said, tears welling in her eyes. "For now, though, the doctors are going to remove the fluid. Then, they'll watch him to make sure the fluid doesn't return."

"I'm sorry," Stacey said, hugging Patty. "It doesn't seem fair."

"I wish all of these complications happened at once. That way, all of this emotional shit would be over in one moment," Patty cried, ending the hug and taking a few steps back. "Instead, it's just fuckin' turbulence that never seems to end. I just want this bad shit over with."

"I know," Stacey said, not knowing what to say next. "Do you need me to come back with you?"

"No, no. You need to stay here with your class. I know the route to Truckee like the back of my hand. I'll be fine," Patty said. She wiped away her tears. "Do I have mascara smudged on my face now?"

"No, you're as cute as ever," Stacey replied.

"Thanks again for inviting me," Patty said, passing over the compliment. "This field trip has taught me a few things. I had no idea water was so dynamic."

"Hey, thanks for coming," Stace said, quietly. "You were a big help."

Patty offered him a smile and scanned the perimeter of the gazebo. Spotting her backpack, she walked over and picked it up from the table. "I almost forgot my backpack. I'll call you later tonight and let you know how he's doing."

"All right. Sounds good," Stacey said. He gave her a quick hug. "Do you remember how to get back to the parking lot?"

"Yeah. Take this trail about a quarter mile up," Patty replied. She headed toward the meadow.

"Call me as soon as you know more about Jeff's situation," Stacey called out. Patty turned around and nodded. She walked around a curve and out of sight.

Returning to his class at the gazebo, Stacey helped the students with the water experiment. They concluded the field trip by surveying the holding ponds for the water treatment facility. All the while, Stacey's thoughts were on Jeff's prognosis.

* * *

A WEEK LATER, Stacey felt inspired to write a letter back to Anneliese. As rain collected on his bedroom window, Stacey sat down at his desk, took out a piece of paper, and began writing.

Dear Anneliese,

I enjoyed reading your letter. You made me feel so loved. The greatest feeling in the world is when the love you send out to someone is reciprocated. The caring words in your letter reassured my thoughts and actions about our future together. In fact, I can't stop daydreaming about us together – weeks, a year, or five years from now.

The last couple of weeks have been tough for Jeff, Patty, and their families. The latest incident occurred last week when Jeff's lungs filled with fluid. Luckily, the doctors were able to remove it and prevent it from getting worse.

They've been on a scary rollercoaster. They've had their hopes slowly rise and quickly plummet, they've had surprise twists and turns, and their stomachs are constantly queasy with tension and anxiety. The ride has slowed, but it's still a long way from ending. It's been hard on their relationship. I'm trying to keep them motivated and inspired. I've been able to visit Jeff in Truckee once or twice per week. I'm glad I stayed for them.

As for Reece, he's doing great. He has another week at the rehab center, and then he comes home. He's still wearing the back brace, but he's now able to do physical therapy, even swinging a golf club now and again. He's much more positive than Jeff. Reece, though, still suffers from guilt about what happened. I don't know if there's much I can do about that. I guess time will have to heal those wounds. He's still seeing a therapist. It's helped a great deal. He hasn't reconciled with Jeff, yet. Jeff's attitude toward everyone is very frustrating and heartbreaking. I hope he turns an emotional corner soon!

I can't wait to see you. I'm keeping busy here in California, but that's all it is. I'm merely living to survive, instead of living for meaning or purpose like when I'm with you. To be a complete person, I need you close to me. I want to be with you when you're accomplishing your goals, when you laugh or cry, when you need a hug, when you need someone to talk to, and when you need support with the pregnancy. I want to be there. Though we're not married, we already have created a union between us. So, being apart from you makes my soul ache for its other half, its companion, its mate, its lover, and its best friend.

Love Always,

Stacey

P.S.

I printed the sonogram of our baby and hung it on the mirror in my bathroom. I also put a copy in my wallet so I could show everyone. I'm a proud papa already.

Later in the evening, Patty knocked on the door for one of her routine weekly stopovers after visiting her parents. Silhouetted on the living room wall, they sat side by side talking for an hour.

I'm living my life in California and imagining a love in Germany, Stacey thought. It's almost perfect.

CHAPTER 19

Time and distance
Both illusions of the mind
No beginnings, no ends

"For the whole of life is really like that; we are almost always in one place with our minds somewhere quite the other."

— Ford Maddox Ford, *The Good Soldier*

O
VER THE NEXT 23 DAYS, the rain slowly started to subside. With spring officially a few weeks away, the clouds became less saturated, lighter, and rose higher in the sky above California. Not only were the moisture levels changing, but the temperature increased from the high 50s to the low 70s.

Stacey soaked in the warm weather as he and Reece walked into Annadel State Park. With hundreds of acres of oak and redwood forests, surrounded by grassy meadows, and traversed with miles of creeks and trails, Annadel was the crown jewel of the local park system.

Noticing the natural world around him, Stacey marveled at the beauty of the vibrant plant life. A family of five deer apprehensively ate the wild grasses which blanketed the land in a sea of green. Birds chirped their spring songs in the trees that budded new growth. Gliding overhead, hawks searched for young rodents to devour. And it all began with the water. The water provided for the plants, which attracted the animals. Stacey thought this exemplified a heavenly ecosystem.

After traversing up the 1.5-mile trail to Lake Ilsanjo, Stacey and Reece sat down on a couple of boulders near the rippling water. Stacey took off his backpack, pulled out two water bottles, and placed them on the rock. Laying his walking stick down, Reece undid his back brace and took a sip of water.

"How's your back?" Stacey asked, squirting a line of water into his mouth.

"It's okay. I made it here didn't I?" Reece declared. He gave a high five to Stacey. "On the last uphill, I felt it tighten. It's a bit painful, but nothing I can't deal with."

"Good. I don't want you to get injured in the middle of your recovery effort," Stacey stated.

"I don't think a hike will hurt me unless I fall," Reece said. "It's the golf I just started playing that might hurt it."

"I can't believe your doctor agreed to let you play golf," Stacey said, taking out two sandwiches from his pack and handing one to Reece.

"He said as long I begin slowly, I should be fine," Reece explained, taking a bite of his sandwich. "A few holes this week. Six holes next week. By next month, I should be ready for the first nine-hole tournament of the season."

"You think you'll be ready by then?" Concern lingered in Stacey's voice.

"Thanks for the heartfelt support," Reece said, glaring. "I'll make myself ready. Look at all the physical therapy and conditioning I'm doing."

"You know I support you," Stacey replied, playfully patting Reece's head. "I just don't want you to reinjure your back. But, I guess if the doctors agree and you're careful, I'm all for it."

"My doctors and physical therapy coach are both in agreement, so lay off," Reece said sharply.

"How about Wende? What does she think?" Stacey asked, biting into an apple.

"I don't know. I don't think she has an opinion," Reece said. "She wants me to play golf in Germany, or on the European tour. She keeps sending me websites for tournaments over there."

"Why don't you? It'd be an excellent opportunity. Play golf. Travel. Learn more about Wende," Stacey said.

Reece shook his head. "I don't think so."

"Listen, you two love each other," Stacey began, offering some chips to his brother. "She got freaked out about the accident. Cut her some slack. I'm sure she'd come back to visit if you asked."

"Nah, I already asked her," Reece said. "She didn't like it here. I think the accident tarnished her experience. She wants me to move to Germany. She said that if you came back that I should come with you."

"Yeah, you could fly over with me or after me," Stacey said, enthusiastically. "That'd be cool. We could ride our mountain bikes all over Bavaria and take German classes together."

"It might be okay for a while," Reece said, hesitating. "I've thought a lot about it. I love Wende. She's great. But I don't wanna leave California. Traveling through Europe was cool, but I enjoy my life here. I'd miss baseball and basketball games. Seeing movies and TV shows in English. My friends and my job at the golf course. I can't do all that for a girl. You're a better man than me, Stace."

"Yeah, I am, but not because of that," Stacey mocked. They laughed. "Initially, living in another country was difficult, but you get used to it after a while. Come on, Reece. No harm in giving it a try for a few months."

"I know, but it's not gonna happen. Sorry, Stace," Reece apologized. "I can find another woman like Wende without the complications. I don't need to throw away my life for a woman."

"Is that what you think I'm doing?" Stacey asked, smirking.

"I don't think you're throwing your life away, but I *do* believe you are drastically changing it for Anneliese," Reece explained. "You love teaching, and you love your life here with us. And now you're giving all of that up. We're here, and you're leavin'."

"I am changing my life," Stacey began, taking a few deep breaths before continuing. "But, I'm leaving to better my life with Anneliese. I'm gaining a companion that I'll have for the rest of my life. If this takes a few years of compromising, then I'll do it. I can't imagine living here without her, even if it means living far away from you guys."

"That's you. I don't see that for me," Reece said.

"Well, to each his own, then," Stacey said.

"Yep," Reece agreed. "To each his own woman . . . and may I have a few of them."

"That's the attitude," Stacey said, adjusting himself on the boulder he sat on. "Hey, Jeff's been back for a few days. I guess he's doing well with the physical therapy already. When are you going to go see him?"

"That's right, I meant to tell you about that," Reece recalled. "I went to see him this morning."

"You did?" Stacey asked, putting his sandwich down. "How'd it go?"

"It didn't begin very well," Reece chuckled. "I walked into his room, unbeknownst to him. When he saw me, he shouted at me to leave. He was visibly upset. He was shaking and stuttering. He was so loud that a nurse came in. My heart was racing. It was like I was a criminal who had broken into his room. The nurse asked me to leave in a very stern voice. She took me firmly by the arm and began to lead me out."

"Wow. That's crazy. He's our best friend," Stacey remarked, wide-eyed.

"So, as I was walking out, I didn't see the wheelchair by the door. I stumbled into it, lost my balance, and slid into the chair. I didn't hurt myself, but Jeff thought it was hysterical. He chuckled, and then roared with laughter. He was laughing so hard; he began tearing up.

"I sat there for a few minutes. I was stunned. I didn't want the moment to end. Anyway, that broke the ice. After that, I was able to apologize to him. He accepted my apology and forgave me."

"I'm so relieved, bro," Stacey sighed. "I know how much that was weighing on your mind. It was probably a relief for Jeff, too. Hatred is so stressful."

"Yeah, he was definitely more like himself. We talked for a long time. He showed me some of the things he was working on in rehab. I left there feeling so much lighter, like the Force has calmed."

"Great. I'm so happy for you," Stacey said, eating a bag of carrots. "Let's polish off this food, and then we'll head on back."

Laughing and talking about sports, Stacey and Reece finished their lunches. They watched a fisherman perched atop a boulder that jutted from the water. Mountain bikers zoomed past, and Stacey and Reece told their favorite biking stories.

"So, when are you gonna tear open that envelope that's been in your backpack and read the letter from Anneliese?" Reece asked, grabbing Stacey's backpack and pretending to rifle through the pockets.

"I don't know. I don't want to read it when you're around," Stacey admitted, swiping the backpack away from Reece.

"You mean, you don't want to weep with love tears in front of me," Reece teased, nudging Stacey.

"Something like that," Stacey said.

"Well, I know you're excited to read your love letter 'cause you've been talkin' about it the whole way up here, so here's what I'm gonna do." Reece gobbled down the last of his sandwich. "I'm gonna hike down the trail, find a tree off the beaten path, and take a piss in private. That should be enough time for you to enjoy your reading."

Reece stood up and patted Stacey on the back. He walked down the trail and out of sight.

Quickly rummaging through his backpack, Stacey found Anneliese's letter and tore open the envelope.

Dear Stacey,

I cried after I read your letter. You write wonderful words. The words make me miss you. You can imagine. But, the words you write does not make me feel bad. The letter makes me think of hope.

I hope in my heart for you to come to Germany quickly. I hope to be with you soon. I hope to be kissing you and hugging you. I hope to talk and breathe the same air. This is my hope.

My last hope is you not read this letter because you are not in California to read it. You will be here in Germany and the letter will be alone in California. I hope for you to come very soon. I think of you coming back much in every day. Three or four weeks have passed. You said you would come back to Germany soon. I am happy you think of München but I am sad to think you not come for more weeks.

I did not want to write such sad feelings from me. I think helping your brother and friends is wonderful. I am happy to know Reece and Jeff do wonderful in hospital. I thank you for telling them that I think of them. Please tell Jeff I read much about paralysis. I want to help. I have wonderful talk with Patty last week. She is very nice. Please tell Reece that Wendeline misses him much like I do you. She will write to him soon.

I am wonderful. I do well in classes at university, but my thinking is on the baby inside of me. My body changes much now. The baby pushes my stomach so it looks like a kangaroo pouch. I give our baby the name "Joey". I think the name is cute. I first felt our baby move inside. I do not think you feel on outside. Maybe when baby grows more big. I hope you are here soon to feel our baby. Please come soon.

I ride the train to my parents' house on weekends. I stay at the house so I am not so lonely. Mom and dad say hello for you. My family and friends miss you also.

Please come back soon to Germany for I am not as happy until you are here. Call me when you buy the airline ticket. I always love you and think for you to be happy. I am excited to see you very soon. You can imagine!

Love,

Anneliese

Biting his lower lip in apprehension and contemplation, Stacey reread the letter and then tucked it back into a pocket of his backpack. Feeling anxious about his situation with Anneliese, Stacey couldn't remain idle as he waited for his brother's return. He stuffed his lunch into his pack and sauntered along the lake. Movement soothed his worries, so he zig-zagged his way beside the water and hopped across rocks strewn in his way.

Returning from his errand, Reece called out, "How was the letter? Did she profess her undying love?"

"Of course, she did. She wrote that she loves me and misses me," Stacey said, as Reece traversed his way through low-lying bushes to meet Stacey at the water's edge. "But, there was also a hint of desperation to her writing. I don't want to hurt her feelings. And I don't want to lose her, either. God, what do I do?"

"Well, you have two choices, bro," Reece said, as he reached Stacey. He leaned on his walking cane. "You could try to get that German teacher to switch back with you again. If the schools agreed, you could probably be back in Germany with Anneliese by next week. Jeff, Patty, and I are all doing better. We'll miss you, but we'll get by.

"Or, you can stay here until school is out in late May. You could be here to bring Jeff home and set him up. You could hang out with Patty and take care of her some more, and continue your long distance relationship with Anneliese."

"Shit, why can't this be easy?" Stacey declared. "That's the thing. A relationship should be easy. People's lives should fit together as smoothly and perfectly as a pre-cut puzzle. All of my relationships with women seem to be difficult. I try to find ways to put awkward pieces together. Sometimes I think that if it isn't easy, the relationship is flawed. That might be why I get out of them so quickly."

"Not as quick as me," Reece observed. They both laughed. "What about marriage? Have you two discussed it?"

"Sure. Luckily, neither of us are in a rush to get married even though she's pregnant," Stacey said.

"When are you planning to propose?" Reece asked.

"Probably sometime after I get back to Germany," Stacey answered. "Speaking of that, I had a question for you."

"Yeah, what?" Reece asked.

"I'm going to have an engagement ring made. But, I was wondering if I could give Anneliese Mom's wedding band when we get married," Stacey said, resting his hand on Reece's shoulder. "What do you think? If it offends you, or you want the wedding band for your marriage, just let me know."

"Stace, I think it's perfect. It couldn't go to a more fitting woman," Reece said, bursting out in tears.

"I'm sorry. I don't have to give it to her," Stacey said, scooting closer to his brother and putting his arm around him.

"No, no. I want Anneliese to have Mom's wedding band," Reece said, wiping the tears away with his sleeve. "I just had a flashback to when they gave us Mom and Dad's rings after the accident. It was a terrible time. You never knew this, but I slept with them under my pillow until we decided to put them in the safe deposit box."

"I didn't know that," Stacey said. "Are you sure you still want me to give the ring to Anneliese?"

"It belongs with you and Anneliese," Reece said, gazing over the lake.

"Thanks. It means the world to me that you approve and that Anneliese will wear it," Stacey said.

Focusing his attention on the water's edge, Reece observed, "Check out that group of water striders. It's kinda cool how they can walk on water."

"Water's got skin. That's why those water striders can walk on it," Stacey explained. "I took my class on a field trip to the water agency at the Russian River last month, and we did a cool experiment. We learned that water has surface tension because the molecules are all drawn in toward each other. That's like me. I can't leave yet because I feel like I'm being pulled toward you guys. I'm stagnating like the water in this lake."

Mesmerized by the water striders skimming across the water, Stacey and Reece stood in silence along the edge of the lake. At times, it looked as if the insects skated across the clouds in the water's reflection.

"What are you gonna do about Anneliese?" Reece asked, staring intently.

"Ah, hell, I already know what I'm going to do," Stacey said. "I'll extend this as long as possible, and then I'll go back. I'll have to explain to Anneliese that I need a little more time."

"I don't think you can do this to her much longer, especially since she's pregnant with your child," Reece said.

"I know, it's just that I'm living in between my two favorite worlds, and I can't let either one go, yet," Stacey stated.

Leaning against a nearby tree, Reece said, "Sorry, bro, but I need to start headin' down the trail. My back is beginning to ache, and the tightening is getting worse."

"All right. Let's head back to the car. We can take Spring Creek Trail for a faster trip down," Stacey said.

Stacey helped Reece climb over a few yards of treacherous terrain to get back on the main trail. The two brothers strolled along the path through the various Sonoma County environments: riparian, evergreen, and oak woodlands.

When they got home, Stacey wanted to write Anneliese, but he was too tired, and he didn't know what to say. Instead, he waited, filled with apprehension.

* * *

LATER IN THE WEEK, after Stacey sorted out his thoughts and feelings, he wrote to Anneliese. By the light of the table lamp on his desk and the presence of the dying rains, Stacey wrote a letter hoping to appease Anneliese.

Dear Anneliese,

I went for a good hike today. You would have loved it. The trees and grass sparkled in the misty rain. The creeks hissed with running water. Squirrels and deer dashed around. It was a great time to be in the park.

You'll be happy to know that I thought about you the whole time. Most of the time, I thought about the times we've spent together. Or sometimes, about the new experiences we'll share in the future. I'm hoping for a long kiss. I can't wait to see you and the baby growing inside you. The pictures you've sent to me are precious. I know you said that you are the only one right now who can feel the baby kicking, but I cannot wait until I feel him/her kicking. I want to tell the baby my name and let him/her hear my voice. I get so excited thinking about you and our baby. I've almost talked myself into flying back to Germany any day now.

While I walked, I considered how I could be feeling so good now with you so far away. The truth is that I'm pretty sad. I miss you a lot, and I wish I could be with you in person, talk to you, and touch you right now and for the rest of my life. There's nothing I want more than to be with you. You are the woman I have searched for my entire life. I have found my soul mate. And, I miss you terribly. So, why am I still here in California and so happy to be holding a mere letter from you?

I guess it's the knowledge that the girl of my dreams is in love with me, even though we are apart. Distant love holds a mystique for me. The romance of a long-distance relationship is looking forward to the upcoming reunion. I think we have the best of both worlds. We are living where we need to live, and we are in love.

I've been trying to decide when I can realistically return to Germany. I know that the sooner the better for both of us. Believe me; I know we cannot wait to see each other.

But, I have to tell you that I'm not quite ready to fly back right now. The main reason is that I am still taking care of things in my life that I can't do while I'm in Germany. I still feel Reece, Jeff, and Patty need my help and guidance. The characteristics that I value in myself make it important for me to help my brother and my friends. I must be the optimist who inspires them to full recovery. I've had to nurture them as if they were my students. I am their greatest advocate and protector. I spend my time teaching them how to live in new bodies and training them to regain their old bodies. I am devoted to getting them through this trial. I can't be disturbed or distracted in my job as their caretaker. When I am with you, I will take care of you.

The truth is, Anneliese, my presence would still be better served here. Every day my mind acts like a scale. On one side are Reece, Jeff, and Patty. On the other are you and the baby. And, as of this moment right now, they need me more than you do. Although, each day that passes, the scales tip in your direction. You're still in your second term of pregnancy, taking classes, and getting around well. Plus, your family is around to help.

Reece doesn't have any close family except for me. He's doing much, much better. Like I told you, he's able to do most of the things he could do before the accident, except that he does them with a large back brace. He is so much more confident about his situation than when you were here, especially since he is now back at home. No more hospitals or rehabilitation centers for Reece. Also, since he and Jeff reconciled, Reece's guilt is slowly fading. Time is healing his wounds.

Jeff, on the other hand, is still in the middle of his rehabilitation. The physical therapists work with him on strengthening his arm and shoulder muscles, so that he can maneuver his wheelchair. They are also trying to stimulate some of the nerves and muscles in his legs, but it hasn't been very successful. Thus far, it doesn't look as if he'll be able to walk again.

Though Reece and Jeff are mending their relationship, the same cannot be said for Jeff and Patty. She is struggling to connect with Jeff on any kind of emotional level. She is becoming more and more frustrated with his inability to show her any affection, sympathy, or even simple gratitude. I have tried to persuade Jeff to action concerning Patty, but it's been to no avail.

I don't know if this triage approach is the best, but it's the way my mind works. I want to know that I have done the best I could for all the people I love. It's important to me that everyone feels important, cared for, and loved. I can't feel guilty for causing anxiety or pain to anyone I love. I can't. So, once you inform me that I have caused your heart to ache, let me know, and I will make it so that your heart aches no more. I will take absolute care of you and our baby. I will shine the light of my love on the two of you.

Love,

Stacey

Stacey folded the letter, put it into an envelope, and addressed it. He felt sad and guilty about what he had written. He wished he could write a letter informing her that he'd be coming home soon. But, the timing didn't feel right. He still had more to do with his brother and friends in Santa Rosa. He wanted to stay until Jeff was stable and had returned to his house. Reece needed to be able to drive again. He also wanted to make sure Patty moved through more of the grieving process and could take care of Jeff when he came home. Stacey knew that all those things would happen soon, just not soon enough.

Stacey and Anneliese called, emailed, and Skyped each other on a weekly, if not daily, basis. Stacey felt pressured to fly back to Anneliese each time they connected. He knew that she would not be pleased with this letter.

But just as time healed Reece's wounds, time will also heal my guilt, Stacey thought as he glanced out of the window into a misty night.

CHAPTER 20

True love is indifferent to time and distance
The heart rules the mind

"Come live with me, and be my love;
And we will all the pleasures prove
That hills and valleys, dales and fields,
Woods or steepy mountain yields."
— Christopher Marlowe, "The Passionate Shepherd to His Love"

IT WAS NEAR THE TOWN of Guerneville on a warm, spring day that Stacey crossed paths with the Russian River again. He had come out of the thick brush on a narrow, hidden path. Wearing a white polo shirt with black swimming shorts and a pair of Keen sandals, he struggled as he carried a large storage box in his arms and a stuffed backpack over his shoulder.

Once he got to the river's edge, he looked for a place where Jeff could maneuver with his wheelchair. Jeff could now sit up in bed, move his arms, and use the upper half of his body to perform daily tasks. Now able to move out of his bed and chairs into his wheelchair, he had become independently mobile over the last month. He learned to maneuver the wheelchair around the rehab facility, up and down small ramps, and over short obstacles. He'd been on a couple of outings in the public, in which he had to handle the wheelchair along sidewalks, around people, and over slight drops and climbs.

Patty was driving Reece and Jeff to the river, and Stacey's job was to get the area prepared for their arrival. Stacey knew that they wouldn't have any trouble getting Jeff down the trail because it was wide and the dirt was packed hard. The problem would come when they neared the sandy river. Stacey chose an area next to some rocks where they wouldn't have to push Jeff very far off the trail into the sand.

Next, he prepared the site for the picnic. He opened his pack, took out the five towels, and flung them open over the sand. Opening up the box, he took out a medium-sized cooler and bag of food. He placed a towel over the box and spread the packages of food on top.

Stacey had some extra time before the group arrived, so he sat down and peered at the river. The wind seemed to dance on the water. He couldn't see the body of the wind, but he could see its footsteps as it glided across the liquid floor. Sometimes the wind would carve up the dance floor in twists and turns, disappear for a few moments, and return again twenty feet away.

The wind on the water is graceful, Stacey thought. It's as if God is writing a message to me. A clue to the meaning of life. If I could only figure it out.

As hard as he tried, Stacey couldn't connect all of his ideas about the mysteries of life. It was as if he was lost in a familiar place. His mind was a maze, and his thoughts kept returning to the same places.

If I could just find the path that connects all the other paths, I would find my way out, Stacey thought. But, I keep going down the same paths in my mind. I always feel I'm on the verge of a breakthrough and that some insight will lead me to enlightenment about the universe, life, death, an afterlife, and God. But, it's always a few synapses beyond my grasp.

Already entranced, Stacey took Anneliese's latest letter from his pack. He then opened and read it.

Dear Stacey,

I love you. I love you much, much, much. I like having the letter from you. I keep all the letters and emails in a folder special for you and me. You can imagine. I read your words each day. It makes me happy. I feel in the words you write that you miss me and love me.

I am good in Germany. I do good in new course at university. I saw my sister for two days. She stayed here to visit me. The apartment is full of people. How wonderful!

But I need for me to write another kind of letter. I need for me to write words of how I think and feel.

I do not think you are right for not coming back to Germany. I think you are wonderful for helping your brother and friends in the last months, but no more. I feel very sad and lonely and scared you do not come back yet. You say you will be back in one month, but now it is three months later and you do not leave. The time away is too long. Our baby needs you to come to Germany. You are missing how it feels for our baby to kick inside my stomach. I think for much time that you love me and our baby, but now I do not know.

Stacey, I need to know you love me and will come to Germany or no. If you write yes, I need to know when you will come. Soon, please. If you write no, I don't know. I cannot think about it. Please write soon.

Love You Always,

Anneliese

Stacey read it only once and then put the letter in his backpack. Tears welled in his eyes. Drop by drop, the tears released and fell until he began to sob.

She must be so lonely without me, Stacey thought. I haven't helped her through the pregnancy. I haven't been to any doctor appointments. Haven't felt the baby kick or listened to its heartbeat. I *have* listened to her fears about childbirth and possibly raising a child on her own. And to think, I am the only one that is to blame for her sadness.

His guilt overtook his emotions. He cried for hurting Anneliese and the possibility of losing such a special woman. He cried for his parents and how they weren't around to guide him.

He felt deflated as if no life were left in him. He had no thoughts. He couldn't feel himself breathing. His feelings were insensible. Stacey sat in a teary-eyed daze without thinking of the time. At that moment, his soul became void of thought or emotion.

After walking to the edge of the water, Stacey snapped out of his thoughtless trance when his feet touched the water. Feeling the coolness of the water as it encased his warm feet, his soul instantaneously sprung back to life. The contrast of temperature between his feet and the water sent a shiver trembling through his body. He watched the sunlight sparkle off the river's skin. He could smell the purified rain water mixed with the upended river-bottom scum and wet sand. He heard the water lapping over a rock close by, random bird cries, and an occasional plane overhead.

The crying. The disappointment. The heartbreak. All of his sadness mixed with the sun generated intense heat upon Stacey. Taking a few long strides further into the river, he walked into the water up to his thighs. He stopped when the water flowed just centimeters from his groin. Stacey debated whether he wanted to go into the water further.

If I go in the water, I might as well go all the way in, Stacey thought.

Not wanting to overload his nervous system, Stacey hesitantly stepped forward one slow, searching step at a time. The cold water pricked his stomach, burned his chest, and then sawed around his neck. He took off swimming. Keeping his head out of the water, he swung his arms out and around. Cutting through the river, he swam out to the middle and treaded water for a while. The cool water felt refreshing now that he had done some physical activity. As he floated, his legs dangled down, and he could feel the water sliding over his skin like tiny waterfalls.

He caught sight of a log lodged in the river's bottom and sticking out above the water about four feet. He swam over to it and grabbed a short stub protruding from the log. After holding on for a few minutes, he wasn't too sure what to do next until his leg bumped into the submerged part of the log. He swung his leg up and over the log. A layer of algae made the wood slippery and his feet couldn't grip it. He tried again and on his third try his feet stayed. Stacey pulled himself up and carefully stood balanced on the log. He looked around to make sure no one was watching him. He felt silly being a grown man balancing on a log in the river.

Getting a sudden urge to jump, he bent down. His leg muscles tensed, and his arms tucked to the side of his body. In one fluid motion, he jumped off of the log. Splash.

Stacey burst feet-first into the river. The explosion sent water pulsing away from his body causing a brief pocket of air between him and the water. But, instantaneously, a wall of water surged back around his body. The bubbled air forced upward across his skin.

Damn, that was fun, Stacey thought as he bobbed in the river. I'm going to do it again.

Stacey climbed back onto the log. He looked around and didn't see anyone. This time, he dove in head first. The water skimmed over his body as he remained underwater for a few seconds. He swam back to the log and did it again, and again, and again.

Each time he climbed onto the trunk, he took a quick glance around the river. Before his last dive, he wondered why he felt a presence. His mood changed from playful to introspective as he pondered the question. He realized he hadn't been nervous about someone watching him. On the contrary, he wished that someone would be watching him, admiring his swimming and diving abilities, and cheering him on. He wanted Anneliese to be with him. He needed her.

He dove one last time into the water. At first, his senses were overloaded with an explosion of fizzing and splashing sounds. Large and small bubbles slithered over his body as they tried to make their way back up to the surface of the other air molecules. The shock of the coldness zapped his skin.

Only seconds later, he glided to a stop under the water. He sensed only calm . . . silence . . . darkness . . . solitude . . . peace.

Under the water is like another world, Stacey thought. It's like being transported to a new planet. Sometimes, I need a new environment to gain a different perspective about my own life.

Contentment rushed over him. The problems and chaos of the world above just disappeared.

Stacey rose to the surface, filled his lungs with air, and sank below the water again. Opening his eyes to look around, he couldn't see much because of the murkiness of the river, but when he flipped himself upside down in the water, he was able to see the sunlight streaking through the top of the river. He noticed the rippling view of the blue sky and the dark shadows of the trees. Stacey admired the beauty until he ran out of breath. Again, he swooped to the top, took a deep breath, and returned underwater.

This time, Stacey let out a few breaths of air from his lungs, which made him sink lower into the river. Reaching a calmness and clarity of mind, he felt his parents' presence in the water. He ached to see them, hug them, and talk with them.

Mom and Dad, wherever you are, I love you, Stacey thought. As I'm sure you already know, I've been taking care of Reece since the accident. I've also been helping Jeff and Patty get back on their feet. I've been away from Anneliese for a few months now. She has been pushing me to come back and rightfully so. I told her that I'd return, but I keep postponing the trip. I can't seem to make a decision. Now, she's despondent, and so am I. She gave me an ultimatum.

Stacey shot up through the water to reach the surface. He went up for air again, came back down after a few breaths, and continued with his thoughts.

So, I'm going to go back to Germany, Stacey thought. I've decided to go, and I hope you think it's okay. Reece will be all right. I hate to leave him, my friends, and you, but I can't lose Anneliese. Being at the river today has made me realize that I want to be with her, rather than without her.

Stacey shot up to the surface to breathe. He scanned the area. No one was around. He took a few breaths and vanished underwater.

Who knows how the future will turn out? Stacey thought. What I do know is that I want my future to be with Anneliese. And whatever feelings or problems we have, we'll be together to work it out. I love her, Mom and Dad. She cares about me, and she makes me happy. Wherever you are, I hope you're as happy as I am.

With those last thoughts unleashed through his mind, Stacey popped his head out of the water. He shook the drops of water from his face and swam to his towel as fast as possible.

When Stacey reached the beach, he climbed out of the water and grabbed his towel. After drying himself off, he found his backpack and took out his binder, a copy of *To the Lighthouse*, and a pen. He felt it necessary to write his final letter to Anneliese right then and there.

Dear Anneliese,

I finished reading To the Lighthouse *by Virginia Woolf. I remember my mom talking about how much she loved the book, so I thought I'd give it a read. Many passages moved my soul, but none more than this. "Distance had an extraordinary power; they had been swallowed up in it, she felt, they were gone forever, they had become part of the nature of things."*

It has been too easy letting distance form a chasm between our souls. Like digging a hole in the sand, the walls crumble in no time at all. I don't want our separation to be the nature of things. I want us to transcend the gap in distance.

I've decided to fly back to Germany. I am in the process of finding out what it will entail. But, I'm hoping that I can fly back next week for spring break and begin teaching the week after that.

I'm coming home to you because I love you, and I think you are the most loving and caring woman in the whole world. I treasure your kindness, caring words, sense of adventure and spontaneity, conversation, and your company. And now that you're pregnant, I worship you. I can't wait to see you.

We've only known each other for five or six months, but I've missed you as if you were my wife of 50 or 60 years. I miss waking up next to you, spending the day doing things with you, even the most mundane of things. I miss talking to you in person. I miss kissing you. I miss sleeping next to you. I think about these moments every day.

When I lived in Germany for those few months, I was homesick at times, especially for Reece, Jeff, and Patty. I missed them, but it didn't make me depressed or lonely. I was truly happy living in Germany with you. The only time I felt I had made the wrong choice about moving to Germany was the day of the accident. I felt guilty that I wasn't in California when it happened. But, even if I was living in California at that time, I might not have been around anyway. I cannot live my life based upon the past or the future. I have to live it in the present.

Presently, living in California with my family and friends hasn't been easy. My heart aches without you. I think about you all of the time. I am so utterly homesick for you. This pain that I feel gnaws at my soul. As time goes on, the loneliness grows deeper. This longing to be with you is so much stronger than the annoying itch I felt missing Reece. Before I met you, something was missing in my life. I wanted to share my life with someone. Then, you came along and brought me a happiness that no one back in California could provide me; a partner with whom I will share all the intimate moments of life.

I thought that we might be able to satisfy love's needs by writing letters and talking to each other on the phone. These are romantic notions, yes, but not sustainable for an extended period or a lifetime. Receiving letters from you inspired me in a way that warmed my heart. I thought I had everything I needed if I merely had your love on paper. The problem with love on paper is that the love is only two dimensional. You can see it and feel it in your soul, but you can't touch it, hug it, smell it, or taste it. Paper fades or is destroyed over time. I don't want that with you.

I realized that I would rather be away from everything and everyone I know than to be without you. Life will be difficult for me in Germany. I know. I will have to give myself to learning the language and getting a teaching job I love. It will be hard, but I will do it to be with you. And, I know it will get easier, and it won't be forever.

I told you when I met you that I want a love similar to Patty and Jeff's. When life gets tough or problems arise, they compromise, and their love rises as they go through it together. That's what I want. I want to go through life and all its difficulties with you. I want to stand by your side as we admire our accomplishments, face adversity, solve problems, and live life for years and years to come.

Anneliese, I want to spend the rest of my days and nights with you. I used to think that love was like a cloud of fog. I could see it clearly and felt I could just reach up and grab it. But every time, it slipped through my fingers. Now that I've fallen in love with you, love no longer feels like that. Love is now the water that surrounds me. Your love is tangible. I can feel it. It's transformed my world. I have a similar feeling of spiritual happiness and optimism when I am with you as I do when I am near water. You have such a rare, serene beauty to your soul that I want to remain in your presence forever. I know this may seem quick because we only met a few months ago, but to me, I've waited my whole life for this moment.

Of all the things I've ever wanted, you are what I want most. I see that now, and I'm not going to lose you. You've made me so happy. I want to do the same for you. I want us to be a happy family together.

I will see you soon.

Love Always,

Stacey

P.S.

I hope you and the baby had a wonderful time in Elba, Italy.

Stacey pulled an envelope out of the binder, put the letter in the envelope, addressed it, and sealed it. He knew that Anneliese was in Italy with her family, so she wouldn't get the letter until she got back. And, he might get to Germany before the letter even arrived. Though the letter seemed useless, he cherished it. The letter was something tangible that Anneliese could keep as a memento of their romance and eventually show to their children.

As Stacey placed the letter in his pack, his hand nudged a small velvet box. He grabbed it and slowly opened it. A trillion-shaped diamond sparkled above a string of tiny diamonds that trailed off around the wavy band like a shooting star atop the golden engagement ring. Stacey had purchased the ring weeks ago in anticipation of his return to Germany. For safety and symbolic reasons, he had grown accustomed to carrying the ring everywhere he went, sometimes storing it in his backpack, pants pocket, or even a money belt around his waist.

I would love to fly back to Germany and propose to Anneliese on Easter. It'd be a perfect symbol of hope and rebirth, Stacey thought. She's vacationing on the Italian island of Elba with her family this week. They're getting back on Saturday and Sunday is Easter. It'd be so cool if I could be there when they get home.

Depositing the ring box into a hidden pocket of his pack, Stacey pulled out his cell phone from another pocket and dialed the long distance call to Anneliese. He was excited, yet a little nervous about telling her he would be with her soon.

The phone rang once and went straight to Anneliese's voicemail. He realized that it was late at night, and she might have turned off her cell phone. Or, since she stayed in a simple home on the island of Elba, she might not get cell phone service. There was a good chance she might not get the message until she got back home.

After the beep, Stacey burst out, "Hi Anneliese. I should probably wait until I can tell you in person, but I'm too excited to wait. I have to tell you now. I'm coming home to you. I realized that everyone was doing well, except me. I miss you so much, so I'm going to try to coordinate another exchange with the same German teacher. I need to take care of a few things, but I'm going to try to leave on Saturday and be there on Sunday for Easter morning.

"Again, I can't wait to see you, the baby, and your family. Hope you are having a great time in Italy. Love you always."

Ecstatic that he'd finally made a decision about what to do and feeling the stress lift off of his shoulders, Stacey hung up and shouted, "Yes!"

I get so stressed when I am undecided about something, Stacey thought. But now, I'm so relieved I made a decision and a good one, too. I can't wait for Patty to get here with Reece and Jeff, so I can tell them the good news.

CHAPTER 21

Water, like God, sustains life
Indifferent as to what lives and dies

"Black smoke I would be, nearing the clouds of God,
All unseen, soaring aloft, as dust without wings I would perish.
Oh, for a seat high in the air, where the dripping clouds turn snow,"

— Aeschylus

STACEY RECEIVED A CALL from Patty that they were close to the river. On the way up the path, Stacey felt anxious about this outing with Jeff. It was only Jeff's third trip away from the rehab facility since they let him travel in a wheelchair. In his two previous trips, Jeff had gone to his parent's house for dinner and then to his house with Patty.

Stacey, Patty, and Jeff's dad had spent a couple of days building ramps throughout both houses. They lowered shelves and installed railings in the bathrooms. Jeff's visits to both houses were extremely emotional for everyone. The realization of how much things had changed for Jeff struck everyone as he wheeled himself around his room, the kitchen, and the bathroom. Most of the objects in the rooms he could now reach, but some items still needed to be moved. The bathroom mirrors were too high, he couldn't reach the sink in the kitchen, and they still hadn't built a ramp from the house to the garage.

Stacey wanted Jeff's excursion from rehab to be light and fun for everyone. He knew Jeff couldn't swim without professional assistance. Yet, he hoped he and Reece could wheel him down to the edge of the river where they could splash him with the cool water, and he could be a part of the outing.

After Stacey met them in the parking lot, Patty carefully helped Jeff out of the van. Everyone carried more backpacks, towels, bags of food, and personal items with them. Stacey pushed Jeff in his wheelchair. The access trail was a smooth dirt path that led from the street to the edge of the river. Stacey didn't have any problems getting Jeff to the spot he chose by the river.

Once Jeff was situated and all the bags were brought down to the river, everyone began helping to set-up.

After pushing the sun-umbrella into the ground and raising it, Stacey announced, "I'm glad we're all together because I wanted to tell you all at the same time that I've decided to move back with Anneliese."

"Dude, we all knew you were gonna go," Reece said, busy extending the legs of a small, portable table. "We were just waiting for you to figure it out. I mean, come on, you thought you'd be able to live in California while the nicest, prettiest, and smartest girl in the world is living in Germany. We all knew you wouldn't last forever with the love letters and phone calls."

"I know. The thought of having a long distance love affair seems like a lame notion, now," Stacey said.

"No, it wasn't lame. It's romantic the way you wrote to each other and called each other every night," Patty replied, smiling at him as she took out the food and organized the plates and napkins.

"That is exactly why I'm glad you're leaving and not a moment too soon if you ask me," Jeff teased. "I don't need you hanging out with Patty and talking about love and romance anymore."

"Well, if I knew you all felt this way then I would have left weeks ago," Stacey joked, moving Jeff underneath the umbrella. "Seriously, though, I'm really going to miss you all. This isn't easy for me. I know my visit wasn't under the best of circumstances, but I wouldn't have missed being here for anyone or anything. I really enjoyed being able to help and, in a way, you helped me, too."

"Well, Stace, I owe you a big thanks for being here for me. I love you for that," Patty said. She hugged Stacey.

Taking out a few beers from the cooler and placing them on the table, Reece announced, "Hey, if anyone wants a beer or Coke, they're now on the table."

"And the food is almost ready," Patty added, placing containers of food on the table.

"Great, I'm thirsty and starving," Stacey said, walking toward the table. "Jeff, can I get you a plate? Do you want everything on the table?"

Scanning the food on the table, Jeff replied, "Sure, it all looks good."

Stacey dished out a plate of three varieties of salads, chips, and a sandwich. He then brought it over to Jeff. Everyone followed suit and served themselves. Forming a circle around Jeff, they took seats on their towels and began eating.

"Stace, I owe you a big thanks for taking care of Patty." Jeff reached out and shook Stacey's hand. "You took care of her when I couldn't, so thanks. And thanks for helping me, too."

"You're welcome," Stacey replied, reaching up and fist-pumping Jeff. "When I got the call from Reece, I felt so helpless in Germany. I knew I had to be here."

"I forgot about that call 'til now," Reece said, sprawling across his towel with his plate. "Such a hard call for me to make. I didn't wanna bother you, but I didn't know what to do, especially since Jeff and Patty were in such dire straits. So, I owe you some thanks for being incredibly supportive, especially to me."

"Well, I'm sure you would have done the same," Stacey said, eating his chips first.

Spotting the drinks still sitting on the table, Reece asked, "We forgot drinks. Can I get everyone a beer?"

"Not me. I'll have the Coke," Patty replied, raising her hand as if she were ordering at a restaurant.

Reece handed out the drinks. He made a quick toast and they clinked bottles.

Stacey turned to Jeff and said, "When I got here, I didn't think I could ever help you. I thought you had already given up. I was worried about you and Patty."

"Yeah, I was definitely in a bad place," Jeff replied, adjusting the plate on his lap. "Those first months were hard, really hard. I thought my life was over. I can see how paraplegics have a high rate of suicide. I mean, it's a fucked up reality to face when you can't walk anymore. It's still shitty, but at least I know I still have Patty."

Looking lovingly at her, Jeff reached out and held Patty's hand. A tear fell from Patty's eye.

Jeff continued, "At least, I can still use my upper body. And, I think I'm going to play basketball in a few months. It's going to take getting used to doing things differently. Shit, I can still drive and pleasure my woman."

With Patty kneeling by his side, Jeff wrapped his hands around her breasts. Patty let out a yelp in delight and put down her drink.

"All right, all right," Patty pleaded, pushing his hands away.

"So, when did you two kiss and make-up?" Stacey asked. "This is the most affection and love I've seen you give Patty since the accident."

"Do you want to tell him, or should I?" Jeff asked Patty.

"I'll tell him," Patty said. "A few days ago, Jeff had an outburst, and it was directed at me. I wasn't the cause, mind you, just the recipient. After months of being neglected and, if I might say, emotionally abused, I took off my engagement ring and put it on Jeff's dresser. I told him that I loved him, would always love him, and felt fulfilled as his partner caring for him. But, I was not going to spend another day listening to him berate me or ignore me. I was completely done with him, and I left."

"My god. How come you guys didn't tell us this earlier?" Stacey asked.

"I was embarrassed about the way I'd treated Patty, especially in front of friends and family. And Patty was just distraught. Neither of us wanted to talk to anyone," Jeff began.

"That's crazy. How did you get from there to sitting here copping a feel?" Reece asked.

"I loved every minute of her standing by my side and helping me through this ordeal. I realized how much of an ass I'd been by not telling her how much I'd appreciated her and loved her," Jeff explained. "Plus, I knew Patty was bluffing about the engagement ring."

Everyone laughed, and Patty playfully slid her engagement ring off and on.

"So, you guys are still getting married, huh?" Reece asked.

"Of course we are. As a matter of fact, the next day after our fight Jeff called and invited me over. As I walked in the door, he had the ring out and proposed to me again," Patty said. "I didn't even hesitate with my answer."

"Nope, no hesitation whatsoever. She still loves me. What can I say?" Jeff exclaimed, proudly.

"I love you now more than ever before," Patty responded. She leaned back and kissed Jeff. "This experience has strengthened our relationship. We've bonded through hardship. We're two pieces of clay that have been fused together in the fire."

"So, Stacey, are you really going to propose to Anneliese right when you see her?" Patty asked.

"Assuming she still says yes," Reece teased, taking a bite from his sandwich.

"Funny," Stacey snickered. "I don't quite know all the details. I haven't really thought about that yet. Maybe next summer we'll get married. In a year, I would guess. I don't think we could get married this summer because she'll be in her last term of pregnancy."

"I know I wouldn't want to get into a wedding dress in my last months of being pregnant," Patty exclaimed, sipping her Coke. "No, I'm pretty sure she'd want to wait until after she's had the baby, and she's lost the baby fat. Well, unless she's extremely religious, and then you'll have to get married before the baby so that you can say the baby wasn't born out of wedlock."

"No, she's not that religious. We already talked about that, and she doesn't care if the baby is born before or after we're married," Stacey explained.

"Where do you think you'll get married? Germany? Here?" Patty asked.

"I don't know. I guess wherever she wants to get married. I'd assume somewhere in Germany. You guys would all come, right?" Stacey asked

"Stace, I gotta be honest, I don't think I can go if Wende's gonna be there," Reece said, winking at Jeff.

"Yeah, Stace, I don't think we'll be able to make it, either," Jeff said, finishing his sandwich. "You know the doctor said I couldn't travel for at least a couple of years."

"You guys are fucked up. After taking care of you shitheads for a few months, this is what I get?" Stacey roared. He found a water bottle nearby and squirted them all.

"Dude, of course, we're comin'," Reece said, kicking sand on Stacey's legs. "I wouldn't miss a chance to see Wende again. Or, maybe Anneliese has some other hot friends who'll attend."

"And, yes, we'll come too," Patty said. "Don't make it in December of this year, though. That's when we're getting married. I always wanted a winter wedding. Plus, Jeff's rehabilitation will be over, and I'll have about seven months to plan the wedding, which is enough time."

Reece finished his beer and stood up. "Anyone want another beer?" he asked.

Stacey and Jeff shook their heads.

"Okay, more for me," Reece said, grabbing another beer from the cooler.

Patty also stood up and collected the garbage into a bag.

"Stace, I wish you and Anneliese all the best," Jeff said.

"Thanks," Stacey replied. "I look at you two and see two people totally in love. I admire what you two have. That's why I'm going to emulate whatever you do."

"Everything but the wheelchair, okay?" Jeff kidded. Everyone laughed.

"Okay," Stacey said. "Anyway, your wedding in December will give me an excuse to bring Anneliese and our baby back to California to spend some time with you."

"That's going to be so damn crazy, Stace. I can't wait until Anneliese gives birth. I want to be there for it," Patty said, closing the food containers and putting them back into the coolers. "Can you believe you're going to be a dad?"

"I know. I've been so caught up in thinking about Anneliese and moving to Germany that I haven't thought about being a dad," Stacey admitted, taking a moment to reflect on the idea of fatherhood. "But yeah, I'm fucking stoked and a little anxious. I love teaching, and I love kids, so I would think the Dad thing will come naturally to me. But babies are all new to me, so there's going to be a learning curve. Luckily though, I couldn't have a better partner to share the experience with than Anneliese."

"I'm sure you'll make a great dad," Reece declared, giving his brother a high-five. "You had such an incredible role model."

"Thanks, bro," Stacey said.

"So, when are you leaving?" Patty asked.

"Well, I have to contact the exchange coordinator," Stacey explained. "I spoke to her about a month ago, and she said that the administrators at both sites are willing to reinstate the exchange. And, as long as the German teacher still wants to come back to California, then everything should move forward. I was going to go online tonight to get an idea about how to redeem the ticket I had from Christmas. I was hoping to arrive on Easter Sunday morning."

"That's cool. We'll still have a few days to hang out," Jeff said.

"Yeah, I'll be busy taking care of some things, but I'll be with you guys every day," Stacey reassured everyone.

"I don't know about you all, but I'm hot. Let's get in the water," Reece declared, quickly changing the subject. They all agreed.

After moving Jeff closer to the water, Reece and Stacey threw a ball back and forth to him. Still wearing a back brace, Reece didn't want to swim, so he only stood in the water up to his waist. Patty spent the time taking care of Jeff's needs. She assisted him with maneuvering his chair and getting items from his pack. Trying to keep Jeff cool, Patty moved the sun umbrella over his chair.

Later in the day, Stacey convinced Patty to swim to the middle of the river. He wanted her to see the tree lodged in the water. He thought Jeff and Reece would enjoy seeing Patty jump off the log. He dared her until she agreed. Patty floated leisurely down the river, while Stacey competitively raced toward the log. Being the first one, he quickly lifted himself onto the log and waited for Patty to get closer.

"I hope no big fish are swimming near me. It'll freak me out if I get touched by one," Patty shouted.

I should dive in and grab her leg from underwater. She'd be so scared, Stacey thought.

When Patty floated within fifteen feet, Stacey dove headfirst into the water. The noise, the bubbles, and then the calm came over him. He glided through the cool water with his arms out in front of him. He could feel the pull of the river as the water flowed around every part of his body. He opened his eyes, but quickly closed them because the water was too murky to see much of anything. It didn't matter anyway because he knew Patty floated straight ahead of him.

Stacey's speed ran out, and his body began to rise. He didn't want to come up to the surface too soon because he wanted to surprise her. So, he pulled his arm forward and kicked his feet. He aimed his body down deeper into the river. He figured that Patty should be along in a few seconds. He let his legs hang down and waved his arms up, which pushed him farther down. His feet fluttered as he tried to find the bottom of the river.

Suddenly, both of his feet brushed past a web of wood. His feet and lower parts of his legs entered into a submerged system of roots from a tree that lay completely hidden at the bottom of the river. He had heard of people getting caught in these traps, and he knew that he'd better get back up to the surface.

Stacey immediately pumped his arms and tried kicking his legs. His legs wouldn't move because his feet were lodged between thick, twisted root sticks. He let out a couple of air bubbles. They rose easily to the top about four feet over his head. Stacey tried again, thrusting his arms to swim upward, but his lower legs kept him firmly lodged. A few more air bubbles escaped from his mouth. He felt his lungs tighten and his heart rate increase.

I need to move the roots, he thought quickly. He reached both arms down to the multiple strands of roots. Each hand searched blindly below until they gripped a root. Stacey pulled with all of his strength.

The root moved slightly, but he couldn't bend it far enough to get his foot out.

That's not the root that's holding me, Stacey realized. It's another one. Find it quick.

Stacey craved a breath of air, and the situation became an emergency. He frantically searched for another root. His right hand found it, and his left hand instantly came to help. The root lay over the previous one. He pulled it up slightly and tried to pull his legs up and out, but they wouldn't budge.

I have to move the piece of wood sideways, Stacey decided. He tried to push it one way and then the other. It still didn't move in either direction.

"Fuck!" he yelled into the water. Bubbles of precious air shot out of his mouth. They floated quickly to the top. Panic now overtook him, and adrenaline shot through his body, which increased his heart rate even more. This chain of events ultimately led his body to use more oxygen in his lungs. His lungs burned for a breath.

I have to get to the surface! Stacey thought. I can't leave Reece alone. I need to be with Anneliese.

He quickly raised his arms, but he couldn't reach the surface. He swung his arms this way and that as he tried to make some splash or wave on the surface for Patty to see. But, he was too deep in the water to make any sign of help. No one saw him motioning in the water. He stopped. His lungs were on fire. They begged for air, and he fought an overwhelming urge to breathe. He needed to breathe.

Don't breathe, don't breathe, don't breathe, he told himself. He tried one last time to free his feet. He kicked his legs. He tried to move the roots. Nothing.

Mom and Dad! Stacey pleaded. I'm going to die.

Without thinking, his body instinctively made his lungs contract to take in a breath of air. Stacey opened his mouth, and his lungs sucked in the water. The water rushed into his mouth, flew down his esophagus, and flooded into his lungs. Stacey's body reacted to the water by forcing his diaphragm to flex as if he was throwing up. He heaved weakly but then sucked in more water.

With no thoughts at all, Stacey lost consciousness in seconds. Patty swam a mere few feet over him. Reece and Jeff joked about Stacey wearing a Speedo for the high school swim team.

As the minutes wasted away, the scene became more tense and urgent. Puzzlement turned into questions, which in turn became panic. Patty searched the water while Reece called 9-1-1 on his cell phone.

Simultaneously, the scene in Germany was one of jubilation and excitement. Only minutes before this accident, Anneliese had listened to her voicemails and came across Stacey's voicemail telling her that he would come back soon. She became instantly ecstatic with happiness. Anneliese called Stacey on his cell phone. Stacey's phone rang, but Reece, Jeff, or Patty didn't notice. Anneliese also called her family and friends, including Wendeline, and happily proclaimed that the "love of her life" was coming back to her and their unborn child.

All the while, the water in the river kept flowing through the natural and spiritual world as it had done for thousands of years.

PART 5

FOG

Fog, rain, snow, water
Perpetual, powerful, fluid, divine
God

"This grand show is eternal. It is always sunrise somewhere; the dew is never all dried at once; a shower is forever falling; vapor ever rising. Eternal sunrise, eternal sunset, eternal dawn and gloaming, on seas and continents and islands, each in its turn, as the round earth rolls."

— John Muir

MONTHS LATER, the heat of a mid-summer sun evaporated water all over the northern hemisphere. The water molecules rose from the ponds, lakes, streams, creeks, rivers, and oceans. An invisible vapor floated upward through the atmosphere. It wasn't until the warm, moist daytime air collided with the cooler nighttime air that the water vapor became visible in the form of fog.

Over the course of the night, a light, wispy fog mysteriously appeared and hovered translucently over the ground in southern Germany. It materialized over the deepest valleys and largest bodies of water. Where there had been nothing, there was now something. It was as if a spotlight illuminated the evaporation process; water vapor caught being reborn. In life there is death, and from death there is life.

The fog arose above the vast pasture lands that surround Rosenheim. It also found its way into city streets where it hovered around houses, office buildings, and the local hospital. It was in this hospital where the fog's ghostly form slipped through the open window of the room where Anneliese gave birth.

CHAPTER 22

There's no difference between death and birth
Perpetual reversal

"Everything teaches transition, transference, metamorphosis: therein is human power, in transference, not in creation; and therein is human destiny, not in longevity but in removal. We dive and reappear in new places."
— Ralph Waldo Emerson, *Journals of Ralph Waldo Emerson*

SURROUNDED BY HER MOM AND SISTER for support, Anneliese gave birth to a healthy, beautiful, baby girl on a foggy night in August. The birth was normal, except for the fact that Anneliese chose to have a water birth, which surprised her friends and family. They all asked questions as to why she wanted that type of birth, but she refused to answer the question until after her daughter was born. Meanwhile, her dad and four friends waited outside in a cramped hospital hallway.

Quite focused during the last minutes of the birthing process, Anneliese sat in the bath with her hands gripping her knees as she pressed her legs apart. Submerged in water from her waist down, she got into a rhythm of five breaths and then two strong pushes, five breaths, two pushes, and so on.

Completely inside of herself, Anneliese and her baby were the only people she was aware of. The other people in the room could tell her what to do, and she'd do it, but it was only an unconscious recognition on Anneliese's part.

As the baby girl's head crowned, the warm water washed her head clean. Her face emerged, and the water gently brushed over her tiny cheeks, touched her nose, and kissed her lips. Once the baby's body slipped completely from its previous womb, it floated in a new womb. The water held her for a few brief seconds. The baby took water into its lungs as it had done with the amniotic fluid of its mother. The warm water, the muted silence, and the gentle sway of rocking gave the baby a calming respite between the chaotic birth and the new, sensory overloaded world she was about to enter. Within seconds, the doctor reached down and swept the baby girl out of the water's grasp.

Twenty minutes after the birth, Anneliese's mom walked out into the waiting area where Anneliese's dad and friends anxiously awaited the news. Teary eyed and overcome with the emotion of the event, Anneliese's mom cried out the news of her granddaughter's arrival onto this earth and fell into her husband's arms. She summarized the hardships Anneliese underwent during the birth but concluded with how happy and proud she was of her daughter. She told her captive audience that her daughter had already become a wonderful, loving mom.

About 45 minutes after the birth, Anneliese's dad was allowed back to the birthing room. Father and daughter kissed and hugged. Teary eyed, Anneliese's dad congratulated her on her accomplishment and exalted pride on his daughter. Then, Anneliese's family walked over to where the nurses cleaned, weighed, and tested the baby. They watched the baby girl in astonishment and amazement.

Anneliese and her family were together in the delivery room for over an hour. They huddled around Anneliese as she cradled and nursed her baby daughter. It was as if Anneliese and her daughter were the fire that warmed their souls, like a good book you can't put down or a conversation you don't want to end. They could not leave, nor take their eyes off of the newly bonded mother and daughter. They realized the miracle as it transpired.

Later, the nurses moved Anneliese to her recovery room down the hall. It looked like a typical hospital room with a television, dresser, movable nightstands, and a telephone. But since it was a room in the maternity ward, it also had a rocking chair, a bassinet, and wall murals of animals. Stacks of diapers, baby blankets, and infant clothes spread over the dresser.

After almost two hours of waiting, Anneliese felt ready to see her friends. She asked her family to leave so that she could spend a half hour, or so, with her friends. Her family obliged and went out to notify Anneliese's friends of their invitation to visit the new mom and her baby daughter.

Being the first to enter, Wendeline saw her best friend sitting in bed cradling a baby girl in her arms. It brought Wendeline to tears even before she said anything to Anneliese. She crept in with her arms raised high into the air as a symbol of victory for Anneliese. She kept saying over and over, "Ya, you do it. You do it!" She kissed Anneliese on the cheek, bent over the sleeping baby, and stared at her for some time. She repeated herself by continually saying in German how beautiful the baby was. Wendeline and Anneliese spoke in German about the birth, her daughter, and their emotions.

Waiting patiently outside the door until Wendeline came out to get them, Reece and Patty tiptoed across the room over to the bed, while Jeff rolled his wheelchair silently. They crept along in fear of waking the baby. Carrying a large, flat package, Patty placed the gift on a counter by the door.

"Thank you so much for flying over last week. You were much help for me. Thank you. I am happy you are here for birth," Anneliese whispered to Reece, Jeff, and Patty.

"This is exactly why we came to visit," Patty said, admiring the baby. "Oh, she's so beautiful. I'm so happy for you."

"Yeah, she's angelic. It's like looking at God," Jeff said. Patty gave him a nudge. "No, I mean it. Her features are so tiny, yet they're so detailed and refined. She's so perfect. I have this feeling that I am somehow closer to God. It's a divine moment for me."

"I can imagine what you say. I can only stare and think of God or angel, or Stacey," Anneliese said, quietly.

"Ya, she comes from heaven. I see that," Wendeline agreed.

"I can already see a blend of Stacey and you in her features," Jeff observed.

"Oh, I see it, too," Patty acknowledged. "It's amazing. We know somewhat how she was physically created. But, her soul? Where did her soul come from? Is she a new soul or an old one? What are her personality traits going to be?"

Pausing in conversation, everyone gazed down to soak in the spiritual beauty of Anneliese's sleeping baby.

Reece stood on the outskirts. He remained uncharacteristically quiet, as his gaze hovered between the promise necklace clinging around Anneliese's neck and the baby she clutched in her arms. Tears soon streamed down his cheeks.

Anneliese was the first to notice Reece's anguish. Looking at Reece released the same emotion that Anneliese tried to contain. She wanted to be overjoyed at this miraculous child, but she had conflicted feelings. She was so sad that Stacey was not present. She knew that Reece felt the same emotions.

"Reece, I also feel pain in my heart," Anneliese told him. "I miss Stacey much. I look at her, and I see him. He is part of her. She is from him always, and it makes me both happy and sad. She brings me close to Stacey."

"I look at her and all I see is my . . ." Reece paused, too consumed by emotion to speak. After taking a few deep breaths, he continued.

"Stacey's in her somewhere. I want to wake her up and ask her where he is. I know it sounds funny, but I want to somehow go inside of her and find him. I feel him so strongly standing here next to her. I know he's here. Sorry, I haven't felt these emotions this strongly since he died."

"Much people ask why I have baby in water. I tell you now," Anneliese said. "I have her in the water because Stacey died in water. I think that he is part of the water now. He loved to swim in water, play in water, and be near the water. Stacey's soul is water. I think that a birth in water might bring Stacey close to us. I also feel Stacey is here. You can imagine."

Reece took some time before he answered. He let the tears fall before wiping them away. Anneliese's words sunk into his consciousness. Then he answered by saying, "Yeah, I know what you mean, Anneliese. I know what you mean. Stacey did love everything about water. Whenever I see a river or the ocean I think of him. The water took him and made him a part of it."

"When my brother died, I had the same thoughts about the whole water thing," Patty said. "They say humans are made up of about 60 % water, which is close to the same percentage for the Earth. I've always thought it to be a strange similarity between the two. So, in some ways, we're all living in water.

"But, when we die the water that makes up our bodies evaporates. We are lifted up into the heavens. My brother was raised to the skies to be reborn again. That's my theory anyway. So, I can see now why you had the water birth."

"You never told me that," Jeff stated.

"It was a thought I had deep in my head after Brian died," Patty explained. "My religion didn't seem to have all of the answers for me, not when I needed answers that made sense. So, one night Stacey and I had a conversation about it all. After that, my mind started wandering—where could my brother have gone after he died? It struck me that we are made up of water and that all the water on the earth is recycled after some time. That must mean that we are recycled in some way, too. And then I thought of how scientists always try to find water on other planets because water is what makes life. So, water must have something to do with living, who we are, which direction our lives take, and where we go after we die.

"I believe that water is the closest thing to a god we have here on Earth. We are in awe of its power and majestic beauty. We are drawn to it as if it's a magical, healing force. We gestate in water, are made of water, and need to drink water to live. We are living in water."

"Wow honey," Jeff replied. "How come you didn't share that with me?"

"I haven't thought about that since Brian died, and you were busy recovering. I remembered it when Anneliese mentioned it," Patty said.

"When we speak of Brian and Stacey, it reminds me that you don't know my baby's name," Anneliese said. "Do you want to know her name?"

"Oh yeah, we don't even know her name. How come no one asked about a name?" Jeff asked, looking around in astonishment.

"I name her Anastacia Brianna. She is named for Stacey and Brian, Patty's brother," Anneliese announced, tears forming in her eyes.

"That is so special. I love it," Patty whispered as she broke into tears, as well. "You don't have to do that."

"Ya, I name her for the special people in each of our lives. I feel much power for name," Anneliese explained. Patty gave Anneliese a long embrace with the baby gently in the middle.

"Well, wherever my brother is, whether it's in heaven, the water, or being reborn, you have a gorgeous daughter who will always be connected to her dad," Reece said. "And, I vow to be the best uncle that this little girl could ever hope for."

"I know you will be a good uncle because you passed the first exam," Anneliese said. "You moved here."

"Before Stacey died, he wanted me to move here with him. I didn't feel ready for it then," Reece explained. "But, after he died, what choice did I have? There wasn't much left for me in California.

"I took a look at myself and my actions, especially involving women, and realized I was an immature asshole. I've had to grow up and face my responsibilities. I had to move here for Wende, for you and my niece, and for Stacey. But, largely, I had to move here for myself."

"I am so happy you moved here, also," Wende said, reaching for Reece's hand.

"Well, we've had the tragedies with Brian and Stacey's deaths. But now, hopefully, we'll begin to have some happy occasions to celebrate," Jeff began. "The birth of Anneliese's daughter being the first in a long line of joyous events, including Reece's first golf tournament next month and our wedding in a few months.

"I say we toast this moment for Anneliese and her beautiful, newly-born daughter. May you and Anastacia Brianna live in health and happiness."

Everyone raised their fake glasses. Instead of tapping glasses together, they all gave each other hugs and European kisses.

"Since we're talking about happiness, we brought something from back home to give to you," Patty stated, retrieving her gift from the counter and placing it on the edge of the bed. "Each of us brought you something. Not really baby gifts, though."

"Okay. I am much excited to see what it is," Anneliese said, sitting up higher in bed. "You can help me open gift, ya? I have arms busy."

"Of course," Patty replied, tearing open the paper to reveal two framed pieces of art. "The painting is from me. I don't know if you remember, but when I was here last fall, I began working on a series of paintings about the weather. So, here is one of those paintings, straight from my gallery show."

"Oh, it is beautiful," Anneliese praised, studying every detail of the painting. "I like how you make the eyes in water and different colors of blue make it seem alive. It feels like a place of heaven. Warm. Inviting. It is wonderful. Thank you."

"You're welcome," Patty said, flipping around the second framed piece of art to reveal a collage of pictures.

"This one is from me," Jeff said, maneuvering himself closer to the artwork. "When we were here in Europe last year, I took hundreds of pictures. I just recently had some time to go through them. There were so many that reminded me of the good times—I came up with the idea of a collage."

"I love it. I live how the picture are placed in an outline of Europe," Anneliese announced, perusing the pictures. "Ah, Wende and I are in Germany. Very clever. Everyone seems very happy and such wonderful views you see on your trip. It brings a smile to remember Stacey in these pictures. It will be a treasure for Anastacia to see her dad. Thank you."

"I also have a gift for you," Reece began, taking out a green, ring box from his coat pocket. "I see you wearing the promise necklaces that Stacey gave you. He felt overwhelmed with joy having you wear our grandparents' necklaces. I didn't tell you this, yet, but when they found him he was clutching the necklace in his right hand."

"The necklaces have much power. He sent me his love," Anneliese said, tears coming to her eyes.

"Well, I have this for you," Reece began, showing the ring box to Anneliese. "I couldn't give you this at the funeral. I don't know why. Maybe I didn't think you'd be able to handle it. I didn't want to make you cry. I think, though, that I wanted to keep it because it meant so much to him. But, it doesn't belong to me. Stacey wanted you to have it."

Reece opened the box and presented it to Anneliese. Looking down into the box and seeing the engagement ring, she burst into tears.

"Stacey went to a professional jeweler, and they designed the ring together," Reece said, taking out the ring.

"You put it on me, ya?" Anneliese asked, arranging the baby in her right arm and holding her left hand out. Reece tried the ring on her ring finger, but it wouldn't fit. So, he slipped it on her pinky. "I just give birth, so ring not fit. I get ring to fit soon."

"Stacey loved you so much and couldn't wait to propose," Reece said.

"Thank you. It is a wonderful gift," Anneliese explained, admiring the ring. Suddenly, tears again fell from her eyes. "I am happy you wait for after Anastacia is born to give me ring. After much time passes, I can appreciate it more."

"I think Stacey would agree," Reece stated.
"I wish he was here. I not know what I will do without him," Anneliese said.

"I don't mean to pry too much, but Jeff and I were wondering what your plans were for the upcoming year. Are you going to go back to school? Are you going to stay home with Anastacia Brianna?" Patty asked, remembering her brother as she spoke the baby's name.

"It is okay to ask," Anneliese said. "I asked the university and they gave me off one year. I have Anastacia for one year. She and I will live in the apartment. I will have much help from my mom, dad, sister, and Wende. Then, I will go to university again and work to be doctor. When I am in university, my mom will care for Anastacia. She does not work, so Anastacia is my mom's new job. She loves the job of caring for Anastacia. You can imagine."

"Oh, that sounds like a great plan, Anneliese," Patty said. "That little girl is going to have so many people to love her."

"Hey, don't forget about me," exclaimed Reece. "I'm gonna babysit her a lot, too. I'm gonna teach Anastacia everything she needs to know about her daddy. And, when I'm done teaching her about Stacey, I'll teach her what she needs to know about American music and sports, and when she gets older, I'll teach her everything about guys."

"Oh, we know you will," Jeff joked.

At that moment, a nurse came into the room with a tray of food. She told Anneliese that she had better get some rest. Anneliese said good-bye to her friends and told them that she'd see them tomorrow. As everyone left the room, Anastacia gave a quiet, squeaky cry. Anneliese held her in her arms.

As she held her daughter, Anneliese whispered to her, "I hope you live like your father. You are a river of divine water that makes a difference in the world. You can imagine."

THE END

ACKNOWLEDGEMENTS

I'd like to thank my family for supporting my writing. My mom introduced me to writing and journaling at an early age. My sister provided ample literature to read as fuel for my creative spark. My wife and dad read the book and gave me valuable feedback. My two boys motivated me to finish the novel.

I'd also like to thank my editor, Robbi Bryant. I couldn't have completed the novel without her amazing assistance and advice.

Some others who helped along the way are Eileen Quacchia and Tiffany Bronzan. They were my first beta readers and gave wonderful comments. Dr. Marie Mallory translated the German passages and offered insights into various aspects of the German culture.

Lastly, the one part of the novel that is loosely based on my own life is the scene on the train between Stacey and Anneliese. Therefore, I want to appreciate that young German woman who entranced me into a long conversation on a European train, ultimately inspiring the story. During that same trip, I was also lucky enough to be captivated by John Irving during his book reading at an Amsterdam book store. That meeting would later spur me to pick up a pen and write this novel.

STUDY GUIDE QUESTIONS

1. What significance and influence do the various forms of water have in the story?
2. Does water have divine qualities? Why or why not?
3. Are the characters' choices believable according to your experiences? Site the important decisions each character makes and discuss how your choice would compare or contrast with the character's.
4. How do the male characters regard relationships? Analyze the arc of each couple's relationship.
5. What are the major themes? Explain how the themes are manifested throughout the story.
6. How do the various settings influence the plot of the story?
7. Why do you think Stacey stays in California for almost four months? Do you think his decision was appropriate considering all of the circumstances?
8. Do Stacey, Reece, or Jeff represent strong masculine characters? Are either Patty, Anneliese, or Wendeline strong feminine characters?
9. Do you agree with how the author ended the story? Why or why not?

www.ingramcontent.com/pod-product-compliance
Lightning Source LLC
Chambersburg PA
CBHW020718130726
47899CB00011B/415